ST. DUNSTAN'S & JOHN

By

Charles E. Pattillo III

ISBN 978-1-934666-20-3

Cover Drawing by Charles E. Pattillo III
Cover Design by John Ropp Art Studio
Drawing of Capt. J. J. Dickison with permission of the San
Marco Bookstore

Published and distributed by:
High-Pitched Hum Publishing
321 15th Street North
Jacksonville Beach, Florida 32250

Contact High-Pitched Hum Publishing at
www.highpitchedhum.net

This is a work of fiction. The literary perceptions and
insights are based on the author's experience. All names and
places not historical, characters and incidents are either
products of the author's imagination or are used fictitiously.

High-Pitched Hum
Publishing

St. Dunstan's & John is dedicated to:

My wife, Sarah, the most special person in the world. Her nickname describes her as "Sassy", which she certainly is not. The love, encouragement and comfort she has given to me will always be the treasure of my life (plus two days).

My family: Britton, Chase, Susan, Mike, Peyton, Jessica, Jimmy and Quinn, Uncle Jimmy, Hazel and Big Pat.

I think of each one of you every day and smile.

Preface

This story grew from my involvement as an architect in church design, an interest in liturgy and church history, a fascination in the story of Jacksonville, and the extraordinary St. Johns River, particularly during the Civil War. Upon retirement, I decided to combine all these interests in a book. Originally planned as a guide book on the history of small wood frame Episcopal churches built along the river, I decided a novel would be more interesting and enjoyable than a dry recitation of architectural design facts. Also, in my story, I can more easily tell you about the treasure of the Confederate States of America.

Charles E. Pattillo III
Jacksonville, Florida

Acknowledgements

With appreciation and pleasure, I would like to thank:

Jill Sprunt, my original typist, critic and friend. She did more than put my words on paper,
Judy and Bill Morrow for providing access to the Archives of the Diocese of Florida,
Edward A. Mueller for discussions and information about steamboats on the St. Johns,
Claude Bass, Clay County Archivist, for discussions and insight to the history of Green Cove Springs and Clay County,
Ron Gordon for advice and information on gold coins, ingots and bars of silver,
Mark Boyles of Hygema Movers for history and techniques of moving buildings,
Matheson Museum, Gainesville, Florida for access to old files and photographs,
Dick Mueller, Evergreen Cemetery for information on burial traditions,
Douglas Lee, Rockland, Maine for detail information on sailboats,
All of the clergy, secretaries, custodians, wardens and vestries of the river churches for access to these wonderful buildings,
Kenneth Smith, Architect for encouragement,
H. Lamar Drake, my architectural partner and good friend, for keeping me in line for forty years,
Sheldon Gardner who took my words through cyberspace to the next level,
And my friends who lent their names to many of the people of Magnolia and St. Dunstan's.

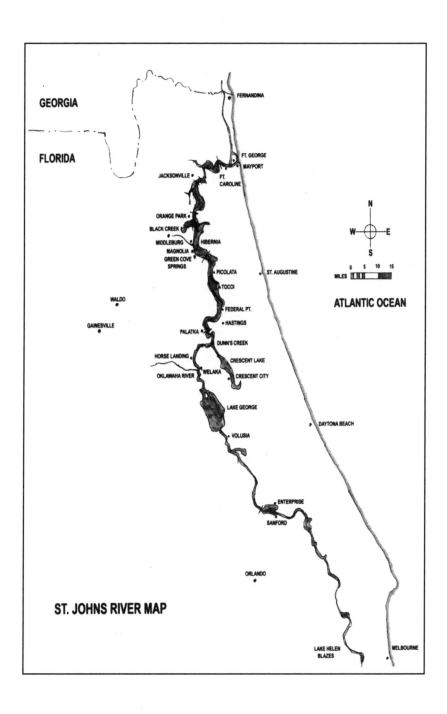

GEORGIA

FLORIDA

FERNANDINA

FT. GEORGE
MAYPORT
JACKSONVILLE
FT. CAROLINE

ORANGE PARK
BLACK CREEK
MIDDLEBURG   HIBERNIA
MAGNOLIA
GREEN COVE
SPRINGS
PICOLATA   ST. AUGUSTINE
TOCOI

WALDO

FEDERAL PT.
HASTINGS
GAINESVILLE
PALATKA
DUNN'S CREEK
HORSE LANDING   CRESCENT LAKE
OKLAWAHA RIVER WELAKA CRESCENT CITY

LAKE GEORGE

DAYTONA BEACH
VOLUSIA

ENTERPRISE
SANFORD

ORLANDO

N
W   E
S

0   5   10   15
MILES

ATLANTIC OCEAN

LAKE HELEN   MELBOURNE
BLAZES

ST. JOHNS RIVER MAP

Long shadows have been created by the setting sun. Whispers of wind bring ripples of movement to the dark water. Pilings and planks on the dock disappear in the fading light. In the distance, a side-wheeled steamboat belches smoke as it heads south.

Leaning on a piling, a thin, gaunt, old man, dressed in a shapeless coat and baggy trousers along with a scruffy hat, seems to be part of the wood piling. Clouds of smoke from a corncob pipe send signals of his presence.

"That's a mighty big river you got here," says a voice from the landside, startling the old man. "How far does it go?" Looking back toward the town, the smoker sees a well-fed young man; his stiff collar and soft cap suggesting his recent arrival.

"Well, son," says the old man, "I don't rightly know but I heard tell she goes all the way to hell 'n blazes."

Chapter 1
The Present

The early morning sun danced with reflections on the St. Johns River as Charlie Gallagher drove his old Volvo station wagon along the winding road that followed the north bank. After leaving the approaches to the Dames Point Bridge and the access roads to the port facilities, Charlie lowered the windows of his car to inhale the fragrance of the marshes with a hint of salt air of the Atlantic, a few miles ahead. The road formed a barrier between the flowing river and a maze of creeks and tidal channels, and Charlie thought of one day exploring the oak, cypress, and pine island hammocks. On the river, boats of all sizes: container ships, sleek cabin cruisers, sailboats, schooners and outboard-powered boats headed to the ocean.

Just as the Atlantic came into view, Charlie turned onto a narrow road leading to Fort George Island. Following the winding road through the marsh, he passed the ruins of an old building built of tabby, a mixture of burned oyster shells that produced lime, crushed oyster shells as an aggregate, plus sand and water. The ruins always appealed to Charlie. Why wasn't the building finished? What happened to the owner? To add to his sense of mystery on arriving at Fort George, Charlie remembered a nearby shell road with its avenue of tall palmetto palm trees curving through the oaks and pines for about a mile. Piercing the canopy of overhanging oak limbs, the palm trees, spaced about twenty feet apart, acted as sentinels guarding the approaches to the Kingsley Plantation House at the end of the road. Who planted these trees with such a sense of arrival? Did the symmetrical original floor plan of the plantation house and the semi-circle of the slave quarters which were bisected by the entry road, suggest knowledge of classical design principles?

Aside from these familiar and welcome thoughts, Charlie wondered aloud, "What am I doing here? Why isn't it raining to match my mood?" He had agreed to meet the Reverend Sam Wood, an Episcopal priest, at St. George Episcopal Church on Fort George Island, presumably to act as a tour guide. Not that he had a lot to do as a retired architect, but Charlie was sure the meeting would result in a standard guide book explanation of the "carpenter gothic" design and construction of the small church. St. George, built in 1883, was just one of seventeen small wood-framed Episcopal churches built along the St. Johns River before and after the Civil War. Charlie had visited each, taken pictures, made sketches, shared the floor plans and construction techniques with other architects, and thought the buildings were fascinating. But this effort had become a private knowledge not necessarily to be further shared. Others had written descriptions, but no one had combined these small buildings with the many local legends surrounding their development. With communication between congregations and different builders, why do they look alike? Who planned each location? Did the mission churches have a building committee, for heavens sake? Or was there a strong, dedicated individual at each church? Here he was, going to act as a tour guide for a recently-arrived priest, when actually he would rather be playing golf. In fact, Charlie was dressed in a bright colored golf shirt and cotton slacks just in case he had time to play nine holes after this meeting.

Charlie's mood brightened slightly as the shadowed road and canopy of trees became a sunlit grass lawn with very white walls of a building and a tin roof glistening in the sunshine. Pointed lancet stained-glass windows and a belfry confirmed the presence of a small church. As he turned into the graded oyster shell parking lot, Charlie figured the stocky gray haired man, dressed in a black shirt with a clerical collar, had to be his client.

The Reverend Samuel Wood pushed away from his car door to watch the approaching station wagon. "Maybe this will be a good start," he murmured aloud. The Reverend Sam Wood had been in Florida only a few months, having left a prestigious church in Richmond, Virginia, to follow a search that had begun a long time ago. As a student of the Civil War, Sam focused on the end of the war and what had happened as the Confederate Presidential Cabinet left Richmond ahead of the Union troops. As his readings and research led him through the south toward Florida, he became focused on Northeast Florida, and the St. Johns River. When the opportunity came to move to Jacksonville, Sam answered the call. His wife could not believe what he had done.

After all, when you are rector of a large church, approaching retirement, comfortable in your surroundings, to give that up is crazy. "Why?" his wife continually asked.

"I followed one call to the ministry many years ago", Sam had answered. "Now I have an opportunity to follow a dream to find out what has been lost. The answer lies in Florida, and I am going!"

Second thoughts, difficult talks with church leaders, hours of painful discussions with family and friends resulted in Sam's acceptance of a relatively minor position with the Diocesan church office in Jacksonville. With access to church archives and involvement with local and regional historians, Sam's interest multiplied with every new discovery. Six months later, standing in the parking lot of St. George Episcopal Church on Fort George Island near the mouth of the St Johns River, Sam was anxious to meet Charlie Gallagher.

Charlie was not a casual selection to begin the first step. Sam had asked staff members and other priests to recommend names of local, perhaps retired, architects who had designed a variety of churches and who were interested in church architectural history.

"I'm Sam Wood. Thanks for coming, Charlie."

"Glad to meet you, but I'm not sure what you want or what I can do for you", said Charlie.

"Did you see Fort Caroline on the south bank? Did you know the first use of the prayer book of the Anglican Church in America happened right over there on John Hawkins' boat in 1565?" exclaimed Sam.

"I know about Fort Caroline, and I've read about John Hawkins. If you know that much about this area, what do you need me for?" asked Charlie.

Sam replied, "Charlie, I moved here to learn more about north Florida and the St. Johns River during and after the Civil War. I want to learn about the small churches along the river, and I figured St. George was a good place to start."

"Okay," Charlie said as the two men walked over to the church. "You sound like you already know about the river churches, but I'll tell you all I can. Each one of the buildings has its own story. To many observers, they all look the same. All have a common heritage, I believe, but part of the appeal to me, is the uniqueness of each one."

"Who located the churches?" asked Sam.

Charlie looked out over the marsh and thought about all the difficulties of just living in those days, much less how a church would get built. "The first Episcopal Bishop of Florida, Francis Rutledge, did his best to encourage church growth, but the population of Florida in 1861 did not justify a whole lot of missionary activity. As settlers, then businesses, saw opportunity and moved into Florida, wagon trails became roadways, with railroads following. Steamboats replaced sailboats on the St. Johns and John Young, second Bishop of Florida, visited families and potential congregations. Winter resort hotels opened at Fort George, Hibernia, Magnolia and Green Cove Springs attracting winter visitors from the north. Local churches, with only one layman to lead the services, welcomed visiting Episcopal clergy, who added missionary enthusiasm by bringing a full range of church services."

"Are all the churches the same size?" asked Sam.

"St. George is approximately 21 by 48 feet, or about 1,000 square feet, and I would say the others are close to that," replied Charlie. "The consistent use of a wood structural frame, vertical wood siding with small triangular wood battens to cover the joints, the slope of the roof, the pointed or lancet windows appear to be from a standard plan."

"Would that be from Richard Upjohn's book?"

"For sure, said Charlie. "John Young brought the book of standard designs for buildings with him when he came to Florida as the second Bishop of Florida. A former Union cavalryman, Episcopalian lay reader and architect, Robert S. Schuyler, helped the Bishop by designing three of the river churches, including St. George. His work, I believe, was strongly influenced by the pattern book of Richard Upjohn and the affection of Bishop Young for Gothic architectural design he felt were appropriate and necessary for church architecture."

Charlie hesitated and then added, "Charles Haight of New York, who was associated with Upjohn's firm, designed St. Mary's in Green Cove Springs. He also designed Good Shepherd in Maitland, not on my list but an outstanding example of the style."

The two men walked around to the church doors, protected from the elements by a small gable roof. Recent renovations had created a grass-covered mound with ramped access to the entry doors to comply with local requirements for the handicapped. "Some of the churches have entry porches and steps on the end of the building and others have entrances on the side", said Charlie. "If you place the altar in the traditional east, these side entries would be on the north side of the building—not always, but generally."

"Wait a minute, Charlie," said Sam. "You mean to tell me that the river churches always had an altar oriented to the east?"

"No, not at all," replied Charlie. "The east location of the altar is a traditional, mostly symbolic orientation. The congregation faces the altar and the east, toward the rising sun, as a symbol of a new life. The priest, until lately, stands at the altar, facing east, in behalf of the congregation, ready to receive the gifts of God."

"I agree with your symbolism," said Sam. "I have heard the metaphor of the flowing river of life, moving east to west, with the priest and congregation individually and collectively facing the current."

"Sounds more like a cathedral than a small church, but I like the thought," mumbled Charlie.

Opening the double narrow entry doors, the two men entered the church and stood silently in the back, near a small, carved stone baptismal font. Sam walked over to a wooden pew, caressed the straight back, and knelt to say a prayer.

The delight Charlie felt in visiting the small churches came back again. He imagined the aroma of recently extinguished altar candles and could hear faintly the fading notes of the last hymn. The proportions of the building dimensions, either based on an experienced eye or a published dimension, were just right

A simple system of wood roof trusses supported by 6 x 6 posts divided the rectangular church interior into equal spaces or bays. In the center of each bay, a pointed (lancet) stained glass window brought glorious colors into the room as the morning sun reached the east wall of the church. White plaster walls, pine wood floors, and a light blue painted ceiling of wood boards complimented the dancing colors. Eight rows of pews on each side of the center aisle formed the nave where worshippers gather for services. On one side up front, two rows were formed to set aside seating for a small choir.

"Charlie, what are the small openings under each window?"

"I believe the openings were ventilation," said Charlie.

"As a practical matter, opening the stained-glass could cause problems. I'm also sure many a young boy went through the opening during a particularly long sermon."

One step divided the nave into a chancel, which contained a piano, prayer desk, and a lectern, where the word of God is proclaimed. A second step formed a sanctuary, where a wooden rectangular altar was placed against the outside wall of the church. On either side of a large, brass Latin cross, candelabra and flowers completed the setting for worship.

"Sam?" Charlie asked.

"Be quiet, Charlie" Sam said. "God is here."

Just as the silence was beginning to feel uncomfortable, Sam asked, "How many of these wonderful churches were built?"

Containing the locations in his mind, Charlie replied, "Between the Atlantic Ocean, Jacksonville, and up the river to Sanford, seventeen Episcopal churches were built on or near the St. Johns River: all in the style described as Carpenter Gothic, influenced by the architect Richard Upjohn, and through the leadership of John Young, second Bishop of Florida. I would describe twelve as river churches."

"Charlie, my research indicates eighteen," said Sam, "and thirteen on the river, if your criteria agrees with mine. Some churches burned, some were moved by barge to another more populated area, and others closed."

Charlie sighed with exasperation. He had been in Florida all his life; studied, visited, and admired every one of these churches and now this guy comes to town and has the total wrong from the start! Thirty minutes into the tour, and we'll have to compare lists!

"I don't know where your number eighteen comes from. I'll go back to my car and get my list and you get yours," said Charlie, jamming his hand into his pocket for his car keys.

"I realize this is not a historical documentation visit today,

Charlie, but what I would like to learn about these buildings is dependent upon an accurate number. I'll get my notes and see what they say," Sam sighed, as he also headed to the parking lot.

The two men gathered their notebooks and folders, returned to the church, and settled into adjoining pews in the back.

Charlie said, "I'll go first with my list, starting from the Atlantic Ocean, and moving up the river:

1. St. George, Fort George Island, built in 1883

2. St. Paul's By the Sea, Pablo Beach [now Neptune], 1887. Relocated many times. Now serves as a small auditorium for Beaches Chapel Christian School on Florida Boulevard.

3. St. Paul's, South Arlington, 1888, moved to the Children's Museum, and then to San Marco on Atlantic Boulevard.

4. Grace Church, Orange Park, 1880

5. Our Saviour, Mandarin, 1883. Built under the leadership of Harriet Beecher Stowe and demolished by Hurricane Dora in 1964. A new church was built in 1967 and includes a chapel that placed the repaired stained-glass windows in approximately the original locations and includes salvaged furniture. The original building did not qualify as a Bishop Young mission or a Richard Upjohn design but was built directly on the bank of the St. Johns in a style similar to the others.

6. St. Margaret's, Hibernia, 1875. Mrs. Margaret Fleming was responsible for the establishment and construction of this small church. Used by her family and guests until St. Margaret's became a church of the Episcopal Diocese of

Florida 1886. From the floor plan and construction details, it is
obvious that Mrs. Fleming consulted with Bishop Young and
followed his architectural preferences.

7. St. Mary's, Green Cove Springs, 1879

8. St. Paul's, Federal Point, 1882

9. St. Mark's, Palatka, 1854. Designed by Richard Upjohn,
closed during the Civil War, reopened in 1866

10. All Saint's, Huntington, 1891. Moved twice, presently
located in Jacksonville as Nativity on Normandy Boulevard.

11. Emmanuel, Welaka, 1881

12. All Saints, Enterprise, 1883

"That's my list of river churches," said Charlie. "I don't
know what all this is leading to, but all these churches are
worth a visit. I have five others that met my standards, but
are not around today.

"1. Our Saviour, Fulton, on the south side of the river,
west of the Fort Caroline National Memorial and the Ribault
Monument. [Sam, I think this church was moved to Mayport in
1914 and subsequently burned.]

2. Our Merciful Saviour, New Berlin, an old community
located just west of Blount Island and east of the Dames
Point Bridge.

3. Grace Mission, Chaseville, at Reddie Point, across from
the entrance of Trout River into the St. Johns.

4. Holy Cross, Sanford, based upon the designs of Richard

Upjohn, destroyed by tornado in 1880 and rebuilt on a modified Upjohn plan.

  5. St. Matthews, San Mateo, 1880"

"That's seventeen", said Sam. I have eighteen that I believe agree with your criteria."

"What's the name of the church you have that I don't?" asked Charlie. "I feel comfortable with my list, and I can't believe I've missed a church on or near a river."

"St. Dunstan's, at Magnolia, north of Green Cove Springs," replied Sam, looking up from his notes.

"Come on, Sam. I've researched, visited, and worked on these churches, and I've never heard of St. Dunstan's!" said Charlie.

Sam looked at Charlie, smiled and said, "One day, while still in Richmond, I read in a Confederate soldier's diary about the visit of Robert E. Lee to a small church on the St. Johns after the war. I also came across references to magazine articles that described a number of Confederate organizations searching from Arkansas to Florida for the lost treasure of the Confederacy. I was eager to know more. What happened to the treasure? Why did Robert E. Lee come to Florida after the war? Why visit a small church named St. Dunstan's that doesn't appear on any list of Florida churches? Would you like to know more about the gold?"

Chapter 2
New York, 1859

A hum of conversation, occasionally interrupted with a loud question or comment directed to the entire drafting room, disguised the fact that serious architectural work was in progress. The clatter of wooden T squares and triangles with the crinkle of paper added to the noise as draftsmen were busy translating architectural sketches into carefully drawn building plans, elevations, and details of construction. In one corner of the room, a talented young man mixed watercolors in preparation for applying a light coating, or wash, of color to a building elevation drawing that would indicate shadows and give an appearance of depth to a flat drawing. Nearby, another draftsman was carefully copying an original construction drawing that would be given to the client and later, perhaps, the builder. Since the technology of drawing reproduction into blueprints was on the distant horizon, the distribution of original drawings or copies was carefully monitored. A young apprentice moved from board to board, sharpened pencils and delivered properly mixed India ink for use in ruling pens. Each man, from time to time, would stand from his hunched over drawing position, stretch, and visit other boards with a suggestion, if his senior status permitted. Sketch books, pattern books from England, Italy, and France were available for reference and perhaps, inspiration.

Conversation ceased abruptly with the entry of Richard Upjohn, architect and principal of the firm. Dressed in a fashionably cut suit and white collared shirt, his tie or cravat hidden behind a black beard and heavy mustache, Richard

Upjohn presented a picture of a successful architect. Twirling a pencil in his fingers, he moved about the room, apparently more anxious to draw than to answer questions. After working alone, the idea of draftsmen to assist in the preparation of drawings, not to mention the luxury of an apprentice, was a source of pride to Upjohn.

Originally hired by Trinity Church, New York, to plan roof repairs for the existing church, Upjohn had foreseen that more extensive work would be required. The walls and roof structure were found to be defective, and replacement was necessary. Upjohn was prepared for this decision and presented the design for a new church.

When opportunity arose for this important commission, Upjohn was able to demonstrate a clear understanding of a new direction of American church architecture. Through extensive readings and study of the publications of the Ecclesiological Society of New York and the Cambridge Camden Society in England, Richard Upjohn had developed an enthusiasm for this new vocabulary of design and had gradually incorporated elements in his earlier designs. Started as a theological movement at Oxford, the Society advocated a return, in Anglican churches, to a more Catholic form of ritual, with the English parish church as a model. In the opinion of the spokesmen, all "High Church" advocates, Anglican churches had become too Protestant in practice, denying their Catholic heritage. As a result of the Reformation in England, churches had become "preaching halls", a wide auditorium with no center aisle, a dominant elevated pulpit and small altar table both placed in a narrow chancel with the congregation close to the preacher.

Upon completion in 1846, Trinity Church became the ideal expression for all churches in America. The architectural floor plan reflected a rectangular nave, with center aisle, two side aisles, and an altar area, or chancel, raised above seating for the congregation. A square tower, on the long axis of the plan, defined the entrance and terminated in a richly detailed spire topped with a cross (in opposition to the Building Committee who advocated a weathervane). Stone columns, separated by pointed arches, defined the interior of the nave. Above, a clearstory contained lancet, or pointed, windows with colorful stained glass, subdivided by stone tracery. Gothic architectural building forms were beautifully detailed by Upjohn. Masonry piers, terminated as pinnacles, rose above the two levels of pitched roofs. The Gothic Revival was launched in America with this glorious building. Architectural commissions flowed into the office of Richard Upjohn. Every denomination, large and small, wanted their own Trinity Church. As his practice grew, Upjohn had to graciously decline small churches; he decided to limit his practice to a single small church commission per year.

The many requests for architectural services from mission churches, hardly able to afford the construction cost, much less a professional fee, led to his publication in 1852 of Upjohn's Rural Architecture, subtitled Designs, Working Drawings, and Specifications for a Wooden Church, and Other Rural Structures.

In the preface Upjohn stated;

"My purpose in publishing this book is simply to supply the want which is often felt, especially in the newly settled parts of our country, of designs for cheap but still substantial buildings for the use of parishes, schools, etc. In the examples given I have kept in view the uses of each building and endeavored to give it the appropriate character; while at the same time, care has been taken to make the drawings as plain and practical as possible. A perspective view is given of each design, with general plans and full working drawings and specifications. Bills of timber and lumber are also added for the Church and Chapel. With these, any intelligent mechanic will be able to carry out the design."

Before Trinity, many of Upjohn's houses and churches were constructed of wood, generally for economical reasons. Simple in form, with a minimum of applied decoration, the book presented wood frame walls and roof trusses for the chapel and church with detailed drawings for appropriate church furniture. The two buildings expressed a stylized English parish church in simple forms, well detailed in proper proportions.

After a lengthy and productive visit to the drafting room, Upjohn reluctantly put away his pencil and returned to his office. Waiting for him, hat in hand, was a new friend. During the planning and construction of Trinity Church, lengthy discussions about church liturgy and correct architectural expressions had drawn Upjohn and the Reverend John Young, assistant at Trinity, into an emerging friendship.

"John, this is a pleasant surprise," said Richard in greeting his new friend.

"Richard, I know you are busy, but I received two letters yesterday from the first Bishop of Florida, the Right Reverend Francis H. Rutledge. You may not know that, in my early priesthood, I served in Florida and was slightly acquainted with Bishop Rutledge who was elected in 1851. Under his leadership, St. Mark's in Palatka, on the St. Johns River south of Jacksonville, was constructed with, I am sure, the guidance of your book. I do not know the contents of Bishop Rutledge's letter, but I suspect he is seeking professional help for another church. Perhaps by my delivering his letter, some doubtful credibility is achieved. In any event, I felt I should bring his letter to you."

Upjohn smiled and opened the letter.

Jacksonville, July 16, 1860

Richard Upjohn, Architect

Dear Sir,

I have taken the liberty of asking a fellow clergyman to deliver this letter with the hope you might more readily consider my request. For the past few years, I have served as Bishop of Florida, attempting to bring the message of the Church to a beautiful wilderness, a task made more difficult by the lack of church buildings. Small groups of people assemble under trees or in cabins or tents, many of whom left familiar church buildings to come to Florida. It is my prayer to build a small church on the St. Johns River, between Jacksonville and Palatka in the village of Magnolia. Access by steamboat and across the river, a road east to St. Augustine make this location ideal. There is now, in Magnolia, a group of men and women who have organized a mission and I feel a proper expression of faith is desirable and necessary.

St. Mark's Church in Palatka followed the direction and plans so well stated in your book, but I am asking that you consider a more direct form of professional service by sending plans and specifications for this church.

The site is elevated above the flowing waters of the river, a pleasant open space looking east across the river. Pine, oak, magnolia, and palm trees surround the cleared area. The Vestry, with my concurrence, would like a building to seat 30 worshippers in an adequate nave plus a raised chancel, built of wood in a manner suited to the Episcopal Church and costing about $900. The parish is to be named St. Dunstan's, after the blacksmith who became Archbishop of Canterbury.

Please allow me to request of you a special effort

toward this mission, praying that God will bless you,

I am, Respectfully Yours,

Francis H. Rutledge, Bishop

Upjohn placed the letter on his desk and turned to his friend. "Well, John, what do you say? Have you ever been to this place?"

John replied, "Before I accepted the call to come to Trinity, I served a number of mission congregations in Texas, Mississippi, and Louisiana. Before that, I was assigned by the Board of Domestic Missions to St. John's in Jacksonville as the only clergyman for many miles. Before he was elected Bishop, Francis Rutledge was in Tallahassee, 200 miles to the west.

"And yes, I have been to Magnolia. The river is wide and beautiful, with an amazing abundance of plant life. Palm trees stand as sentinels at the edges of the river, large oak trees dripping with Spanish moss on every branch, and pine trees taller than you can imagine are at every turn of the river. I think Magnolia would be a good place to build a mission church. For it to be an original architectural design by Richard Upjohn would make St. Dunstan's even more successful."

New York
August 5, 1860

The Right Reverend Francis H. Rutledge

My Dear Sir,

Your interesting and challenging letter was delivered to me by John Young, as you requested.

John and I have developed a strong friendship over our mutual interests in music and Gothic architecture. He described to me the difficulties for missionary work in Florida, and I am certain rewards are few and are, in no way, a measure of your efforts.

Since it has been my practice to provide professional services to a single mission parish each year, I have decided to listen to your appeal from a far away place. St. Dunstan's in Magnolia, Florida is of great interest to me and I will provide a set of plans for a small church of good architectural proportions to be constructed of wood on the banks of the St. Johns River. I hope that my humble concepts of architectural design will result in a proper expression of our shared beliefs and a building that will assist you in your ministry. May God bless you and the people of St. Dunstan's.

> With the Greatest Respect,
> Your Most Obedient Servant
>
> Richard Upjohn

Upon receiving a copy of this letter, three weeks later, John Young bowed his head with a silent prayer of thanksgiving, not realizing the impact this small church would have on his ministry.

Chapter 3
Magnolia, Florida, 1861

After the noon meal, just before the usual rainstorm, the steamboat whistle was heard in the distance; a sharp exclamation of sound that was more in anticipation of arrival than a mournful wail of a train whistle.

Caleb Hopkins, owner of the general store, hollered to his son, Jeb, to get the wagon out and hitch up the mule so any passengers on the steamboat could be taken to the hotel and any freight unloaded.

From a clearing on the west bank of the river, a long wood dock extended into the dark slow moving water. At the end of the dock, log-built small buildings and a few wood-framed white painted houses were gathered around a larger two-story building. South of the dock, a flowing stream ran to the river fed by an active spring beside the larger building. Two large magnolia trees stood beside the bubbling waters, giving the name to the small village.

Nathan Benedict, M. D., and his wife Dorothy, visiting Jacksonville from Maryland, enjoyed a trip to Magnolia. He decided to move to Magnolia, open a small hotel and offer his services as the town doctor.

Caleb Hopkins, his wife Sarah and son Jeb, had also come up the river and decided to leave Jacksonville and opened a general store. Thaddeus Washington came along to open a tavern. Thomas Hendricks was appointed Postmaster as the Hibernia post office was relocated to Magnolia.

The Reverend Harold Alexander and his wife Kate from Virginia, were so attracted to the weather and the river, that he built a house and barn and stayed year round. Then his

brother David, and his wife Deborah, came soon after.
Thomas Hunter of Jacksonville saw an opportunity to plant
orange trees. Up the river, J. J. Dickison, had a large ranch,
where he, his wife Mary Elizabeth, and their son, Charlie,
raised cattle and tended a small orange grove. With other
settlers and ranchers scattered in the woods and farmers
nearby, Magnolia grew into a small village.

The tavern was empty in the afternoon heat, but a second
sharp whistle woke Thad Washington from his nap and
brought most of the village to the water. Cypress, magnolia,
and oak trees hid the steamboat as it approached the dock
that extended out into deeper water. You couldn't see the
boat through the dense growth, but you could certainly hear
it as the paddle wheels slapped the water and then pushed the
boat through the water. The Darlington, a two-deck steamboat
with paddle wheels on each side, over 100 feet long and 25
feet wide, had left Jacksonville this morning on her regular
run to Palatka and Lake Monroe to the south. Passengers on
the upper deck began to gather their belongings. Three
couples from the north and two other men watched the
docking procedures as handlers on the lower deck moved to
unload what appeared to be stacks of bricks. The shorter of
the two men, bearded and dressed in a long coat over faded
gray trousers, looked from his vantage point at the village of
Magnolia. During his early years in Florida, Francis Rutledge,
first Bishop of Florida, had traveled this way many times. To
his companion, Bishop Rutledge pointed out the hotel and
springs, the general store and tavern framed in logs, with
wide front porches under sloping roofs. Obviously newer
houses could be seen grouped around large oak trees to
capture the shade, so important in the spring and summer.
These houses, clad in wide boards with narrower boards or
battens covering the joints, also boasted wide porches and
sloping roofs of cypress or heart pine roof shingles. All were
built on cypress posts above the ground as protection from
rising water, snakes and other unwanted animals.

Bishop Rutledge turned to his companion and said, "This is a good place for a new church!"

Caleb greeted the three couples as they stepped ashore and directed them to his wagon for a ride to the hotel. He then turned to the smiling, bearded visitor, "Francis, I'm glad to see you. I received your letter describing the response from Mr. Upjohn in New York and I'm anxious to see what he has planned for us!"

Bishop Rutledge extended his hand. "Caleb," he said, "I have high hopes for what is going to happen here in Magnolia. Not only do I have the plans for St. Dunstan's, as promised by Richard Upjohn, but I have also brought with me Mr. Ed Foley of Jacksonville, an experienced and trustworthy man, who I have commissioned to build the church. Since I have confidence in the funding for St. Dunstan's, I have also purchased the bricks for the foundations."

Ed Foley, a stocky red-head with a bushy moustache, stepped forward to shake Caleb's hand. "If you'll bring that wagon up to the dock, I'll see that our bricks are properly unloaded. You and the Bishop know where it's going so I'll follow your lead."

Eight trips by the wagon brought bricks and mortar mix to the church site. In a previous visit, with axe in hand, Francis Rutledge had selected the location, south of the dock, near the stream. A very large oak tree simplified his wish to place the church on an east/west axis and also be visible from the river.

Anxious to have a church after services in Caleb's house and the hotel, the people of Magnolia had cleared the heavy underbrush while waiting for the Bishop's visit and now stood watching today as if the building could be completed in one day.

In the next few days, Ed Foley, following the drawings of Richard Upjohn, laid out the building with stakes at the corners. With two workers, brought along from Jacksonville, he then began excavations for the building foundation. On the long sides of the church, brick piers, twenty inches square, were placed about seven feet apart. Another row of piers was planned down the middle of the building. On each end, a single brick pier was planned at the center. On the north side, a nine by nine extension for a robing room was indicated by Upjohn. On this same side, at the corner of the robing room, a foundation for a chimney was planned. The church entry on the east side completed the layout.

The hole for each pier was about eighteen inches deep, down to undisturbed soil. After roots and other debris were cleared, the bottom was tamped down. A thick layer of Spanish moss was also tamped in place with a lattice, or grid, of thin cypress strips placed on top, ready to receive the first course of brick. Lime, made from burned oyster shells crushed to a powder and combined with sand was brought from Jacksonville. Mixed with water from the nearby stream, a mortar was created for the masonry work. After the height of each pier reached the level of the ground, dirt was placed in the hole against the brick and tamped down. Each pier, twenty inches square, was laid in brick courses to approximately sixteen inches above the ground.

After completion of the masonry work, Ed Foley sent word to the lumber mill at Hogan's Creek in Jacksonville, that he was ready for the framing lumber. A small water-powered sawmill owned by Joseph Brooker was in operation, but Ed felt the quality and quantity of the framing timbers could best be furnished by a mill in Jacksonville. Richard Upjohn's documents included a "bill of timber and lumber" that described the length and width of each framing member as well as the quantity needed. Ed Foley, being experienced in similar specifications prepared in far away places, decided to make the final cuts for length on the site. Splices would be necessary at the sill beams, wall plates, and other major pieces of the structure. Ed believed in the old saying, "Measure twice and cut once". A circular saw, powered by a steam engine was brought from Jacksonville, along with the framing lumber and four additional carpenters. Appropriate hand tools, one and two-man crosscut saws, axes, chisels, framing squares, hatchets, boring tools, block and tackle and ropes were brought along as well; all necessary to build St. Dunstan's. The timber frame of the church would be joined together by connections, complicated by description, but standard for skilled carpenters, literally joiners. Variations of a single type of joint connection would hold the timbers together, a mortise and tenoned joint. Mortise describes a rectangular hole cut into the wood that would receive a tenon, or tongue, shaped by saw and chisel at the end of the post, beam or rafter. Occasionally a wood pin, called a tree nail, is inserted into a hole bored through the two pieces as they are joined.

Across the completed brick piers, around the perimeter and down the center of the building, eight by ten inch sill beams were placed in a bed of mortar. Depending upon the length of the timber, a lapped joint was made at a pier and at each corner. After careful measurement, a rectangular hole, or mortise, was made in the center of the sill beam, above each brick pier. Each eight by ten inch post was cut to a height of ten feet, with a tenon at each end, and guided by hand into the mortise cut in the sill beam. Diagonal braces, approximately three feet long, were attached to the posts and the sill beam.

As this work was progressing, Ed Foley located two trees tall enough and, based on his experience, strong enough to handle the weight of the wall plates and roof rafters. The trees were cut, bark was removed and block and tackle attached to the top. Multiple ropes securely anchored supported the rig, call a "gin pole". (A contraction of the word engine, or a device for lifting heavy objects). Using the lifting capacity of the block and tackles attached to the gin pole, eight by ten inch plates were raised, and with tenons or the posts carefully matching the mortise holes, the plates were lowered into place. Four by six inch wood studs were inserted on either side of the windows and doors and spiked to the plate and sill beam. Diagonal braces were added to give lateral support to the structural frame.

The schedule of erection now called for the placement of floor joists. These timbers, three by eight inches, were laid from one sill beam across the church building to the sill beam down the center of the building, (occasionally called the "summer" beam). A second joist would be placed along side the first to continue across to the other sill beam. The floor joists were spaced sixteen inches apart with two by four inch diagonal braces, called cross bridging, nailed between each joist. At the west end of the church (the chancel), additional short posts were added from the sill beam to raise the floor two steps or about fifteen inches.

Floor boards, one and one half inches thick were laid across the floor joists and securely nailed. During the next stage of construction, the floor of the church would serve as a working surface to assemble the principal roof rafters and to make all necessary mortise and tenon cuts before erection.

To span the twenty foot distance between the side walls, Upjohn's drawings indicated two inclined eight by ten inch timbers, or rafters, meeting at the apex of a triangle, that would be placed on the wall plates about eight feet apart. A collar beam about halfway down from the point of the triangle kept the two rafters from spreading apart. A notch, or bird's mouth, was cut at the foot of each rafter to also help resist the outward thrust. Mortise and tenoned joints, with wood pins [tree nails] connected the three pieces together, forming a rigid, strong frame.

As each frame was assembled on the floor, ropes from the block and tackle mounted on the gin poles lifted the heavy timbers. Workers using push poles, with iron spikes at the end for better control, guided each frame into place. Temporary braces were added until all frames were in place. Across the top of each frame, mortised into the inclined rafter, six by six inch purlins were set.

During construction, the people of Magnolia brought lunch to the workers and were thrilled to see St. Dunstan's slowly take shape. As the last frame was put in place, Caleb watched Ed Foley walk out of the woods with a large branch of a pine tree in his hands.

"What is that for?" asked Caleb as he watched Ed climb to the top of the first frame and attach the branch.

"This branch is to symbolize the 'topping out' of the structural frame", Ed explained as he climbed down. "Caleb", he said. "I think we should gather your folks together and give thanks to God for the gift of trees and all they provide."

Caleb walked back to his store looking for his son, Jeb, to help him gather as many people as he could find.

From his porch, the Reverend Harold Alexander had been watching the construction of St. Dunstan's. He knew what was ahead. When he had retired and moved from Virginia to Magnolia, he thought his days of parish concerns were over. Bishop Rutledge had asked him twice and he had politely declined once to take charge of this new church. He told his wife, Kate, that he had to help. "I can't just sit on the porch and not answer this call". He was curious when he saw Ed Foley climb up the frame of the church and attach the branch. As he saw Caleb walking toward his house, Harold Alexander felt his ministry at St. Dunstan's Episcopal Church in Magnolia, Florida, was about to begin.

"Almighty God, we gather this day to give thanks for Your creations. We see around us every day Your gift of trees, accepting them without thankful hearts for the important place trees have in our lives. Open our eyes to all Thy works, that we may learn to use them to serve You more. We give thanks to these men who have joined together each timber with the skill and knowledge that You have given them. Show us, with Thy presence, the way we may use this church to spread Your Word. In our joy today, may we feel Thy hand laid upon us and abide in peace; through Jesus Christ, our Lord. Amen."

Chapter 4
Northeast Florida, 1861

The scrawny cow watched the approaching rider wind his way through the pine trees. A swirling whip snapped with a sharp pop, startling the cow into a trot. The rider slapped the flank of his horse with a battered hat as he followed the cow. J. J. Dickison coiled his whip and murmured, "At least he's going in the right direction."

J. J. had left his plantation earlier in the day with four men, including his son Charlie, four dogs, and a wagon full of supplies to start a round-up of his "cracker" cattle. In this part of Florida, open dry prairies are rare; cows and calves are collected, branded, and turned loose. On small horses, well-adapted to heavy underbrush, clumps of palmettos, oak hammocks as well as pinewood flatlands and swamps, cowboys became cowhunters. Running ahead of the cowhunter, dogs were trained to catch a cow by the ear and to hold until the rider appeared. Cracking his whip, the cowhunter would move the cow toward the herd and the dog would trot off to find another wandering cow.

As his horse trotted down a sandy trail, J. J. could hear whips cracking and dogs barking as his men guided the cows toward the north. He rode out of the trees, urging the cow by his whip, toward a small pond where he saw his son and three other riders waiting. It was hard to tell them apart. All four men had broad-brim, sloppy-looking hats, all were dressed with baggy shirts and faded cotton trousers with a long knife in a leather sheath hanging from a leather belt. Each man carried a rawhide braided whip about twelve feet long, with a buckskin cracker at the end. These whips, known as drags, swung overhead and snapped with a loud pop, were used with great skill, to keep the herd moving with the crack of a whip rarely touching a cow, or to kill a threatening rattlesnake. Slung from all four saddles were twelve-gauge double-barrel shotguns, with the long barrel cut down to about twenty-four inches for more effective use in heavy stands of saw palmettos and wire grass.

"Charlie, take the cows on. Let 'em graze along the way", J. J. said. "I heard the boat whistle for Magnolia, and I'm going to hear for myself what Caleb and Harold Alexander been telling me. They say newspapers and letters from Savannah and Charleston tell us trouble is coming. I don't know what I'm gonna do about it, but I want to learn more."

In Magnolia, Ed Foley had started the process of cutting shingles for the church roof. From straight pine trees ten or twelve inches thick, he cut short logs about eighteen inches long. Using a hatchet and a tool called a froe, a wedge-shaped cleaving blade with a handle attached at right angles, it was a sit-down job. The worker sat on one upright log as he split the shingles from a second pine log.

On the roof frames, perpendicular to the purlins, one and a half inch thick boards were nailed in place, to serve as a base for the roof shingles. At the exterior walls, across the eight by ten posts and the four by six studs, three by four inch furring strips were attached, like rungs of a ladder, to receive the board siding. The walls were then covered with one and a half inch planks, ten to twelve inches wide. Each board had a tongue on one side and a groove cut on the other. At the bottom of the wall, a board was angled out at forty-five degrees to direct rainwater away from the brick foundations. Each joint of the vertical boards was covered with a triangular cover, called a batten, split from a three by three inch section of pine.

The boat whistle stopped all work and, as usual, the whole community headed for the river, watching the Darlington ease up to the dock. Bishop Rutledge was the first off and headed toward Caleb, Harold Alexander, and Ed Foley.

"Got bad news", he said. "Ft. Sumter in South Carolina has been fired on. In Tallahassee, a convention called to discuss our political future has voted to secede from the Union! There are rumors of gunboats at the mouth of the river and I am afraid war is imminent! Ed, I'm going to ask you to stop work on St. Dunstan's. I just don't know what lies ahead for the Diocese, but I am sure we will need the money I set aside for the completion of the church. Please finish the siding and roof shingles and pray that we can start construction again soon."

Caleb and Harold shook their heads; Ed Foley slammed his hatchet to the ground. "Bishop", he said, "you've got to let me do more than just stop! I've got to paint! You know how long exposed wood will last around here, and I've got to close up the window openings. The folks here can use the church if I hang the doors."

"Alright, Ed, I understand. Go ahead with that work, but I repeat, I believe war is imminent."

J. J. rode up to the group and heard only the words "stop construction and war." "Come on, Francis," he exclaimed, "we have waited and worked hard for St. Dunstan's. We have worshipped at Caleb's, Harold's, my house, Nathan's hotel and even in Thad's tavern - and just like that you say 'stop!' With just a few words, our world has come apart!"

"J. J., I have not closed St. Dunstan's. What was to be is postponed. I pray that you will continue to worship together under Harold's leadership, even in the incomplete church. And, yes, your world and mine have come apart with the thoughts of war."

Chapter 5
Magnolia, Florida, 1861

Ed Foley finished his work at St. Dunstan's as limited by Bishop Rutledge and, with regret, headed back to Jacksonville. Newspapers and visitors brought word of the surrender of Ft. Sumter and the establishment of the Confederate States of America.

As work on the church stopped, the people of Magnolia expressed their displeasure and frustration, turning then to a deep concern over the prospects of war coming to their community. But life went on; the steamboats and visitors from the north came and went. The hotel, Caleb's store and Thad's tavern were busy. On Sundays they gathered in the shell of St. Dunstan's; the hot days of summer were ahead.

Down the river in Jacksonville, it was business as usual. The town was growing; new homes, boarding houses and hotels were being built, expressions of support for the Confederacy appeared everywhere. Along the riverfront, steamboats and two and three-mast schooners unloaded and loaded commercial products. Sawmills were active, answering an increasing demand for lumber and naval stores in the north, Cuba, Spain, and England. Several owners offered their slaves for sale and advertised for the return of those who had fled in fear.

The Union blockade at the mouth of the St. Johns began to take effect. With the presence of Federal gunboats at Mayport, commerce with other Southern seaports, the north and Europe came to a halt. Lumber remained stacked for shipment at the sawmills, citrus and vegetables spoiled on the docks, and most business came to a standstill.

J. J. Dickison was concerned about the war coming to

Magnolia. He knew about Ft. Sumter and had read and talked with others about states rights and the problems of slavery. Whatever could happen to Florida, he felt it was important to organize some kind of protection for the town. Notices were posted and word was circulated calling for a town meeting at St. Dunstan's.

J. J. was surprised at the turnout. All of these men and their families were fiercely independent but depended on Caleb and his store. On Saturdays they would bring animal skins, alligator hides, oranges and vegetables to trade for flour, coffee, salt, tobacco, ammunition, and occasionally whiskey; but if there was nothing to trade, they came for talk. Most Sundays they came to church.

J. J. stood up at the front of the church and waited for silence from the gathered men and women. Caleb, Thad, Nathan, Joe and Harold were there along with farmers, settlers, ranchers, citrus growers, and cowhunters from up and down the river from Magnolia.

"You have heard the news about war coming to Florida. I have no idea what the future holds for each of us and our farms, ranches, and groves; but I believe we should be prepared. I propose to organize a home guard to protect us until we receive some kind of official word from the state or Jacksonville. There will be no uniforms or drill; what I propose is for each family to take turns sending a circuit rider or wagon once a week to make regular contact with each family. This rider would pass on any news. Caleb's store will be headquarters for us and he would inform each rider what should be passed on to our neighbors. If the steamboats stop coming, my son Charlie and Caleb's son Jeb could alternate taking our boat across the river to seek out any news from over there. We will try to send a rider to Palatka and send a boat down the river to Jacksonville to see about mail and pick up any newspapers."

The Reverend Alexander, Caleb and Thad each spoke in turn; sharing J. J.'s concerns but urging caution. Dr. Nathan

Benedict and Joe Brooker did not endorse any thoughts of secession from the Union. Any organization like J. J. described could offer some security but the two men felt support of the Confederacy was not in the best interests of the town. The younger men and cowhunters were ready to fight. Many spoke in agreement with J. J. and were ready to get started. J. J. was elected captain, and planning began to start the first rider on a circuit of families.

As Dickison's home guard riders began their circuits around Magnolia, Union gunboat crews at Mayport, were astonished to see a long, slim, two-mast schooner glide past, fully rigged with sail. The racing yacht America, a decade removed from her successful challenge to British racing supremacy, had slipped through the blockade offshore and was on her way to Jacksonville. Renamed Camilla by British owners, she had remained in European waters until the Civil War began. After crossing the Atlantic under the helm of an English adventurer, the yacht stopped in Savannah, where she was purchased by the Confederate government to carry dispatches through the Union blockade. After two trips to Bermuda, it became more difficult to run a more effective blockade, so the sleek boat remained at the docks in Jacksonville. Fearful of any attempts by the Union to take Camilla, it was decided to take her up the river to be scuttled.

From the fantail of the St. Mary's, a side wheel steamboat, rope hawsers were fed through chocks on the deck of the Camilla to wood posts, called bitts, bolted to the frame of the schooner. So a sad voyage began, a sleek black hull with two distinctive sloping masts pulled by a smoke-belching steamboat eased away from the dock in Jacksonville.

Sam Thomas, cowhunter, serving today as a circuit rider around Magnolia, guided his horse through the scrub oaks toward the river. Cracking his whip at low-hanging moss from time to time, he startled a skinny cow that jumped and quickly ran off. Sam followed a faint trail to the bank of the river, looked north and was surprised to see black smoke from a boat coming up the river. He hadn't seen anything like a large boat since the last visit of the <u>Darlington</u> about a month ago. Kicking his horse into a fast trot, Sam headed for the captain's ranch.

J. J. heard Sam's report and ran from his porch through the trees to the river. Looking across the still waters to the east bank nearly a mile away, he could see nothing. Walking carefully on his shaky wooden dock, J. J. looked to the north and saw Sam's smoke. Sure enough, there was a steamboat coming his way pulling a large sailboat. J. J. ran back to the house and called for Charlie to saddle their horses.

"I don't know what it is, Charlie, but let's head for town and see if the steamboat is going to stop at Magnolia."

J. J. and Charlie pulled their horses to a stop behind a group assembled at the Magnolia dock and watched with amazement as the two boats stayed in the middle of the river and went right on by.

"What in the world?" J. J. exclaimed as crewmen on both boats waved in response from greetings from the shore.

"Charlie, you and Jeb take our sailboat and follow. See if you can find out what the two boats are up to. Take what you need for a couple of days and bring us back some news."

Charlie was glad his father suggested taking Jeb. He could handle the little boat better and seemed to understand wind on the water and all that stuff. The two young men packed up the boat and pushed off. Using the oars, Charlie and Jeb headed into the wide river watching astern as Magnolia disappeared from view. As they left the protection of the trees, Jeb raised the single canvas sail and set one of the oars as a rudder. A good breeze from the east soon filled the sail and Jeb began a series of tacks, or a zig-zag course using the wind, up the river in pursuit of the strange convoy.

Chapter 6
Magnolia, Florida

"They did what?" exclaimed J. J.

"Just like I said, Pa; me and Jeb watched while those men on the <u>St. Mary's</u> towed that pretty sailboat past Palatka and "devils elbow", then turned into that big creek leading to Dunn's Lake. They climbed down below the deck, released the lines and left the black boat to sink. The <u>St Mary's</u> went on into the lake and me and Jeb watched as the boat settled down in the mud with only a side rail showing!"

In the late afternoon, J. J. and his wife Mary Elizabeth sat on their porch looking east through the trees toward the river. The setting sun behind them touched the distance shore with the traces of gold and then faded into a dark line of trees. The feeling of pleasure also slipped away into a sense of anxiety about the days ahead.

"The thought of that sailboat being sunk just mystifies me," said J. J. "And then for the <u>St. Mary's</u> to go on into the lake rather than heading south to Palatka; I just can't understand. The hotel is empty and there are no steamboats on the river. I believe the dark days we have been dreading are here."

The steamboats on the river were gone. Some, like the <u>St. Mary's</u> headed for shallow water out of the reach of deeper draft Union boats. Others left Jacksonville and tried, most unsuccessfully, to breach the Union blockade. A few, like the <u>Darlington</u> steamed past Ft. George and Talbot Islands into Nassau Sound and then to Fernandina. Two were confiscated by the U. S. Navy and used as troop transports. Since Jacksonville was occupied by Union forces, gunboats extended the offshore blockade to now include the river

itself. From Mayport to Lake George, 100 miles south of
Jacksonville, Navy gunboats patrolled the river searching for
boats carrying cotton and oranges south to the Indian River
for further transfer to ocean ports. St. Augustine opened their
city to the Union, effectively giving the North possession of
northeast Florida, from St. Augustine to Mayport and
Jacksonville.

HEADQUARTERS PROVISIONAL FORCES, EAST AND MIDDLE FLORIDA DEPARTMENT

[SPECIAL ORDER NO. 48]

TALLAHASSEE, JANUARY 4, 1862

John Jackson Dickison, Magnolia, Florida, is hereby
authorized to raise a company of cavalry, to be
mustered into the Confederate States service for
three years, or the duration of the war, to be raised,
if possible, within the present month.

By Order, Brigadier General commanding

W. Call
Assistant Adjutant General

Magnolia, Florida, March 1, 1862

Colonel W. S. Anderson,
Commanding East and Middle Florida

Pursuant to Special Order No. 48, I beg leave to
report to you the organization of J. J. Dickison's

troop of cavalry, to be designated Company H., Second Florida Cavalry. First and second lieutenants being present with six non-commissioned officers, twenty privates from the counties of Clay, Duval, St. Johns and Alachua. J. J. Dickison elected Captain.

Major R. N. Myers

Adjutant and Inspector General

The circuit riders of Magnolia and others from nearby counties became a troop of cavalry, looking not quite as distinguished as the designation. With their own weapons of varying types, little ammunition, and whips tied to the saddles of their own small horses, J. J. Dickison's troop loaded their wagons and headed for Gainesville for ammunition and whatever supplies that might be available. After three weeks of serving as picket guards and other routine duties, orders were received from headquarters at Camp Milton to proceed to Palatka, "make contact with any enemy lines and attack whenever conditions and terrain are suitable."

A base camp was established northwest of Palatka, away from the river. Some men were allowed to visit their nearby families but each stood ready to assemble when called by a circuit rider or a blast from a cow horn. J. J. felt his system would work for the army so he kept riders or wagons circling the camp day and night. As small detachments of Yankee soldiers were encountered as they searched for beef and escaped slaves, J. J.'s men did not hesitate to attack, even when outnumbered. Union commanders soon learned that standard tactics of the use of infantry were not appropriate in heavy underbrush and thick woods.

Late one afternoon, a courier arrived from East Florida Headquarters in Lake City with orders for Company H. In the order, General Finegan described the saga of the America, renamed Camilla, and how the decision was made to scuttle the yacht. He further noted that a very reliable contact reported U. S. Navy steamboats were en route to locate Camilla and then raise her for service. Company H was ordered to proceed south to Dunn's Creek and block any attempts to raise Camilla. The general further ordered Captain Dickison and his troop to rendezvous with a company of Home Guard sent out from Welaka for the same purpose.

After consulting his maps, J. J. planned to move south around Palatka on horseback, then use small boats to ferry his dismounted men across the St. Johns. Once they reached Dunn's Creek, logs would be cut and placed across the mouth of the creek to prevent access by Yankee boats. After the meeting with the detachment from Welaka, the sunken vessel would be surrounded by Confederate forces to discourage, with gunfire, any efforts by the U. S. Navy.

Upon landing on the east bank, J. J. sent out scouts toward the creek in advance of his main body. After the boats were hidden, signals by whip "pops" were reviewed and an order of march through the woods determined. Pickets were placed front, rear and both sides as the force of twenty men moved south. After five miles of slow progress through swamps and heavy underbrush, whip "pops" were heard ahead. Captain Dickison moved to the front as Corporal Joe Tillman came through the woods.

"We're too late, Captain!" reported the scout. "I found two men from Welaka in the trees ahead and they said they watched the Yankees arrive and begin work but their Captain refused to fire! All we had to do was shoot but Captain Stephens said it would be murder and ordered us to head back to Welaka."

Recalling the passage of the two boats passing Magnolia and the surprise sinking of the boat watched by his son Charlie, J. J. Dickison, Company H, Second Florida Cavalry, slammed his hat to the ground in frustration over a lost opportunity.

The <u>Camilla</u> was successfully raised by the U. S. Navy, returned to Jacksonville, reconditioned, renamed <u>America</u> and was soon a part of the Atlantic blockade.

Chapter 7
Magnolia, Florida, 1863

In Magnolia, Caleb, Thad and the Reverend Harold Alexander had volunteered for J. J.'s cavalry troop but were refused due to their age. J. J. assured each of his recognition of their loyalty but asked for their leadership at home. Nathan Benedict, M. D., felt he should remain in Magnolia to serve as town doctor. One Sunday after church in St. Dunstan's, the few women and children had gone home and the four men stood on the bank of the river and watched with fear as a Yankee gunboat left the center of the river and turned toward shore.

The Columbine, a small side-wheeled steam gunboat with cannons fore and aft, slowly eased up to the dock. Caleb, Thad, Nathan and Harold watched as two men jumped ashore and tied lines to the pilings. A second group of uniformed sailors, with rifles, followed the anchor detail to the dock and headed for shore.

"I don't think we should run, but I sure would like to", murmured Caleb.

"Let's see what they want", said Harold, as the four stepped out from the trees.

A tall young man with sword belt and peaked cap saluted the group. "Ensign Frank Sanborn, of the U. S. Navy gunboat Columbine, at your service. I am under strict orders to not harm you or the residents of this community. My men and I are here to inspect Magnolia, to search for escaped slaves and to make contact with any Union supporters, offering them the protection of the U. S. Navy."

Caleb spoke. "The men of Magnolia, other than the four of us and a handful of older citizens, have gone to war. Even though our political beliefs are not in agreement and you are representatives of the enemy, we will stand true to our heritage of hospitality and welcome you to this community. My store is ahead; there is little food. Thad's tavern is adjacent. The larger building is a hotel, completely vacant and over in the trees is our church."

Ensign Sanborn nodded his head as each man introduced himself and then directed his men to the buildings, repeating his order to harm no one and adding a warning to respect private property. "We are looking for evidence of the whereabouts of the guerrilla, J. J. Dickison. I understand his plantation is nearby." The four men looked at each other and said nothing.

"While my men are searching, I would like to see the famous spring so well advertised before the war. And I would like the Reverend to show me the church, obviously incomplete. St. Mark's Episcopal Church in Palatka has closed and I wonder if this small building will be closed as well. I was raised in Brunswick, Maine and attended St. Paul's Episcopal Church. The church there was built by my father in 1845 and I am instantly attracted to the similarities I see here."

Harold Alexander was dumbfounded that this young Yankee officer could notice the small building and compare it to a Maine church so very far away.

"Is it possibly designed by Richard Upjohn of New York? Or copied from another church? The wood frame, window openings and board siding are very familiar to the son of a builder. I must tell you the triangular wood battens confuse me; St. Paul has rectangular battens. I know about this because I nailed many of them under my father's close supervision."

The priest and naval officer walked over to the church as Caleb, Thad and Nathan hurried to accompany the inspecting shore party. Harold told Ensign Sanborn how St. Dunstan's was designed by Richard Upjohn at the request of Francis

Rutledge, Bishop of Florida, and how he stopped construction as the war began.

"Why is a horseshoe hanging above the door? Isn't that irreverent to have a good luck symbol at the church door?" asked Sanborn.

"Not at all," replied Harold. "This church is named for St. Dunstan, a blacksmith before he became Archbishop of Canterbury. Legend tells us that one day, while working at his anvil, the devil appeared and asked to have his cloven feet shod. Dunstan grabbed the devil, lashed him to his anvil, and beat him until the devil cried for mercy. Dunstan made him promise to never enter a door where a horseshoe was hung; always with the open side up so as to catch the mercies of heaven."

Sanborn smiled and reached up toward the head of the doorway as the two men entered the church. "I can see Upjohn's hand in the design of the building and I very quickly see the skill of the builder. The joinery of the posts and roof trusses is a pleasure for me; it is almost like a visit home to enter this church. I would enjoy being here for a regular service but I know that is impossible. May I ask you, Sir, to remember, in your prayers, all the men who are far from home? Will you ask God for His protection over them?"

Frank Sanborn, of Brunswick, Maine, walked up the center of the church, laid his hand on the altar for a brief moment, then turned and headed for the door at a brisk pace. Replacing his peaked cap, Frank Sanborn walked out the door, once again captain of the U. S. Navy gunboat Columbine.

"I see my men have requisitioned a cow and chickens and helped themselves to the oranges on your trees. We will not enjoy the benefits of your famous spring. My visit to Magnolia has been rewarding to me personally but since we have found no evidence of your support of Mr. Dickison, we will leave. If any support is revealed, I will return to destroy any such facilities." said Ensign Sanborn as his men headed for the boat.

"Dadgum it." said Thad. "That cow was hardly worth taking. One of J. J.'s men drove it over here, tied it up back of my barn for us for slaughter to feed our families and that bunch took it away! They didn't take all our chickens and the oranges will grow again, but I wish I could've stopped 'em, somehow. Darn right we support J. J. but that bunch won't get any thing from me!"

Caleb and Thad walked out to the dock, watching black smoke belch from the stack as the <u>Columbine</u> headed downriver toward Jacksonville. "I think we made it easy for them to come to Magnolia," said Caleb. "Maybe we should burn our dock so those Yankee boats can't get to the shore so easy. After we run the Yankees out of Florida, we can build it again!"

Traces of black smoke from the gunboat lingered on the horizon as the first clouds of white smoke from the Magnolia dock rose into the sky.

Chapter 8
St. Johns River, 1863

The small fleet of U. S. Navy gunboats, <u>Columbine</u>, <u>Ottawa</u>, <u>Uncas</u> and <u>Norwich</u>, effectively stopped all traffic on the river. Gunboat crews destroyed all boats that were found while also searching for Union sympathizers and any larger Confederate boats attempting to move up or down the river. Shallow draft boats headed for cover up small rivers and creeks, with boat owners occasionally placing log booms at the entry from the St. Johns to discourage gunboats. Claiming that this destruction kept Confederate raiders from crossing the river, Yankee sailors managed to anger residents, Union and Confederates alike, on both sides of the river, denying them easy access, by small boats, to an abundant food supply of a variety of fish and water fowl.

South of Magnolia, on the east bank, the village of Picolata developed as a result of an old Indian trail, loosely called a road that connected the port city of St. Augustine with the St. Johns. George Bollinger and Chester Dorsey, two old friends of J. J. Dickison and occasional visitors to Caleb's store, had decided to stay on their land, near Picolata, trying to protect their farms and small groves as best they could. Too old to be conscripted into military service, Chester and George love to fish and shared a leaky old rowboat. One day before the Yankees were searching for small boats, the two men made a surprise contact with one of J. J.'s circuit riders near a favorite bass fishing spot on the west bank. News was exchanged and a plan established to meet again regularly.

Two days later, George and Chester reported to Harry Byrd, Corporal, Company H circuit rider, that a shipment of supplies from Palatka had arrived by a Yankee steamboat. Corporal Byrd told the two men he would report the information to Captain Dickison. When he learned that George had overheard soldiers describing the contents of wooden boxes as Spencer repeating rifles with ammunition and gunpowder, he put spurs to his skinny horse.

Company H had made raids across the St. Johns attacking Yankee detachments in brief encounters. Taking horses back and forth across the river by raft was difficult at best. In the woods, fighting from horseback was not effective. On making contact with Yankee soldiers, J. J.'s men would dismount, leave their horses tended by two or three men and proceed on foot according to a plan of attack. So J. J. continued to send his men dismounted as raids were made on the east bank. When J. J. received the report from Corporal Byrd, he was tempted to ferry enough horses across the river and strike Picolata. As he and his staff made their plans, the idea of moving a sufficient number of horses for that size attack was abandoned.

"Charlie," he told his son, "take three men and head for Six Mile Creek by boat. We have seen some regularity in the movements of those gunboats and I think if you leave at sunset and ease on down the ten miles, you'll be okay. If you can, tow another boat so we can bring home some of those rifles. Hide during the day and at dark, light a lantern for ten minutes every hour. I'm gonna start our boats on their way at sunset and I want them to be able to find that creek. Pop your whip when you see us coming. After we hide the boats, we'll wait till morning to start south for the road."

Lt. Harvey Stringfellow, U. S. Army, charged with the delivery of the weapons to St. Augustine, believed in the standard army procedures taught at West Point. A single scout on horseback was sent out one hundred yards ahead of Lt. Stringfellow, well mounted, leading an advance guard of six cavalry troopers also on horseback. On each flank, Stringfellow set a single trooper, seventy-five yards out.

Three wagons pulled by Army mules followed the advance guard. Eight infantry men on foot, in a column of twos, brought up the rear. Twenty yards behind rode a single trooper. The "road" through pine woods and palmetto-spiked underbrush did not make the wagon train move very easily. An hour after leaving Picolata, the company was spread over a mile and steadily growing further apart. After two more hours, Lt. Stringfellow called a halt to rest the horses and men. Scouts from ahead and on the flanks reported the usual difficulty in moving through heavy woods and reported hearing occasional "pops", not as loud as gunfire but like a sharp crack. Two hours later, after hearing the noises himself, Lt. Stringfellow signaled another halt. Riders sent out to find the flankers found no trace of the outriders. Stringfellow decided to double the riders on the front and flanks, reducing his force by eliminating the advance guard. With increasing apprehension, infantrymen were brought up to walk alongside each wagon, rifles held across their chests, ready to fire.

Rounding a curve a short while later, the train was stopped by a large pine log dropped across the road. Soldiers were ordered into defensive positions around the wagons; Lt. Stringfellow dismounted and stood in the bed of the lead wagon, pistol in hand. Pops on all sides led to gunfire by the Union soldiers. Rebel gunfire followed and the fight was over in a few minutes with two dead and six wounded Yankees and one dead and two wounded Rebels. Lt. Stringfellow and his men were astonished to see men step out from bushes close to the wagons, some materializing, it appeared, from thickets of palmettos and others dropping out of gum and oak trees.

Lt. Stringfellow offered his saber formally to Captain Dickison who accepted the sword and then drove it deeply in the sand. "When help arrives, you may have your sword back, Lieutenant. You may tell your superiors that Company H, Second Florida Cavalry will visit you again."

Four men mounted four captured horses, tied two

additional bridles to their saddles and headed south to a predetermined rendezvous on the river where men and animals would be ferried across. All wounded were treated as best they could, offered water and placed under a large oak tree. Other prisoners were gagged and then bound tightly to each other and to the tree. One wagon was emptied to hold the two wounded troopers and the body of Private Robert Waterston of Ocala. The remaining two wagons were loaded with the cases of Spencer rifles, ammunition, gunpowder plus all of the captured weapons. J. J. Dickison saluted Lt. Stringfellow and led his men toward the river.

Arriving at Six Mile Creek, the mules were turned loose and the three wagons destroyed. The loading of the boats with two wounded, the body of Private Waterston and the valuable cases of rifles, was carefully completed. Two round trips in the dark were required to return to the west bank; traces of black smoke appeared on the horizon downriver as the sun crept over the east bank trees.

HEADQUARTERS
NEAR MAGNOLIA, FLORIDA
April 20, 1863

Captain W. G. Barth, Assistant Adjutant-General
Camp Milton, Lake City, Florida

CAPTAIN: After crossing at night to the east bank of the river, I have successfully captured 200 Spencer repeating rifles with ammunition and a large quantity of gunpowder. Six good horses were brought to my headquarters by another route. One brave private trooper was lost and two wounded. Every man displayed remarkable coolness and bravery. As you request, save for the replenishment of equipment under my command, all captured property will be turned in to the chief of ordinance.

Picolata remains occupied by Union forces; gunboats <u>Columbine</u> and <u>Ottawa</u> continue to patrol on the river and have begun to respond with gunfire to any perceived movements on the western shore.

I am, Captain, yours respectfully

J. J. Dickison, Commanding

HEADQUARTERS
MILITARY DISTRICT OF FLORIDA
Lake City, Florida
May 1, 1863

Captain J. J. Dickison, Commanding

CAPTAIN: Your dispatches of the 20th instant received and the major general commanding tenders you his sincere thanks for the handsome captures you have made. Continue in your good work. He cannot commend too highly the gallant conduct of yourself and the brave men under your command.

He directs me to notify you, that under separate orders, Lieutenant Mortimer Bates, with one section of artillery, one twelve-pound howitzer and one Napoleon gun with twenty-five men, has been ordered to your headquarters for your use as you determine.

Very respectfully, your obedient servant,

H. Goldthrate
Major and Assistant Adjutant-General

Chapter 9
St. Johns River, 1864

U. S. STEAMSHIP <u>PAWNEE</u>
Mayport, Florida
May 2, 1864

TO: ENSIGN FRANK W. SANBORN, U. S. Navy
Steamer <u>Columbine</u>, St. Johns River

SIR: A report of the capture of two hundred
Spencer rifles near Picolata, by a detachment of
cavalry, led by the rebel leader, J. J. Dickison, has
been received by this command. You are directed to
proceed up the river for the express purpose of
locating and removing any evidence of support for
Confederate forces with a particular effort toward J.
J. Dickison and his company. A similar order, under
separate cover, is being sent to U. S. Navy Steamer
<u>Ottawa</u>, Lt. C. R. Rogers, Commanding.

Very respectfully,

George Balch, Captain, U. S. Navy

Ensign Sanborn was not surprised to see the dock burned
down to the water as <u>Columbine</u> approached Magnolia. From
his pilot house, he could see no activity on shore. Up and
down the river, he had noticed, and reported to headquarters,
that most individuals living along the river had abandoned
their homesteads, destroyed their docks, and the citizens of
Magnolia had done the same.

Gun captains from his two cannons were directed by Ensign Sanborn to open fire on the buildings of Magnolia that could be seen from the Columbine. "However," he said firmly, "I want that small building on the south side of town to be spared. I cannot fire on a church! Particularly that one", he murmured to himself.

When the smoke from the guns cleared after numerous rounds, Magnolia was in ruins; Caleb's store, the tavern and hotel were gone, but the church, as Ensign Sanborn noted, still stood.

To challenge the gunboats, Confederate artillery batteries would be moved to the river to fire on Yankee gunboats as they moved, with apparent ease, up and down the river. Navy captains realized that any occasion to stop their vessel was best accomplished by anchoring in the middle of the river. At places where the river narrowed, rebel snipers fired at gunboat pilot houses and gun crews; both efforts meeting only marginal success. Determined to continue any type of attack, hoping for a more positive result, Confederates began to place mines [referred to as torpedoes, by both sides] in the river floating just below the surface of the water with a suspended weight to keep the explosive device upright. Some mines were made in Confederate arsenals, others were home made. Seventy pounds of gunpowder were placed in a round wooden container, not unlike a beer keg, and bound with iron straps. Most were two feet long, eighteen inches in diameter. At each end, wood cones made of pine were attached for buoyancy and coated with tar. The gunpowder was ignited by a percussion cap exploded by a spring actuated hammer. Some mines contained gunpowder carefully mixed with mercury and acids that would explode on contact.

Near Mandarin Point, approximately fifteen miles north of Magnolia on the east side of the river, Captain E. P. Bryan, on detached duty from General P. T. Beauregard's staff in Charleston, placed twelve mines, manufactured in the Charleston arsenal, in the river. Early in the morning of April

1, 1864, <u>Maple Leaf</u>, a side wheel paddle steamer, struck a mine off the point at Mandarin. Operating as an army transport with twenty-two crewmen and thirty-four passengers, including four Confederate prisoners aboard, <u>Maple Leaf</u> was en route from Palatka to Jacksonville with the camp equipment and baggage of three Army regiments. Four crewmen were killed in the explosion, fifty-eight passengers and crew were loaded into lifeboats and headed for Jacksonville. The four Confederate prisoners were refused space in the lifeboats and were left on board and swam for freedom to the shore. At dawn, Confederate artillery fired on the remains of the <u>Maple Leaf</u> and a detail, led by Captain Bryan, boarded the sunken vessel, set fire and watched her burn to the water line. Nothing was saved.

Three other steamer troop transports were sunk by these "infernal machines of devilish ingenuity" as described by reporters of the day. Only a few days after <u>Maple Leaf</u>, <u>General Hunter</u> struck a mine near Mandarin Point, killing a single crewman as no troops were on board; <u>Harriet A. Weed</u> and <u>Alice Price</u>, armed transports, struck mines further down the river with a total loss of five crewmen with passengers suffering burns, concussions and broken bones.

The <u>New York Times</u> urged abandonment of naval operations on the St. Johns.

Chapter 10
St. Johns River, 1864

On Columbine, tied to the rickety dock at Picolata for the night, Ensign Frank Sanborn sat in his small cabin thinking about home and the church he had seen in Magnolia. The Richard Upjohn design, here on the St. Johns, was almost too much of a coincidence. His father, in Brunswick, Maine, would be as surprised, he imagined. As his thoughts returned to the war and Columbine, Sanborn smiled to himself with pride, as captain of a gunboat of the U. S. Navy. A loud knock startled Sanborn, bringing him back to 1864, as he opened his cabin door.

"Delivered by courier just now, Sir," offered a sailor as he handed Sanborn an envelope.

Once again, Columbine was ordered to join Ottawa in protecting two troop transports as soldiers were landed on the east bank of the river, across from Palatka. Ottawa and Columbine would then proceed up the river to Volusia, delivering dispatches to a small detachment.

As Columbine moved away from the dock, Sanborn worried about the latest weapon of the Rebels. From his pilot house he noted mine sweepers his crew had rigged. If a mine was snagged and brought to the surface, gunfire from a sharpshooter could explode the "infernal machine".

Not too far from the river, in his camp, Dickison sat in his tent listening to the soft rain on the canvas. Although he realized the Yankees were in control of the St. Johns, the mines must have resulted in a slower and more careful movement of the gunboats. Caleb had brought word of the bombardment of Magnolia as the survivors moved into J. J.'s camp.

"For some reason, the <u>Columbine</u> spared St. Dunstan's," reported Caleb. "Everything else is gone."

J. J. instructed his riders to be on the lookout for all boats but to be very aware of his particular interest in <u>Columbine</u>.

From a cypress tree in a swamp near Palatka, Private Seth Barnes watched as the troopships unloaded on the east bank and then, with <u>Ottawa</u> and <u>Columbine,</u> moved south. Jumping to the ground, Barnes untied his horse and headed for camp. On hearing the report of his scout, J. J. directed Lt. Bates to move his artillery battery to Brown's Landing, south of Palatka, in hopes of intercepting the two gunboats in a narrow section of the river.

"I'm going ahead with twenty men. It's getting towards sunset. Can you move your wagons and guns and get all set up ready to fire?"

"Yessir," replied Bates. "The gun carriages, the caissons and the ammunition wagons are loaded; my men are hitching up the two six-horse teams and we are on the way!"

As he approached the dock at Brown's Landing, J. J. heard the familiar slapping of the paddlewheels as a boat drew near. Hiding behind heavy bushes, J. J. popped his whip as a signal to hold all rifle fire and to stay hidden, as he watched the gunboat go by.

On <u>Columbine</u>, Ensign Sanborn was uneasy in the approaching darkness. <u>Ottawa</u> was behind him, but in the narrowing river, the gunboat had to move at the speed of the transport. Standing in his pilot house with his crew at full readiness, Sanborn thought he saw movement in the shadows on the west bank.

"I don't see anything certain," he told his First Mate, "but I heard again those strange popping sounds."

<u>Columbine</u> eased around a headland and was lost from sight as Bates arrived and began a standard routine of setting up his guns for a field of fire. <u>Ottawa</u> appeared from the north with a transport nearby. As J. J. and Bates watched with growing disbelief, both steamboats dropped their anchors

and lit their lanterns for the night. J. J. directed his artillery to
open fire and with a loud and practically simultaneous bang,
the two cannons opened fire on the well-lit boats. The
troopship raised her anchor with astonishing speed and
headed back to Palatka. Ottawa received several damaging
hits before her guns could return the fire toward the west
bank. J. J. and Lt. Bates noted the aiming difficulties in the
dark as Ottawa's guns could only fire at the flashes of the
Rebel guns. After watching Ottawa take a few more well-
placed hits, J. J. directed Lt. Bates to cease fire and, at first
light, to move his battery to Horse Landing, about six miles
to the north. The next morning, J. J. directed a squad of
sharpshooters to maintain rifle fire at selected targets on
Ottawa as he followed the artillery with his main force to
Horse Landing.

As dawn broke in Volusia, Sanborn had his sailors and
infantrymen assigned to Columbine at action stations. Crews
at the two cannons, one forward and a second at the stern,
were cautioned to be ready. Rebel fire was certain, he felt, at
Brown's Landing and again at Horse Landing. Passing
Ottawa, anchored near the east bank, Sanborn noted repairs
were underway and the wounded were under care on the
better-equipped gunboat. J. J. had his men well-hidden in the
trees and underbrush on either side of the clearing called
Horse Landing. Lt. Bates had placed his guns so that the
twelve-pounder could fire as soon as Columbine came into
view. The second gun was ready to fire as the gunboat came
past the landing.

Columbine came around the bend in the still waters of
afternoon. J. J. held his order until the gunboat was barely
fifty yards away and then opened fire; two cannons,
sharpshooters and all troopers. Lt. Bates' second shot hit the
rudder control chain turning the Columbine onto a mud
bank. A third round pierced a major steam pipe sending
steam to cover the decks. The bow cannon crew was wiped
out by sharpshooters followed soon after by the loss of the

stern cannon. At this loss, most of the remaining infantrymen jumped overboard and swam to the eastern shore. Columbine's engineer reported loss of steam and Ensign Sanborn slowly realized that surrender was inevitable.

Sanborn's official report concludes:

"...I called a council of my remaining officers, in which it was decided to surrender. I was spared the mortification of hauling down the flag, it having been shot away in the early part of the action."

In less than an hour, Columbine was reduced to a smoking, battered hulk and Ensign Frank Sanborn, U. S. Navy, Commanding Columbine, hoisted a white flag.

Two boats pulled away from shore with Captain Dickison and Lt. Bates aboard. Both officers were pleased that the element of surprise had resulted in not a single casualty on the Confederate's side of the brief encounter. As he stepped onto the wreckage of Columbine, J. J. directed two men to check all small boats aboard and to take the least damaged back to Horse Landing. He also directed a second detail to make necessary preparations for burning what was left of Columbine. The damage appeared to be extensive but Ottawa was on the river nearby and could attempt a recapture.

"I am honored to meet you, Sir", said Ensign Sanborn as he offered his sword to Captain Dickison. "I ask you to help the wounded from my boat, if you can, and bury the dead with the honor they deserve as courageous and brave sailors. Your exploits are well-known. I have been diligent in my search for your band of guerilas."

J. J. Dickison accepted Ensign Sanborn's sword. "I am familiar with your activities on the St. Johns. At sunset last night, I watched, with great anger, as you passed Brown's Landing, hoping to greet your passage with gunfire but waiting until a more favorable opportunity. My orders were to strike the enemy when I had the advantage and I certainly did today. I know that you visited Magnolia. How and why you spared St. Dunstan's on your second visit is beyond my thinking, but I'm glad that you did. We will respect your wishes and care for your men. As you continue in this war, please remember that <u>Columbine</u> was not captured by a band of guerillas but by Company H, Second Florida Cavalry, Confederate States of America."

And so it remains in military history that on May 23, 1864, the United States Navy steamer gunboat <u>Columbine</u>, was captured and sunk by a troop of cavalry.

Chapter 11

Enduring hardships of constant movement and a steady search for food and weapons, J. J. Dickison's troop of cavalry continued their pattern of surprise attacks on Yankee forces throughout north central Florida and on both sides of the St. Johns. His repeated victories, often against a larger number of Union soldiers, led newspapers to create such nicknames as Gray Fox, War Eagle and Dixie in their glowing reports of his actions. The west bank of the river became known as Dixieland, by Yanks and Rebels, alike. As 1864 drew to a close, Dickison's victories were not matched by Confederate troops on battlefields in other states. More battles were lost than won. Food, horses, clothing, salt as a preservative, guns and ammunition became more difficult to find as the blockade of seaports proved increasingly effective. Morale was suffering as some Confederate soldiers deserted and headed home. Sherman marched through Georgia and turned north at Savannah into South Carolina. The Army of Tennessee was broken. Lee's forces were gradually surrounded north and west of Richmond by General Grant.

After interrupting the construction of St. Dunstan's, Bishop Rutledge faced difficult times in his missionary efforts in Florida. St. Mark's in Palatka closed soon after the war started with occupation of the town by Union soldiers and the subsequent departure of the rector. Trinity Church, in St. Augustine, served by Francis Rutledge twenty years previously, proved difficult to visit as the city surrendered to the North, followed by occupation. Elected Bishop while serving as Rector of St. John's in Tallahassee, the dual responsibilities began to affect his strength. Faced with the failing economy of the South as the war progressed, contact with his mission churches proved difficult. Travel by horse, wagon, on foot and occasionally by boat over long distances combined with poor food and constant fatigue led to failing health. One Sunday, Francis Rutledge was helped to the altar at St. John's. Bringing tears to the eyes of the congregation, he could barely be heard as he struggled to complete the worship service. Soon after, the first Bishop of Florida, Francis Rutledge, died, his last thoughts, surely, of concern for the future of the church.

The state of the Episcopal Church in Florida was in neglect, suffering from all the destructive impacts of war upon people and property. The Diocesan Council, recognizing the need to elect a new bishop as soon as possible, selected John Freeman Young, assistant rector of Trinity Church, New York. John Young chose to be consecrated in the Gothic beauty of Trinity, designed by his friend, Richard Upjohn. After a glorious service, John Freeman Young began his life as the second Bishop of Florida.

After a month of difficult travel, Bishop Young arrived in Jacksonville, hoping to make contact with local church leaders and friends he had previously known during his earlier days at St. John's church before the war. As he was beginning to settle in to his new ministry in his large diocese, a letter arrived from Richmond, Virginia.

March, 1865

The Right Reverend John Freeman Young

My Dear Sir:

The Reverend Charles Minnegerode of St. Paul's Episcopal Church, here in Richmond, gave me your name, upon my inquiry, as a person of great trust and integrity, a classmate at seminary in Alexandria and a loyal friend.

We have received word this day from General Lee that President Davis and his Cabinet are to leave Richmond ahead of advancing Union regiments, with surrender of the city soon to follow.

With great humility, I am asking you, a stranger, to serve as my friend and representative in Florida. I believe total surrender of General Lee will be forced in a matter of days and it is my order to remain here as long as necessary and then meet President Davis in Danville, Virginia. Our route of travel from there is not certain; delays are expected as we hope to ask for the assistance of friends and communities as we travel south. President Davis hopes to ultimately make contact with our valiant leaders in Alabama, Mississippi or Louisiana and re-establish the Confederate government. I am certain General Grant will organize a search for President Davis and the Cabinet, and I am asking for your discretion in this matter.

I ask, with great presumption that you travel to Gainesville, Florida to meet me, or perhaps President Davis himself, at the home of Congressman James Dawkins, to receive and hold for me certain items of luggage. I anticipate a rendezvous in forty-five days. With deep appreciation, I remain

Your obedient servant

John Cabell Breckinridge

Secretary of War
Confederate States of America

A few weeks later, at his camp, Captain Dickison received an order:

HEADQUARTERS
MILITARY DISTRICT OF FLORIDA
Lake City, Florida
April, 1865

Captain J. J. Dickison, Commanding

Sir: You are hereby ordered to proceed, with appropriate aides, to Gainesville, Florida and the home of James Dawkins, to meet with a general officer of special identification with our cause.

Place yourself under his direction to perform whatever tasks he may order.

H. Goldthrate

Major and Adjutant General

Chapter 12
1865

On the morning of April 2, during the eleven o'clock morning service at St. Paul's Episcopal Church in Richmond, a note was handed to President of the Confederate States of America, Jefferson Davis, from General Robert E. Lee, repeating with urgency his earlier recommendation that the government of the Confederacy leave Richmond as soon as possible. President Davis left the church immediately as the Reverend Charles Minnegerode attempted to continue the service before a very disturbed congregation.

That night two trains left Richmond bound for Danville, Virginia. One train carried President Davis, his cabinet, staff and important records of the Confederacy. On the second train, commanded by Captain William Parker and under guard of midshipmen of the Confederate Navy, was the treasury of the Confederacy and private funds of the banks of Richmond. Packed in bags, boxes, kegs and chests, the treasury consisted of double eagle twenty dollar gold pieces packed in rolls of $5,000, Mexican silver coins, silver bricks, gold ingots and nuggets, Confederate currency of rapidly declining value and English "Liverpool Acceptances", negotiable in England with a value of 18,000 pounds sterling. The value of the treasury was estimated to be over $500,000. The bank funds were kept separate and were valued at $200,000.

John Breckinridge, Secretary of War and General of the Confederate Army, was left in Richmond to supervise the evacuation of the city. As flour mills, ordinance and tobacco warehouses were destroyed by fire that soon spread to adjoining buildings, black smoke covered the city as order turned to chaos. Deciding to contact Lee and then join President Davis, Breckinridge left Richmond on April 3, accompanied by his staff, headed southwest on horseback.

In Danville, word was received that Union forces were approaching from the west, Davis and his cabinet realized that any attempt to reorganize the government was futile. A telegram from Breckinridge reported he had made contact with General Lee and that "straggling has been great and the situation is not favorable..."

Still under guard, Walter Philbrook, Chief Teller of the Treasury, opened his chests, redeeming an unknown amount of Confederate currency for silver. While the cabinet was still active, anxiously waiting for further word of the war, the chests were closed after three busy days and the treasure train, including the assets of the banks of Richmond, headed south toward Greensboro, North Carolina.

On April 10, President Davis received a message that General Lee had surrendered at Appomattox Court House, Virginia on April 5. Re-boarding their train, the cabinet and President Davis followed the treasure to Greensboro.

The officer responsible, Captain William Parker, decided Greensboro was not a favorable place to store the treasury so he moved on by train to Charlotte, North Carolina where the treasure and the assets of the Richmond banks were placed in the government mint, still under heavy guard. For the use of President Davis, two chests of gold coins were left behind in Greensboro.

General Breckinridge was ordered to Durham Station, North Carolina to participate in surrender negotiations between General Joseph Johnston of the Confederate Army and Union General W. T. Sherman. The generous terms of amnesty for all soldiers and welcoming the state governments back into the Union were rejected by the government in Washington as too liberal. Abraham Lincoln preferred the grant of amnesty to those who took an oath of loyalty to the Union; however, civilian leaders would need a presidential pardon to regain their political rights. Sadly, Lincoln was assassinated on April 12 and his successor, Vice-President Andrew Johnson believed Confederate leaders were responsible for the death of Lincoln and branded Davis and his cabinet as criminals announcing a reward of $100,000 for their capture.

President Davis, uneasy over the earlier terms of surrender, decided to move further south to escape Union cavalry detachments reported in the area. A courier sent by Breckinridge informed the cabinet of the death of Lincoln. Travel by railroad was now impossible as bridges and tracks had been destroyed across Virginia and North Carolina. Wagons were loaded and the government headed for Charlotte.

Captain Parker, unable to find a responsible person to relieve him of his charge of the treasury, moving once again ahead of the cabinet, loaded his wagons, assembled the guard and headed for South Carolina. From Newberry, then Abbeville, Captain Parker crossed into Georgia, placing the Richmond bank funds in a bank in Washington. From there, the wagons with the balance of the treasury, moved to Augusta. Frustrated again with his unsuccessful search for responsible organizations, Captain Parker decided to leave Augusta and rejoin President Davis following the Savannah River northwest toward Abbeville, South Carolina.

Meanwhile in Charlotte, after reluctantly signing the Johnston/Sherman surrender documents, Davis met with his cabinet seeking assurances of their willingness to continue the struggle. Two members resigned. General Johnston, after being ordered by President Davis to move his forces toward Mississippi, decided instead to surrender all Confederate armies under his command. Disappointed, but facing reality, Davis made plans to move south. Gathering all Confederate soldiers under the command of General Breckinridge, the wagon train of the Confederate government, including the two chests of gold coins, headed south again towards Abbeville, South Carolina.

Captain Parker and his midshipmen had moved the

treasure for nearly a month. Reaching Abbeville, he placed the assets in a warehouse, quickly reloading his wagons when word was received of an approaching company of horsemen, assumed to be Union cavalrymen. Soon identified as an advance guard for the wagon train of President Davis, Parker was finally able to discharge his responsibility by turning the treasure over to John Reagan, Acting Secretary of the Treasury, and his assistant, Captain M. H. Clark. Before making his final report, Captain Parker paid and then disbanded the detachment of midshipmen from the Confederate Navy, faithful guardians of the treasure from Richmond, Virginia to Abbeville, South Carolina.

Now under the command of Generals Breckinridge and Duke, the treasure rode in two wagons with a rear guard of nearly 1,000 men. Still under Confederate command and with a promise of pay in Washington, Georgia, the troopers were tired of the war and wanted to go home. Some of these men wanted to surrender to nearby Union forces; others threatened to seize the treasure and take their pay rather than wait.

General Breckinridge, sensing a threat of mutiny and rebellion, stopped the wagons and confronted the troopers. Fearing a complete loss of discipline, he agreed to open the chests for payment. History records that over $100,000 was taken as pay; some narratives suggest much more as troopers grabbed at the contents of the chests and bags. With a small number of loyal cavalrymen remaining and an unknown amount of the treasure, Breckinridge rode to Washington and reported to President Davis.

As home for several Confederate generals and a supply depot in an area of large plantations, Washington, Georgia had felt little impact of the war. The citizens enthusiastically welcomed Davis; the local bank on the public square offered the use of a second story apartment, which Davis, nearing exhaustion, quickly accepted. The next morning, before meeting with his staff and cabinet members, the President received General John Breckinridge.

"General, it distresses me greatly to see you so fatigued from the difficulties of our travels" said President Davis. "Your service as Secretary of War in my cabinet and as a general officer in our army has been exemplary and I offer you my deep appreciation. I am meeting with the cabinet in a while and, although I will not agree with their combined judgment that I anticipate will be rendered, I cannot dissolve the government. I am certain the enemy cannot be far away and the size of my escort makes our whereabouts easily determined. I intend to make my way south with a smaller escort and less baggage hoping to cross the Mississippi and make contact with General Kirby Smith. I have received word my family was recently through here. My heart would be pleased if I can catch up with my wife and children and their wagons."

"Sir," replied Breckinridge, "it has been my honor to serve you and our cause. Some of my men are anxious to continue their service to you, knowing it will be as volunteers. I intend, as your Secretary of War, to honorably discharge all my troopers and release them to go home, on their horses as permitted by the final agreement of General Lee."

"I understand that you, the cabinet officers and I have been the object of an intensive search by Union commanders. Rumors of the amount of our wealth in the treasury have been passed to me; no doubt creating a group of undesirable southerners after the money," said Davis.

"Sir, just east of Washington, faced with unrest of the soldiers and a gradual disorganization of my command, I approved the payment in silver to the troopers. The gold remains intact and under guard here in Washington," said Breckinridge.

After a full accounting by Captain M. H. Clark, recently appointed as Acting Treasurer, President Davis said, "After a disbursement to you and John Reagan for your expenses in moving south and another for each of the officers of my escort, it is vital that a significant amount should be forwarded to Nassau in the Bahamas for the account of the Confederate government. If that proves impossible, it is my direction that you hold the assets for safekeeping until you receive word from me or General Lee. Is that clear?"

"Mr. President, I understand and will follow your orders. I will disperse those men remaining under my command, encouraging them to leave Washington by a variety of routes to confuse our pursuers. I plan then, with the wagons, my two sons and their cousin, General Duke, Colonel Wilson, Tom, my servant, and a few others as guards, to head toward Florida and the Gulf. I have arranged for two gentlemen to meet me in Gainesville, Florida. Captain J. J. Dickison of the 2nd Florida Cavalry who will provide guidance and direction for future routes and the Right Reverend John Young, recently elected Bishop of Florida, recommended to me by the Reverend Charles Minnegerode in Richmond."

"General, I wish you Godspeed," said Davis.

Straightening his tired back, General Breckinridge stood erect, rendered a crisp hand salute and whispered with a heavy heart, "Thank you, sir", turned and left the room.

Chapter 13
May 1865

In Gainesville, Florida, James Dawkins was nervous. General John Breckinridge had arrived last night with six men on horseback and a single wagon. After forty days in the saddle, on constant alert for Union cavalry patrols and sleeping on the ground, Breckinridge gratefully accepted the hospitality of James Dawkins. Pleased to welcome such a distinguished visitor, Dawkins attempted, with little success, to conceal his concerns. He knew of enemy scouts in the area and was somewhat relieved with the arrival of J. J. Dickison and a detachment of his men. The sharp crack of whips was heard as the Confederate riders began a watchful circuit of Dawkins' farm.

Located on the outskirts of the village of Gainesville, Dawkins' two-story wood-frame house with a ramshackle barn nearby, shaded with oak and pine trees, seemed hardly the place for such an important gathering. General Breckinridge was delighted to hear that Bishop John Young was in the area visiting church families and asked that word be sent asking for his attendance.

Dawkins had his kitchen busy early in the morning preparing bacon, biscuits, grits and coffee for his guests. His curiosity increased, later in the morning with the arrival of Bishop Young.

"What in the world is happening at my house?" Dawkins muttered to himself as the clergyman stepped down from his horse, appearing to be a dusty cowhunter rather than a priest and bishop of the church.

"You are welcome, sir, to my home", said Dawkins. "General Breckinridge is here and was pleased to know of your whereabouts. He is in the parlor with his staff. I am told to also expect Captain J. J. Dickison, who has been camped nearby."

"I have no idea of the reason for my attendance, Mr. Dawkins", said Bishop Young. "To hear of J. J. Dickison and his many successful encounters with those who attempted to occupy our land is one thing, but to hear that he is expected here today is a mystery to me also."

In the parlor, General Breckinridge rose to meet Bishop Young. A welcoming smile betrayed his fatigue as he shook the Bishop's hand and introduced his staff.

"As I said in my letter last March, I assumed a great deal asking you to meet me here. Back in Richmond, in what seems as a distant past, the Reverend Minnegerode spoke highly of you. Today, Mr. Dawkins tells me of your continuing efforts to reach out to all Episcopal churches and isolated families in your Diocese. I hope you will understand shortly my need of a person of great trust and integrity. Perhaps the sound of horses I hear outside brings Captain Dickison and your questions will be answered."

James Dawkins watched from his porch as four riders turned off the narrow tree-lined road and pulled up to his house. A single man dismounted and tied the reins to a rail, then turned to the three other men, who remained on horseback.

"McCardell," he said. "Check on our circuit riders. Be sure they are aware that enemy patrols have been seen and they are to remain alert. If contact is made, have them pass the word to you by the usual signals and let me know immediately!"

McCardell said, "Captain, may I ask the reason for your concern? You told us that fighting is to stop in a few days!"

Dickison replied, "Lieutenant, I have indeed, received word that the war will soon be over and I am to parole each of you. However, I am meeting now, a general officer of our army who is being pursued by Yankee cavalry who have been told he is a criminal. Our job today is to protect this man and his staff as I receive detailed instructions." Removing his gloves and a wide brim shapeless hat, Dickison slapped his leg to remove some of the dust, turned and stepped up on the porch.

"Welcome, Captain Dickison. I am glad to see you again," said Dawkins. "The General and others are in my parlor. Please go in."

Four men, seated in the small parlor, stood as Captain Dickison entered the room. As a cavalry officer of company grade, J. J. was aware of the rank of two of these men in their service to the Confederacy. A large man with deep-set eyes, dressed in a dusty hunting jacket stepped forward, extending his hand in greeting.

"Captain, I am pleased to see you. My name is John Breckinridge. May I present Colonel James Wilson, my aide who has been with me since we left Richmond and Captain John Wood who met us in Madison, Florida, bringing news of the unfortunate capture of President Davis and his family in Irwinville, Georgia, ninety miles north of the Florida border."

A fourth man extended his hand in greeting. "Captain, I have followed your military career with great interest. My name is John Young and I am unsure of my place in this distinguished group of soldiers."

In answer to a knock on the door, a servant entered the parlor with a large enameled pot of coffee. Cups in hand and seated around the room, four men looked toward General Breckinridge.

"Gentlemen, the capture of President Davis increases the importance of our meeting today. I left the President in Washington, Georgia on May 3. We decided to take different routes to head south to Florida and then either west to Mississippi or to Cuba, hoping to reach General Kirby Smith. With my two sons, my cousin W. C. Breckinridge, General Basil Duke, Colonel Wilson, James Clay, my servant Tom

Ferguson and two cavalry troopers, we carefully worked our way through South Carolina and Georgia. While we were en route, General Duke and my cousin, James Clay, left to surrender to Federal troops and I sent my sons home to Kentucky. After a stop in Madison, Florida, where we met Captain Wood, we arrived here last night. My wagon with two guards and Tom Ferguson is in Mr. Dawkin's barn. In that wagon is what remains of the financial assets of the Confederate States of America. It is hidden in a pine coffin that I purchased from the undertaker in Washington, Georgia. I hope that any who looked into the wagon would believe we were returning the body of a valiant soldier to his home. From Richmond and through North Carolina, South Carolina and Georgia, money from that treasury has been disbursed toward expenses of travel and as directed by President Davis. I estimate that value of what is left is $100,000 in gold and silver coins, ingots and bars as well as some financial notes that are negotiable in England. In Washington, President Davis directed that a significant amount be forwarded to Nassau in the Bahamas. If that proves impossible, he directed that the funds be held in safekeeping until he or General Robert E. Lee further direct."

Breckinridge paused, looked at John Young and J. J. Dickison and continued. "I have asked Captain Dickison here to guide me to the west coast of Florida where I can find passage or a boat to Cuba or Mississippi. Bishop Young is here to offer, I hope, his trust and integrity to safeguard the treasury."

John Young stared in astonishment at the General.

J. J. spoke up. "Sir, I have received reliable reports that a considerable number of Union soldiers are looking for President Davis and his cabinet. All ports along the Gulf coast are held by the Yankees with patrols on all rivers. I think the east coast would be a better route for you; over to the St. Johns, then south by boat to the Indian River, then to the Atlantic and Cuba."

After considerable discussion, General Breckinridge began to see the logic of this alternate route.

"General," continued J. J., "I have a boat that may serve your purpose. Months ago, I believe divine providence directed me to save this particular lifeboat from the capture of the Yankee gunboat <u>Columbine</u>. It is about twenty feet long with four oars and a place in the bow to receive a mast and sail."

Breckinridge smiled. "Captain, your marvelous accomplishment in the capture of the <u>Columbine</u> was reported to the Cabinet in Richmond and featured in many newspapers. I am pleased that such a boat may be available but how would Colonel Wilson, Captain Wood, Tom and I handle an unfamiliar craft on a river that we have only heard about?"

J. J. thought of his loyal company of troopers waiting in Waldo to receive their parole from military service. "I believe some in my command are more than capable and would respond to my call for volunteers to help you travel south. If you approve I will send Lieutenant McCardell from my staff on to the river to secure the boat from its hiding place and prepare it for your party."

Nodding his head in agreement, General Breckinridge sent Captain Wood to Dawkin's barn to have the horses saddled and wagon hitched, ready for another journey. Under the authority of the General, the two troopers were given their back pay and discharged from their loyal service to the Confederacy. After a handshake and final salute to the general, the two men mounted their horses and headed home.

John Breckinridge turned to James Dawkins. "Mr. Dawkins, once again may I say your loyalty and hospitality are deeply appreciated. I believe the further we travel into central Florida the safer we will be. However, any misdirections you can give our pursuers would be most helpful."

Mounting their horses, the five men; Breckinridge, Colonel Wilson, Captain Wood, J. J. Dickison and Bishop

John Young, with Tom Ferguson at the reins of the horse-drawn wagon, headed east toward the river. Following the lead of Dickison the small group followed a trail of two parallel ruts, barely classified as a road, through pine woods, taking pleasure from the shade of occasional large oak trees. Ever so lightly applying spurs to his horse John Young moved alongside John Breckinridge.

"General, I must confess your letter to me aroused my curiosity and I arranged my travels to be near Gainesville, as you requested. To be asked to safeguard the treasure, as you call it, is beyond my desire or ability. I cannot assume such a responsibility."

John Breckinridge turned in his saddle and said, "Bishop Young, I appreciate your reluctance. I ask you, as a man of courage and strong beliefs, to consider my request. I cannot take these funds with me on a difficult journey towards a yet unknown destination. The war has ended. President Jefferson Davis has been captured. The Confederate States of America are no longer in existence east of the Mississippi, and I fear, not long in the west with only a single army remaining in the field. The loyal men of our army and navy have fought with honor but are anxious to return home. Captain William Parker guarded the treasure from Richmond, through North Carolina, South Carolina and Georgia searching for a qualified official to take responsibility for the funds. He finally made contact with me and John Reagan, then Secretary of the Treasure. As I reported in James Dawkin's parlor, President Davis directed me to forward, what he termed to be, a significant amount to the Bahamas; if that proves impossible, as it now appears, I was instructed to hold the funds in safekeeping until further directed by General Robert E. Lee. It appears that many are after the treasure, Yanks and Rebels alike. I have been branded a criminal by those in Washington, D.C. History will tell our story, written by the victorious. This morning, all that remains is our individual memories, a prayer for our families, the support of each other as we ride and what is in that wagon.

"I need you and Captain Dickison to find a place to hold the remaining assets of the Confederacy and protect them until you are contacted by General Lee or Jefferson Davis. I will take five hundred dollars in coins and the Liverpool Acceptances to help me, with Colonel Wilson, Captain Wood, Tom Ferguson and any volunteers provided by Captain Dickison, as we travel south."

John Young sat back in his saddle as he heard these words from Breckinridge. Looking back toward Captain Dickison, he said, "Have you heard the request of General Breckinridge? Are you willing to accept this responsibility?"

Dickison replied, "Sir, I am under orders to perform whatever the General requests. As he said, the war is over. This afternoon we will stop at my camp near the village of Waldo where I am directed to offer my company of cavalry an opportunity to give their parole; a pledge of honor that they will fight no more. I cannot so quickly cease my service to a cause that I believe still exists. So, yes, I will accept the orders of General Breckinridge. With your help, we can together decide how to protect the money."

Deep in thought and with a prayer for guidance forming in his mind, John Young lowered his chin to his chest and let his horse follow the others.

The sound of horses crashing through the heavy underbrush startled Young. Pulling on his reins, he watched as five men, armed with Spencer repeating rifles, forced the small caravan to a halt. Baggy clothing and soft wide brim hats suggested southerners but saddles, bridles and weapons appeared to be Union cavalry in origin. One of the five, a heavy-set man with a long beard, looked over the captives and ordered them to dismount. Pistols were removed from the holsters of Breckinridge, Wilson, Wood and Dickison; Tom Ferguson was pulled from the wagon.

Dickison looked surprised and angered. "Where are my circuit riders? We are approaching Waldo and my men should still be circling the camp perimeter. How did these riders slip through?" he wondered.

One by one, each man was searched. John Young lost a tug of war with one rider who pulled the cross and thin gold chain from around Young's neck. Hands were tied and the six men pushed into a line.

"I don't see any uniforms or insignia", said the heavy-set man, "but I think we hit the jackpot, boys! Up in Georgia, they got Jeff Davis and I believe we got the rest! Bound to be a reward for these fellows!"

Two men jumped on the wagon and started throwing off bedrolls and bags. Uncovering the coffin, they paused and turned to long beard. "Looka here, Eugene, they're carrying a coffin."

John Young spoke up. "We're taking a young soldier home. He's come a long way from Virginia and I aim to bury him by the river he loved."

John Breckinridge watched the men hoping his face showed concern for the fictitious soldier, rather than a strong apprehension for the real contents of the pine box.

"Leave it be", said Eugene. "We can dump it in a swamp when we head north with these criminals." Dickison and John Young exchanged glances, knowing their responsibilities, accepted by one and undecided by the other, could not end in a swamp.

One of the riders walked over to Dickison's saddle and untied the rawhide loop holding the whip. "Looks like a leather rope with a fancy handle", he said, uncoiling the whip. Pleased with the diversion away from the coffin, J. J. said, "You use it to herd cows. I'm surprised you don't recognize it as a whip. The noise from the pop startles the cow and gets him moving."

Eugene, long beard, grabbed the whip. "It's just a toy, a fancy noisemaker! I'm gonna use it to herd you fellows into that wagon and we'll head north." Awkwardly swinging the whip, he produced a weak pop. "I got the hang of it now", he cried as he swung the whip again. A louder pop was followed by a substantial "crack." J. J. smiled as he heard, very faintly, a whip pop in the distance.

Pushing his captives toward the wagon, Eugene climbed up on the seat and turned to swing the whip again. A startled look appeared on his face as a large splotch of red spread on his chest, the result of a large caliber bullet. Falling to his knees, he looked at his captives as he tumbled to the ground.

Scrambling for their weapons, the four riders looked in vain for targets. Rifle shots from the underbrush on each side of the trail quickly brought an end to the captivity. J. J. grabbed his whip, expertly producing a very loud crack. Ten of his troopers stepped into the clearing.

"Whips talk to men better than cows," said the smiling J. J. "Specially if you know the language!"

Chapter 14
May 1865

East of Waldo, following his ten troopers, Captain Dickison, Breckinridge, Wilson, Wood, Ferguson and John Young headed directly into a thick grove of cypress trees, standing in shallow dark water. Shadows of the trees in the late afternoon sun quickly brought relief from the hot dusty trail from Waldo. An open hammock of dry land appeared ahead, with oak trees sheltering canvas tents, lean-to's and wood-framed huts, each with a smoking campfire preparing for supper.

"The Yankees have looked hard for us," said J. J. "This camp, hidden in the swamp, has served us well. My family and home are southeast of here and another ten miles will take you to the St. Johns. As you will see tomorrow, to get there takes a little wandering. My circuit riders are still around. You should hear their whips occasionally and, I'm sure, a few strange noises from animals during the night, but you should sleep well.

The next morning, under a gray sky and soft misting rain, Breckinridge and John Young watched from under the shelter of a canvas tent as Captain Dickison described the parole process to his assembled company. "By signing the parole form, you agree not to fight anymore against the government of the United States. You are authorized to take your weapon and horse and return to your home. The parole further states that you will not be disturbed by the United States government as long as you observe this obligation."

"We have not been defeated in battle," said one scrawny private. "We have been told the war is over. We have given our word to fight no more so we just shake each other's hand, take our rifle, saddle and horse and go home! I hope someone remembers what we did!

In response to a call for volunteers from the paroled company to guide the four officers of the former Confederacy to safety, J. J. selected three troopers, all skilled hunters and good fishermen. Sergeant O'Toole, Corporal Russell and Private Murphy were directed to lead Breckinridge, Wilson, Wood and Ferguson to the St. Johns and a rendezvous with Lieutenant McCardell and the boat.

"Sir, you may give these men your complete trust," said Captain Dickison. Riders have been sent on to the plantation of Colonel Samuel Owens, south and east of here, for a secure place for you to rest tonight before meeting Lieutenant McCardell the next day."

Breckinridge turned to face Bishop Young. "I ask you again to join with Captain Dickison and safeguard all that is in the wagon. I have no choice but to trust you and J. J. to protect the assets until you hear from General Lee. I do not know how long that will be or in what form; I ask you to please be patient. My destination is unknown, I hope for Mississippi, but I feel Cuba and England may offer me the best chance of seeing my family again." He offered his hand to the Bishop. John Young reluctantly extended his hand in acceptance and offered a silent prayer for guidance and for safe travel for the General and his party.

Handshakes and expressions of praise and gratitude were exchanged all around. General Breckinridge and his command, now numbering seven, mounted their horses and entered the dark waters of the swamp.

"Well, Bishop," said the Captain, "I knew the man before you, Francis Rutledge, fairly well. He started the building of my church, St. Dunstan's in Magnolia before the war, and stopped construction when the war began. I'm sorry he won't be here to see us start again.

"May I call you John? The J. J. in my name stands for John Jackson but J. J. seems to work."

"All right J. J." said John Young. "We have to decide where we should go! What do we do with the treasure, as they call it? Where can we put it so that you and I can go on with our lives, in what I feel will be difficult times, and yet trust each other to leave it undisturbed?"

J. J. said, "Perhaps St. Dunstan's is where we can find the answer."

The two men nodded to each other, tied their horses to the back of the wagon and climbed up on the wagon seat. J. J. took the reins and with a slight flick of his wrist, the Captain and the Bishop and the gold headed east toward the river.

Chapter 15
The Present

Closing his notebook, the Reverend Sam Wood looked up at Charley Gallagher. "Can you understand now why I'm interested in these river churches?"

"Not quite," replied Charlie. "That's a great story, but the only church you mentioned on the river was St. Dunstan's; the one I didn't know about. What about the other twelve? Where did you learn all those tales of J. J. Dickison and Breckinridge and John Young?"

Sam said, "Charlie, my church in Richmond was St. Paul's. One day, in an old file cabinet, I found what was called a letter book, where a hand copy of each outgoing letter was made and held just like we make file copies today. In that book, I found a letter that, in 1865, the Reverend Charles Minnegerode wrote to John Breckinridge, recommending John Young, recently elected Bishop of Florida, as a person worthy of trust. I didn't think a lot about it at the time. My interest in the Civil War followed the paths of Jefferson Davis, John Breckinridge and, of course, Robert E. Lee. Every now and then a report of an activity on the St. Johns River would appear in my readings."

Charlie smiled. He began to feel that his knowledge and affection for the river churches and the St. Johns River were no longer private.

"There seemed to be one fascinating story after another about Florida during the war and shortly after. When I read of the capture of Jefferson Davis in south Georgia and then about Breckinridge eluding his captors to sail down the river in a lifeboat taken from a gunboat of the U. S. Navy, I was hooked. What happened there? Who was J. J. Dickison?

When I was given an opportunity to move to the Diocese of Florida, I did not hesitate. Since I've been here, I have learned a lot. This morning at the church on Fort George Island was terrific, but when I found a copy of the letter Breckinridge wrote to John Young in March of 1865, I had to learn more about Breckinridge, J. J. Dickison, John Young and the treasure of the Confederacy."

"What happened to the gold?" asked Charlie.

"I don't know!" sighed Sam Wood.

"You don't know? How can you not know after all that research and study?" cried Charlie.

"History is not clear, Charlie. Accounts of the treasure vary. Exaggerations, suspicions and few facts confuse the true story. Even the funds of the Virginia Banks, after being placed in a bank vault in Washington, Georgia, have a bizarre fate. Bank officials appealed to a Federal officer who released the funds for return to Richmond. Confederate army veterans thought the money was part of the Confederate treasure, organized themselves and attacked the wagon train at the Chennault farm near the Savannah River. The wagons were looted. Coins and bags of gold disappeared into the night. A local Confederate general, Edward Alexander attempted to recover the stolen funds but was not completely successful. Tales of the success of suddenly wealthy individuals have been circulated but the bulk of the money simply vanished."

"Now what?" said Charlie.

"Perhaps if I tell you more about St. Dunstan's, Magnolia and the visit of Robert E. Lee, you might help me find the treasure!"

Chapter 16

After the bombardment of Magnolia by the <u>Columbine</u> in 1864, the town dock was burned. With only burned wood pilings showing above the water, any landing by Northern boats was discouraged. Concerned with the safety of their families, many citizens left town. His general store and home in ruins, Caleb Hopkins and Thad Washington, whose tavern was gone, packed their belongings and moved inland. Many farmers, cattlemen and citrus growers, like Thomas Hunter, moved away from the river.

Hoping for protection from the U. S. Navy, even without a dock, some residents stayed and began to rebuild. The Reverend Harold Alexander, first and only rector of St. Dunstan's, decided to offer spiritual help and regular church services in the partially completed church. Thomas Hendricks, Postmaster, left no doubt that he was going to reopen the shattered post office. Dr. Nathan Benedict remained in town, built a new small hotel and served as town doctor as well as spokesman for local Union sympathizers.

In the fall of 1864, detachments of Union army cavalry, artillery and infantry occupied the town, erecting defensive earthworks west of town. Nathan's hotel became headquarters and the town soon filled with Union soldiers. Word spread throughout the region and Union sympathizers, seeking protection, took an oath of loyalty to the Union and became residents of Magnolia. In support of the Union, farmers and cattlemen were delighted for the opportunity of selling meat and produce to the Federal troops. But, to the surprise of all and to the disappointment of those who had taken vouchers for their cattle and corn, the Union detachments left Magnolia after only four months. Some thought the departure was a result of the difficulties of resupply while most felt an unsuccessful engagement with J. J. Dickison's men hastened the decision to leave.

Their herds of cattle confiscated and slaughtered, farms depleted of all produce, Union sympathizers left Magnolia with only vouchers of doubtful value and headed for St. Augustine and Jacksonville.

In May of 1865, J. J. and John Young rode their wagon into town, bringing with them their saddles, packs and the pine coffin.

Looking toward the river, J. J. said, "Looks like the dock's been rebuilt. I don't see many people around. Somehow I expected to see more."

John Young said, "When I was first assigned to the Diocese, I visited here as a missionary. St. Dunstan's was only a dream of Bishop Rutledge. I remember delivering the letter from Bishop Rutledge to Richard Upjohn asking him to design St. Dunstan's. I've heard the incomplete church was spared from destruction by the Columbine. The name of Harold Alexander comes to mind. Do you know if he survived the war?"

"I think I hear him now," said J. J., turning the horse and wagon toward the sound of a loud hail.

The Reverend Harold Alexander ran to the wagon, grabbed J. J.'s hand, shaking it vigorously. "I'm glad the war's over and I'm certainly glad to see you, J. J. Your circuit riders have continued to watch over Magnolia. Even while the Yankees were here I could hear 'em popping their whips, and now that the fighting is over, we'll have to get used to them not protecting us."

John Young, Bishop of Florida, was introduced to Harold who dropped to his knee with a look of surprise on his face. "You are welcome, Sir," he said. "St. Dunstan's is not ready to receive you properly, but we will, soon I hope, complete our church and welcome you with appropriate ceremony."

Extending his hand, John Young stepped down from his

seat. "Harold, J. J. and I are here from Gainesville and Waldo by way of J. J.'s camp. I have been trying to make contact with all isolated Episcopalians in the Diocese and hope to return to Jacksonville soon by horse or boat, if there is one here. I look forward to a discussion about St. Dunstan's and your ministry here. But first, J. J. and I have brought a soldier home and we need to bury him soon, hopefully in your cemetery. I hope you will conduct the burial service for the valiant soldier tomorrow."

J. J. looked over to the Bishop, realizing that John Young had decided to bury the treasure. John saw J. J.'s glance and slightly nodded his head. Since leaving Waldo, the two men had talked at great length about their responsibility; as ordered by one and accepted reluctantly by the other. They felt the coffin and its contents should be buried and left alone as they awaited word from Robert E. Lee or Jefferson Davis. John told J. J. that to arrive in Magnolia and not bury the coffin, so obvious in the wagon, would raise too many questions. Harold Alexander could lead the burial service relieving John Young of the pain of conducting a sham funeral service.

The next morning, as the sun rose over the trees on the far bank of the river, the three men, J. J., John Young and Harold Alexander, stood over the grave. The service had been brief.

Slowly at first, and then with growing excitement, families returned to Magnolia seeking to reclaim and rebuild what was left of their property. Steamboats were seen again on the St. Johns; the Darlington was overhauled and resumed her pre-war runs. The Starlight, Dictator and the Hattie, side-wheelers between 160 to 200 feet long, carried freight and passengers to and from Jacksonville, Palatka and Enterprise with regular stops along the way. Tourists enjoyed the medicinal qualities of the springs at Magnolia and Green Cove. The hospital and orphanage in Magnolia, established soon after the war, closed and two doctors bought the property, renovated the building and opened the second Magnolia Hotel, with accommodations for 100 guests, in competition with hotels in Hibernia and Green Cove Springs. Investors saw the opportunity to invest in land and commercial activities; citrus growers, lumbermen, farmers and cattle ranchers returned to north Florida.

One afternoon, the Darlington arrived with guests for the hotel and a man very familiar in Magnolia. As the passengers and guests for the hotel climbed aboard a horse drawn wagon, Caleb Hopkins recognized Ed Foley, builder of St. Dunstan's.

"Ed, is that you? What in the world brings you back to Magnolia?" said Caleb. "Seems like a lifetime since you were last here."

Ed Foley shook the hand of Caleb and said, "Bishop Young found me in Jacksonville and asked me to figure the cost of finishing St. Dunstan's. He has sent missionaries up the river in answer to a growing need for churches and hoped a completed St. Dunstan's would serve as inspiration to other congregations. I thought I'd better see if there was any damage from the war and plan from there."

After the pleasure of seeing Caleb, Thad Washington and Harold Alexander again, Ed walked over to the church. "Looks better than I thought," he said. "Especially after I heard the Yankees shelled the town. I still have Mr. Upjohn's drawings and specifications, so there's no doubt about what to do.

"The foundation is O.K. and I'm sure the wall framing and roof trusses are in good shape. I might have to replace a shingle or two, but I don't see any sign of roof leaks. I blocked up the windows before I left and I see some of that has been removed, no doubt for ventilation. Bishop Young said he had funds available to complete the church and spoke of a gift of windows from a Mr. Frank Sanborn of Brunswick, Maine. I think I have a good carpenter who can build a proper altar, lectern and pews. That old table and the benches have got to go. I'll report to the Bishop and I'm sure I'll be back soon."

Harold Alexander heard the name of the man who gave the windows and looked to Caleb and Thad.

"Could that be...?" he asked, remembering the young man from Columbine who had visited the column and directed his gunfire away from St. Dunstan's.

"Well, I hope he can come back now that the war is over to see how much his gift has meant to all of us."

A few weeks later, Ed Foley returned to Magnolia, with the approval of Bishop Young, carrying the original drawings and specifications of Richard Upjohn. In addition to new windows, doors, paint and carefully selected pine, cypress and oak lumber, Ed brought a finish carpenter and talented woodworker, Will Hendry, who would build the new altar, pulpit, lectern and pews. Following the details on Upjohn's drawings, the men went to work. The window openings required new wood trim, inside and out, to receive the new plain glass with colored borders, hinged at one side for ventilation. The pine pews with a sloping back proved more comfortable than the plain benches.

One day, Will asked Harold Alexander about the altar details. "Mr. Upjohn described the altar carefully, but he didn't show how high it should be."

Harold smiled with the memory of an old professor and replied, "Three foot three, three foot four, never less, never more."

J. J. asked Will Hendry to add trim to the altar containing the design of a horseshoe, reflecting the heritage of St. Dunstan. With the input from Harold, a wide trim piece was added to the altar, carved by Will, with alternating symbols of a horseshoe, open end up, and the Greek letter omega.

Ω℧Ω℧Ω℧Ω℧Ω℧Ω℧Ω℧Ω℧Ω℧Ω℧

A few months later, Ed Foley had completed his work at St. Dunstan's. Bishop Young returned to the church and with proper ceremony knocked, with his pastoral staff, on the closed door. In answer, the Reverend Harold Alexander opened the door as John Young entered. Pausing, he marked the threshold with the sign of the cross. Upon completion of the service of dedication, the Bishop returned to the doorway to assist in the mounting of a horseshoe, open end up, above the door.

As the day drew to a close, J. J. and John Young finally had a private moment. "J. J., I know our shared responsibility remains in place. John Breckinridge asked us to wait for instructions from Jefferson Davis or Robert E. Lee. Reliable sources have told me that Jefferson Davis was released from prison at Fort Monroe, Virginia, went into exile in Canada and was recently granted amnesty. He has become a symbol of the south in hopes of a renewed conflict. We may hear from him but I personally doubt it as I don't believe he knows of our responsibility. I pray that we will soon hear from General Robert E. Lee."

Chapter 17
1870

Lexington, Virginia
April, 1870

Colonel Jaquelin J. Daniel

My Dear Sir:

Your name has been given to me as a leader in the restoration of Jacksonville from the ravages of war. I have reluctantly agreed to a visit to warmer climates in hopes of relieving angina pain. My route by rail will be from Virginia, through North and South Carolina and into Georgia. From Brunswick, on the coast, it is my hope to cross, by boat, to Cumberland Island and pay my respects to the grave of my father at Dungeness Plantation. I will board the steam vessel <u>Nick King</u> on returning to Brunswick and travel on to your city. From Jacksonville, I will go to Magnolia to visit an old friend. I am told the weather has been uncomfortably hot. If I find it so, I will not remain long.

It will be my pleasure to greet you and other leaders of Jacksonville in the salon of the boat. However, I do not plan to leave the <u>Nick King</u>.

I would appreciate your kindness in inviting John Young, Bishop of Florida, to join us on board and then hopefully travel with me to Magnolia.

I remain,

Your Obedient Servant,

Robert E. Lee

Jacksonville
April, 1870

Captain J. J. Dickison

Dear Sir:

It is my prayer that you and your family have continued to prosper and enjoy good health. My missionaries, in their travels up the St. Johns, have reported to me on the growth of Magnolia as visitors from the north discover the attractions of Florida.

Through Colonel Jaquelin Daniel, I have received an invitation to greet General Lee as he arrives in Jacksonville and to travel with him to Magnolia. Any private conversations I may have with him will surely include the disposition of our mutual responsibilities.

I believe it is in our best interest to have that which is hidden, uncovered, so that it may be delivered to General Lee.

I am, Respectfully Yours,

John Freeman Young, Bishop

Belching thick black smoke, the <u>Nick King</u> eased up to the Magnolia dock. With independent engines for the two twenty-six foot diameter paddlewheels, the steamboat produced a large amount of smoke. With her steam whistle blowing, she certainly attracted attention from the residents of Magnolia. Wagons were hitched to mules and taken out onto the dock ready to receive visitors to the hotel.

Today, after the lines from the boat were secured to the dock, a quiet settled over the assembled crowd of citizens and dignitaries. Caleb, Harold Alexander, J. J. and Thomas Hunter stepped forward to greet their celebrated visitor. Looking tired, but distinguished in a long grey coat, General Robert E. Lee stepped onto the dock. Men and women stood quietly on the wood planks from the boat all the way back to the shore. Their silence seemed more of a demonstration of respect and affection than any cheering crowd.

After introductions and words of welcome from the four men, General Lee said, "Gentlemen, there will be no speeches and, I hope, no formal reception. After a brief rest, I hope to meet my old friend, Colonel Robert Coles, who is associated, I believe, with Mr. Hunter in the production of citrus. This evening, I would like to meet with the valiant Captain J. J. Dickison and Bishop John Young who accompanied me from Jacksonville."

Climbing into the hotel wagon, General Lee nodded to the wide-eyed driver, and the wagon moved slowly toward the shore. Admiration and respect showing on their faces, the crowd parted to allow passage for their famous leader.

Later, Colonel Coles took General Lee into a grove of trees bearing clusters of large yellow fruit. Slicing one into sections, he offered the assembled group a bite of the fruit. "From the bittersweet taste," he said, "I don't believe there could be much commercial value. I have named the fruit after the manner in which it grows in clusters - grapefruit."

That evening after supper, as the sun painted the east bank of the river a golden hue, Harold Alexander escorted General

Lee to St. Dunstan's. A table and chairs had been placed beside the church under the widespread limbs of an oak tree. General Lee smiled when he saw the furniture. "Mr. Alexander, I'm flattered that you, or someone here, remembered my dislike of meeting in places of worship. My prohibition is really for military activities. This setting is so pleasant, I believe it will be my choice for talks with Bishop Young and Captain Dickison. I would be pleased if you and I could go into the church for a word of prayer."

As the two men climbed the steps to the entry, General Lee paused. "Is that a horseshoe above the door?"

Harold told him of the legend of Dunstan, the blacksmith, who became the Archbishop of Canterbury.

General Lee said, "I've never paid much attention to horseshoes above doors to barns or houses. I hope to remember the most effective way to mount the shoe when I return to Virginia. Perhaps an old shoe of Traveler's would be best."

Bishop Young and J. J. Dickison were waiting inside as the two men entered. Sitting together in a pew, three heads were bowed as Harold Alexander offered a prayer of thanksgiving and a hope for the future.

"Captain Dickison," said the general after the three men were seated under the oak, "your accomplishments have been well documented. It would be my pleasure to discuss with you, at some future occasion, your mastery of the use of horses and men in heavy underbrush. Would you tell me of your meeting with John Breckinridge and his fate? Bishop Young, please do likewise where ever you enter the narrative."

After J. J. and Bishop Young finished their story, General Lee asked, "Where are the assets now?"

J. J. said, "We buried the treasure in a wood coffin here in the cemetery of St. Dunstan's on our arrival from Gainesville and Waldo. I have moved it to the church if you would like to accept it tonight."

The three men rose from their chairs and re-entered the

church. Bishop Young stepped into the chancel and, with J. J.'s help, pulled the wood altar away from the wall. Opening a drawer in the base cleverly concealed by the carpenter, Will Hendry, he reached in and removed three canvas bags. Opening one, he withdrew an ingot of gold, handing it to General Lee. "Rolls of gold coins, silver dollars from Mexico and five ingots of gold remain in the other bags," he said.

General Lee said, "I will take a single ingot of gold. What I have in my hand is all that is left of the efforts of honorable men to resist those who would force their will on the South. It will most certainly not be used in an attempt to restore the Confederacy but will be used to educate and train young men to do their duty in life. Jefferson Davis is in exile in Canada. We have communicated by mail and he wrote of his plans to move to England so he can support his family. He may plan to return but I cannot say for certain as he continues to urge all southerners to remember the deeds of our brothers. I will attempt to contact President Davis to discreetly inform him or our meeting today. Accounts of his arrest and trial, your description of events in Washington, Georgia and Gainesville lead me to think that Jefferson Davis believes the treasury of the Confederacy is all gone.

"So I ask you to hold the balance of the so-called assets until you hear from me again. As you note, my health is poor. I plan to return to Washington College in Lexington, Virginia where, I am sure my last days will be spent. If you receive word from me to strike the tent, you will know our concern for the treasury is over. There are no more owners of the asset you hold. There is no further distribution possible. You are the last. Take the gold and silver and use them wisely."

The next day, General Lee returned to Jacksonville on the Nick King, invigorated by his visit to Magnolia. To the delight of the citizens of Jacksonville, he left the boat to tour the city and attended a reception in his honor at the home of

Colonel J. P. Sanderson. General Lee departed by boat early the next morning en route to Charleston and on to Lexington, Virginia. Upon returning to Washington College, his inspiring leadership as President for four years was to end as his health faded. On October 12, 1870, at home in his beloved Virginia, Robert E. Lee spoke his last words, "strike the tent" and then died.

Chapter 18
1877

Bishop John Young, in response to a slight shift in the wind, adjusted his single sail as the dock at Magnolia came into view. He smiled with pleasure on being able to handle his boat with a developing degree of skill as he visited his growing mission churches. From Jacksonville, he could travel by railroad to his churches in west Florida and soon, he hoped, by rail to central and south Florida. For communities on the river, travel by his small sailboat or commercial steamboat was the most enjoyable, as well as the most efficient, way to travel.

John Young had arrived in Orange Park yesterday, preached this morning, enjoyed lunch with a small group of Episcopalians and was on his way to St. Dunstan's in Magnolia. Passing Hibernia, on the west bank, he noted the Fleming home rebuilt from the destruction of war and the recently completed small church. Mrs. Fleming, before her recent death, had discussed with him the design of the church, responding favorably to his recommendations of following certain architectural principles of Richard Upjohn. Neither a parish or mission, St. Margaret's, with help from visiting clergy from the north and Bishop Young, was able to hold occasional services for the Fleming family and other visitors.

Approaching the Magnolia dock, John Young turned his boat into the wind, dropped the sail and coasted up to the pier. Holding a line for the bow and another for the stern, he climbed onto the wood planks and secured the lines to two wood pilings.

"I'm impressed with your boat-handling," said J. J. as he

greeted the Bishop.

"If I knew you were watching, I probably would have crashed into the dock," replied John Young, as the two men walked toward St. Dunstan's and their familiar wood bench under the oak tree.

"All the way up the river from Jacksonville, last night in Orange Park and today, I have been thinking and praying about what has been laid before us. I have decided that I cannot accept any of the treasure that we have been offered."

J. J. said, "John, there is no one left. It has been twelve years since we arrived in Magnolia in the wagon and seven years since Robert E. Lee came to see us. From his deathbed, he gave us our final instructions. Jefferson Davis and most authorities believe the treasure is all gone. I have read that John Breckinridge returned from England to Kentucky after President Andrew Johnson granted amnesty to the leaders of the Confederacy. I don't know if he spoke or communicated with General Lee. If he had, I feel certain we would have heard from him."

"He died, J. J.," said Bishop Young, "two years ago after a successful practice of law."

J. J. said, "During the war, I was blessed with an association with many brave, faithful and capable men. As the war ended, it was my honor to meet and experience the leadership and loyalty of General Breckinridge. I am sorry to hear of his death. I hope his story is faithfully told so that others may learn of his role in the Confederacy.

"Since our friendship began in Gainesville on that same occasion, I have admired your courage and conviction to do what you believe is right. I will accept with reluctance what you are telling me this afternoon. Somehow, I am not surprised. However, I intend to keep my share of the treasure and as required by General Lee, "use it wisely." As you serve the church in spreading the word of God, I believe your share could help, if you would claim it, in the building of churches up and down the river. I cannot just bury it in the

ground again under the false headboard. I will place some of
the coins here at St. Dunstan's in that special place Will
Hendry made for us. Do I tell Harold? I haven't decided. If
times become difficult for St. Dunstan's or Harold, then I
probably will. I believe it is in our best interest to protect the
existence of the Confederate treasure. As you have
considered your decision not to take any of the coins, I have
thought about where I could conceal your share, or a portion,
at the churches I'm sure you will build along the river. I
watched Ed Foley as he started the construction of St.
Dunstan's before the war and completed our church five
years later. I know you will follow the architectural
principles you and Upjohn advocate as you guide the
planning and construction of each church. I know there will
be more than one. I will submit to you, in writing, an
indication of where I have placed gold coins. For obvious
reasons, it will not be specific but a location that you will
recognize from our experiences together."

John Young looked at J. J. for a full minute without
speaking and then said, "J. J. that is the most preposterous
idea I have ever heard! Hiding or placing the coins as if it
were a game. I told you I did not want any portion of the
treasury!"

"John, when you receive a letter or word from me that I
have visited one of your churches tomorrow or next year,
then you will know I have initiated my plan. If you don't
need the coins, or for whatever reason you don't want each
church to have the money, the gold will remain there!"

"J. J., if you do hide the coins for some unknown
beneficiary, what are you going to do with your share?"

J. J. Dickison looked at his friend, John Young, Bishop of
Florida, and smiled.

Chapter 19
1882

On the third floor of the Magnolia Hotel, James Britton admitted to himself that once again, he had eaten too much; the hotel dining room had lived up to its reputation of serving the best food on the river. As he prepared for bed, James enjoyed a final cigar and just a sip of port wine. Tempted to move a chair to the open window and enjoy the view of the river by moonlight, he was even more attracted to his bed. One last pull from the cigar and he fell asleep, dropping his cigar onto the bed sheet. The open window and the louvered wood door created just enough cross-ventilation to fuel the cigar ashes. As the smoldering sheet burst into flame, James jumped to his feet, throwing the burning sheet away from the bed, but unfortunately toward the window drapes. As the fire began to spread, James hesitated only briefly before running to the door and into the hall shouting an alarm. On the floor below, the night manager was just beginning his rounds when he heard James' cry. Heading for the stairs, he ran to alert the guests on the upper floors and sent the first night maid he saw to spread the word on the lower floors.

In the dining room, the headwaiter grabbed four of his cleaning men and headed for the fire pumpers stored in a garage near the boiler room. Isaac Cruft, the owner of the hotel, had purchased two pumpers in Jacksonville and had ordered a third after a demonstration. Mounted on a four-wheel wood frame caisson, a fifty-gallon tank was connected by a two-inch hose to a double pump. From the pump a coiled length of two-inch hose was ready to be directed at the fire. The first four men to reach the garage took their place on either side of a projecting tongue and started pulling the pumper toward the hotel courtyard. A bucket brigade was organized at the hotel water tower to keep the pumper tank full, while another group of men pulled the second pumper around to the front of the hotel. A bucket brigade, with water from the river, struggled to keep the tank full. Other bucket brigades did their best, but more water was spilled in haste than thrown on the fire. In the kitchen and office, eight-inch round glass globes of carbon tetrachloride were thrown at the base of flames, displacing the oxygen. Some of these globes, in a newly-patented frame, were mounted in the hotel hallways. When the heat melted a lead connection, these individual globes dropped to the floor, scattering the fire-fighting chemical.

The guests, in night clothes clutching what valuables they could, ran away from the rapidly spreading flames. Employees filled sheets, blankets and canvas bags with what could be carried; furniture was left in the parlors, lobby and reading rooms. The fire spread quickly in the wood frame building. The pumpers had little effect; the bucket brigades contributed even less.

Flames and smoke, illuminated by the fire, were visible for miles up and down the river. Townspeople and neighbors jumped from their beds and ran to help. Harold Alexander's wife, Kate, shook his shoulder, bringing him awake with a start. Pulling on trousers over his nightshirt, Harold ran for the hotel. Heading to the exterior stairs that led up to the second floor verandah, he found a stream of people running for safety. Realizing the need to protect the stairs, Harold hollered for the pumper to direct a stream of water toward the stairs. Looking up, he watched guests on the third and fourth floors gathering on the roof of the verandah, desperately seeking a way to the ground. Harold headed for the lobby and on up the interior stairs to the third floor, looking for ropes or ladders.

James Britton, frantic over what he had started, went from

room to room grabbing sheets and bedspreads to help people reach the ground. He and Harold Alexander literally ran into one another as they moved from one room to the next. Flames and smoke forced the two men away from the hallways and rooms onto the veranda roof. Harold grabbed a length of sheets tied together and threw the makeshift rope over the rail, urging James to climb down to the ground. Reaching safety, James looked back up at Harold, motioning him to follow. Harold put his leg up and over the rail and felt the rail give a little. James watched with horror as the porch roof collapsed onto the burning timbers of the verandah.

Dawn found a brownish gray haze over Magnolia. Tall blackened chimneys somehow remained, standing guard over pieces of blackened stud walls, roof trusses and a mountain of gray ashes, still smoking. Nearby houses and surrounding oak trees were scorched from the fire. Exhausted employees and townspeople who had valiantly fought the blazing hotel, stood silent or slumped to the ground. Hotel staff members braved the smoldering ashes as they searched for guest registers that would help in the identification of those who had died. Some survivors wandered through the remains looking for friends.

Kate Alexander, distraught over the death of her husband, was comforted by her friends and neighbors. Men and women of St. Dunstan's, broken-hearted with the news of Harold's death, offered food, water and shelter to the survivors. J. J. Dickison, notified by a rider sent by Caleb arrived just before dawn and, somehow as expected, took charge.

From Jacksonville, when told of the tragedy, Bishop Young sent condolences and heartfelt expressions of sympathy to Kate Alexander, asking if he could conduct the burial service for his old friend. He had planned to visit churches on the Gulf Coast, traveling on the recently completed railroad between Jacksonville, Tampa and Key West. The railroad offered the Bishop a new convenience in visiting his widespread congregations. After an overnight stop in Magnolia for the funeral, Bishop Young could resume his missionary travels.

During the brief, but sad, service of burial at the cemetery, Bishop Young could not help but glance toward the nearby grave of the "soldier" he and J. J. had brought from Gainesville.

As a temporary headboard was placed at Harold's grave, J. J., with a heavy heart, described his love and respect for his old friend and said, "Kate, I think it would be appropriate to carve a horseshoe on Harold's headstone."

Kate Alexander nodded her head in agreement. "Harold would be pleased at your suggestion. My family and I thank you for always being here for us and for your love and support during difficult times. As the years ahead unfold, you will always be an important part of my memories of Magnolia and St. Dunstan's."

Two weeks later, Caleb watched J. J. dismount from his horse and walk out onto the Magnolia dock. The sun had just started its afternoon dance with the rippling waters of the river and the trees on the distant shore shone with pleasure as the leaves reflected the glow of the setting sun. Caleb felt as if the beauty of the river could not overcome his depression and suspected that J. J. felt the same. J. J. turned as he heard his friend approaching, and smiled.

"Caleb," he said, "when the sun sets like today, sometimes I feel that if I could just get closer to the trees and the river, the sadness within me would go away. Do you remember the day before the war started and Bishop Francis Rutledge came here and stopped the work on St. Dunstan's?"

Caleb said, "Sure I remember. You said our world has come apart."

J. J. looked toward the river and said, "I feel that way today, Caleb. Here in north Florida, we won the battles but lost the war, as others have said. We have lost the hotel, the ashes behind us still smolder; we have lost Harold Alexander, who showed us how to keep the faith in hard times and gave his life helping others. There will be talk of rebuilding the hotel with access to the new railroad, but I don't think it will happen. The signal pole we put up years ago to notify steamboats when we had mail or passengers is without a signal flag today. For a number of years it was not needed. The steamboats brought visitors anyway. We sure didn't need it the day General Lee came to town. Somehow, that empty pole is telling me of the future of Magnolia. The center of the world for you, me, our families and friends has come apart again. I believe it will be the last and final time."

It wasn't long before J. J.'s distressing predictions began to unfold. With the Magnolia Hotel gone, winter visitors selected Hibernia, five miles north. Although the hospitality of the Fleming family proved to be very popular, the number of guest rooms was limited. Green Cove Springs, just two miles south of Magnolia, answered the demand with the construction of numerous hotels and boarding houses, each claiming access to a sparkling spring. In contrast to Magnolia, where the healing waters required consumption, the therapeutic qualities of the water at Green Cove Springs could be enjoyed by bathing in the bubbling spring, surging from the earth at a rate of over two million gallons per day. The healthful waters flowing to the St. Johns were first directed into separate and screened bathing pools for men and women.

When the county seat of Clay County was relocated from Middleburg, about twelve miles to the west, lumber interests, businessmen, ranchers and farmers followed a population shift toward the river. Local churches, formerly supported by winter visitors, found a need to accommodate year-round congregations. St. Mary's Episcopal Church, completed in 1878, designed by Charles C. Haight of New York, followed the architectural style and use of materials advocated by Bishop John Young. A simple rectangular wood framed building, clad in board and batten siding, with lancet topped windows, and a tower and spire above the river front entry delighted visitors and year round members alike. In contrast, St. Dunstan's, struggling without a fulltime priest, slowly lost their congregation.

One Sunday, during a service led by Caleb Hopkins as lay reader, with a congregation of five, a letter from Bishop Young was read.

Diocese of Florida
June 8, 1883

St. Dunstan's Episcopal Church

My Dear Friends,

After long hours of prayer and with conflicting emotions between my heart and practical decisions required by my position as Bishop, I have decided to close St. Dunstan's.

Rather than endure the sadness of watching a very special building fall into disrepair, it is my plan to move St. Dunstan's by barge to a riverfront location in Jacksonville. Our old friend Ed Foley, who built the church, has accepted the responsibility of moving the church. He and I discussed the possibility of dismantling the building, but due to the techniques of construction so beautifully utilized, we decided to basically move the building. There are men who have experience in moving buildings by water and Ed, being more qualified than any other to protect our interests, can make sure any damage is minimal. The small cemetery will remain; the graves of Harold Alexander, an unknown soldier and others will continue to be sacred ground.

The altar, so beautifully built by Will Hendry, has a special meaning to J. J. Dickison and me. To that end, I have asked J. J. to take charge of the altar and to relocate it to an appropriate place. I will be in touch with Frank Sanborn of Brunswick, Maine, who gave the windows, to inform him of my decision. Unless we hear of his wishes to the contrary, Ed will remove the windows and secure them for travel.

May God bless each one of you and your families. With a heavy heart, I remain

Your Obedient Servant,

John Freeman Young,
Bishop of Florida

Chapter 20
1884

The unfamiliar sound of a boat whistle announcing an intention to dock brought many residents of Magnolia to the riverfront. Turning toward the west from the middle of the river was Balsam, a side wheel steam towboat, pulling a wood flat bottom barge loaded with timbers and wagon wheels. Although a shallow draft vessel, Balsam eased as close as possible to the shore and then turned south into the current and dropped her anchors. Crewmen at the stern launched two rowboats and released the lines of the barge. Accompanied by a lot of shouting, the barge was guided to the riverbank with help from men in the rowboats and deckhands on the barge with push poles. Using cleats mounted on the gunwales of the barge, lines were secured to pilings and nearby trees. Unloading began with heavy oak planks that would be used to build a ramp from shore to the barge. Satisfied that the barge was in place, Balsam raised her anchors and steamed over to the deeper water at the end of the Magnolia dock. Ed Foley was first off the boat and was greeted by Caleb.

"I'm not too happy with the reason for your visit," he said, "but I'm glad to see you again."

Ed thanked him and introduced Harry Drake as the salvage contractor. "I've known Harry and seen his work," said Ed. "I know he'll take good care of your church. When J. J. comes around be sure and tell him of my approval of Harry. After all is unloaded, the Balsam will return to Jacksonville but will be back when Harry has the church on the barge ready to go."

Upon completion of the oak ramp from the barge to the

riverbank, materials were unloaded and properly stored. Harry's workers began a planned sequence of steps preparing the church for its move. After clearing the site around the church leading up to the ramp, the crawl space under the building was excavated to a depth of about four feet from the ground up to the bottom of the floor joists. Five pair of eight by eight inch timbers, bolted and strapped together horizontally, with a six foot lap, called "balks" by pontoon building engineers during the war, were then slid underneath the church; one at each end and the other three spaced equally. The ends of each "balk" were prepared to receive wheel housings. With wood blocking built up in stages from the ground up, the crossbeams were slowly raised high enough for three iron screw jacks to be placed underneath. Between each crossbeam, six by six timbers were attached, completing the creation of a strong platform that would support the church as it was moved from the foundation and onto the barge.

Harry Drake carefully checked the location of each screw jack to insure placement beneath the perimeter sill beam and the center, or summer, beam of the church. Before any actual load of the church was transferred to the crossbeams, Ed Foley removed the windows and placed diagonal wood braces from wall to the floor inside the church. Workers were placed at each row of screw jacks; a one-quarter turn was made starting at one end, followed by a similar turn at each row down the building. At the last row, a one-half turn of the screw was made. Quarter turns at each row of jacks back toward the opposite end followed, with hardwood wedges inserted to keep the building level as St. Dunstan's rose slowly from the brick foundation piers.

Wood timbers and wagon wheels on the barge were just part of the materials needed to move St. Dunstan's. Two wagons, loaded with ropes, chains, pulleys, harnesses, and miscellaneous equipment, arrived in Magnolia, each pulled by a team of six mules.

When all appeared ready; the crossbeams, wheels, connections, the ramp and the barge, Harry motioned to his mule skinners. With pulls on the reins, cracks of whips and lots of shouting, the two teams of mules were hitched to wood poles connected by chains to the first crossbeam. Mule skinners climbed onto saddles at the wheel and lead pair of mules. At Harry's signal, with more shouts and pops of whips, St. Dunstan's moved slowly from the foundation excavation, up the ramp and onto the barge.

J. J., Caleb and many citizens of Magnolia watched the mules complete their work. Wagon wheels were blocked; the mules were unhitched and taken back to shore, one at a time down the sides of the building. Harnesses, bits and bridles were removed; additional tie down lines were attached to cleats on the barge. The pleasure felt by Harry's men in the completion of a difficult move was restrained by the sad faces of the spectators.

Early the next morning, a loud whistle announced the return of Balsam. Skillfully using the side wheel paddles, the captain backed carefully to the barge; crewmen caught lines tossed from the barge to be tied to two large bitts located on the stern of the towboat. The oak plank ramp was dismantled for reuse and as lines from the barge to the shore were released, J. J. asked Harry if he could go in the church one last time to return a small item that should go with St. Dunstan's. With his arms raised, ready to signal Balsam to ease ahead, Harry reluctantly gave J. J. permission. Climbing over the braces, J. J. entered the doorway of the church. Standing in the back, J. J. thought of Bishop Rutledge, Harold Alexander, Bishop Young and the "soldier" over in the trees and said a prayer of thanksgiving for St. Dunstan's and his friends.

It must have been quite a sight as Balsam, a side wheel steam towboat headed toward Jacksonville pulling a barge holding a wood church that appeared to have wheels. From the banks of the river you couldn't tell it was a church but as the word spread up the river, people headed for the river to see the "floating church."

In March 1864, Captain E. P. Bryan, on detached service from General P. T. Beauregard's staff in Charleston, had planted twelve mines, also called torpedoes, off Mandarin Point, north of Magnolia on the east bank of the river. The mines proved effective immediately, sinking the <u>Maple Leaf</u> within forty-eight hours and three other troop transports within the next three months. Two of these mines, referred to as "infernal machines" by northern newspapers, broke loose from their anchors and drifted slowly to the west until a line connecting the two snagged on an underwater tree trunk. Years passed before the manila rope line finally rotted and the two mines broke loose. The first mine drifted toward the surface until the anchor line from the second mine hooked another trunk, holding both mines just below the surface.

On <u>Balsam</u> in the wheelhouse, Ed Foley and Harry Drake were discussing the successful transfer of the church to the barge. The captain noted the red day marker ahead locating the wreckage of the <u>Maple Leaf</u> and directed his helmsman to alter course to the west. The portside paddle wheel housing struck the first mine, detonating one hundred pounds of gun powder, lifting the towboat completely out of the water. Seconds later, the bow of the barge, torn loose from the bitts on the stern of <u>Balsam</u>, was raised by the explosion allowing the second mine to hit the barge on the bottom in the middle. The blast blew the wood barge, the wagon wheels and the crossbeams into fragments, and split the church into two pieces. The beautiful and strong wood joinery kept some beams and roof trusses together, but only briefly as they struck the water and broke apart. The rear wall and a piece of a side wall tumbled into the water, floated briefly and then sank. Fragments of the wood structure, the barge and <u>Balsam</u> covered the turbulent waters; the detonation snapped Ed's leg and threw him in the river. Harry hit the water flat on his back, knocking him unconscious. The captain grabbed both men, pulled them to a large floating piece of his boat and waited for help. Crewmen of <u>Balsam</u>, thrown into the water by the explosion, grabbed some of the floating timbers and also waited for help. The towboat <u>Balsam</u>, the barge and its unusual cargo, became the final victims of the "infernal machines."

St. Dunstan's Episcopal Church, formerly located at Magnolia, Florida, was gone.

Chapter 21
1885

J. J. Dickison often thought of the meeting in 1870, with General Robert E. Lee and Bishop John Young. He felt comfortable in accepting the wishes of General Lee, unlike Bishop Young. Even while he remained active in the military affairs of Florida, J. J. followed the missionary efforts of his friend. Occasionally, the two men were able to enjoy a meal together. J. J. would describe to Bishop Young a visit to a new river church where he had left a remembrance of their shared responsibility. John Young would repeat his refusal to accept any of the Confederate assets and would urge J. J. to abandon the game of hiding some portion at each church.

"The money is yours, John," J. J. said repeatedly. "General Lee released the balance of the assets to you and me. I will continue to visit each of the churches you work so hard to develop and I'll continue to write to you after each visit without describing any details of our gift. As I said years ago, the location will be based on our experiences together."

Early one morning in November, J. J. received a telegram that Bishop Young had died in New York, while on Diocesan business. The telegram further reported that Mrs. Young was on her way back to Jacksonville with his body. J. J. packed a small bag and hurried to Magnolia to hoist a flag on the signal pole hopefully in time to be seen by the afternoon steamboat en route to Jacksonville.

In the parlor at the Bishop's home, a group of friends and clergy gathered to offer their condolences to Mary Stuart Young. Their quiet conversations ceased as a thin, erect gentleman in a long gray coat entered the room.

"My name is J. J. Dickison," he said. "I would like to pay

my respects to Mrs. Young."

Escorted by a friend of the family, J. J. was led to a small parlor. Seated on a small settee was a somber slim lady dressed in black silk, holding her hands together in her lap. A bearded clergyman sat next to her and rose to his feet as J. J. entered the room. At the mention of J. J.'s name, Mary Stuart Young smiled and offered her hand. The clergyman introduced himself as John Beckwith, Bishop of Georgia. Shaking J. J.'s hand in a strong grip, he said, "I am pleased to meet you, Sir. Your accomplishments are well-known in Georgia." The Bishop asked permission from Mrs. Young to return again and then left the room.

"My husband thought highly of you, Captain Dickison. He told me of St. Dunstan's in Magnolia as a special place for the two of you, and how he regretted his decision to close the church. When he heard of the destruction of the church by mines in the river, he told me he felt that something special was lost."

"He was my friend, Mrs. Young. Twenty years ago, we met in Gainesville as the war ended. The impact of that meeting and the responsibility we were asked to accept created a bond that became stronger with every year. His influence on me, my faith and my church cannot be measured. There is so much I wish I had said to him. In Magnolia, our church is gone but when John Young's name is mentioned, expressions of affection will always follow. He will always be a part of St. Dunstan's of Magnolia. I don't need to tell you of his efforts to develop mission churches along the St. Johns. I am sure that the architectural principles that identify each church will always be associated with his name. I have written to him of my visits and the sense of his presence at each church. We talked of his work at Trinity in New York and his translation into English of famous hymns from around the world. Silent Night, in my opinion, will live forever as a Christmas hymn."

"Thank you for your very kind words, Captain Dickison.

My husband spoke of you with affection many times, ending each conversation with, I felt, a shared secret of some kind. Occasionally, in his sleep, I have heard the word "tent", possibly reliving his travels with you. What does that mean, Captain?"

"I don't know," said J. J. "The Bishop always had a lot on his mind." He held Mrs. Young's hand an extra long moment, offering his support in any way, then turned to leave as Bishop Beckwith returned to the small parlor.

After the service of burial was completed at St. John's Church, J. J. joined the long procession to the city cemetery. Bishop Young's family, friends and the clergy of Florida stood silently as the casket was lowered into the ground. From the distance, a series of sharp sounds, not unlike a volley of gunfire, was heard. J. J. raised his head and looked across the grave to the veterans from his old command, Company H, Second Florida Cavalry. Smiling, as their heads were raised from the final prayer, they recognized the sound of rawhide whips, so familiar to each man from twenty years ago, snapped in a unique tribute to John Freeman Young, Second Bishop of Florida.

Chapter 22
The Present

"Well, Sam, what do we do now?" asked Charlie Gallagher as he settled into a large comfortable chair in Sam Wood's church office.

"I think it has been interesting to say the least," said Sam. "I know a lot more than I did when I left Richmond, and I think you have gained a little background knowledge of the river churches. I believe that you also share my curiosity and interest in the Confederate treasure. Many pieces of the puzzle are missing that would reveal the location, but we have a unique viewpoint as to where it is. Do you want to keep going?"

"Sure I do," said Charlie, "but you're the one with a job."

"Charlie, there are missionary reasons for me to travel up and down the river. Both of us don't have to run down every clue. There is an advantage on my part for access to Diocesan archives. Don't you think we'll have to feel our way into the search? I'm not happy with the idea of the two of us arriving at St. Whatever, announcing that we are there to search for a treasure. If I can notify the local rector that you, or you and I, are coming for a pseudo-legitimate reason, our visit will be easier. I guess what I'm saying is that we should feel our way into a process."

"O.K., Sam, I agree and, like I said, what now?"

Sam sat back in his chair, raised his hands to form a tent with his fingers and replied, "Let's review what facts we know about the treasure.

"First, most historians of the Civil War acknowledge that the assets of the Confederacy left Richmond by train on April 2, 1865, bound for Danville, Virginia. Eventually, the treasure arrived in Washington, Georgia. From that location, there is no consensus as to its whereabouts.

"Second, we have a copy of a letter from the Reverend Charles Minnegerode that I found in the files of St. Paul's in Richmond, recommending John Young as a person of trust.

"Third, in old records of the Diocese of Florida under John Young, I came across a copy of a letter from John Breckinridge to Bishop Young asking him to serve as his representative and to 'hold certain items of luggage.' I believe John Breckinridge had a portion of the assets with him in Gainesville and asked John Young to safeguard it. J. J. was ordered to Gainesville to meet a general officer and to perform any tasks.

"Fourth, we have a copy of Bishop Young's letter to J. J. Dickison anticipating the visit of Robert E. Lee to Magnolia mentioning the 'disposition of our mutual responsibilities.'

"Fifth, a copy of Bishop Young's letter to the congregation of St. Dunstan's closing the church and giving J. J. Dickison the responsibility of relocating the altar to 'an appropriate place'. I believe the altar, somehow, is a clue to the location of the treasure.

"Sixth, old Diocesan records contain letters from J. J. Dickison to Bishop Young describing his visits to eight river churches. I'm not sure if those are all the churches he visited or what clues each visit would tell us."

Sam continued, "Charlie, I believe the river churches, including St. Dunstan's, will contain a portion of the treasure or give us a clue as to the location of the legendary assets of the Confederacy."

Charlie said, "There's one thing that bothers me. How did you find out about St. Dunstan's that I must have missed completely? From what you tell me, the church was started in 1861 by Bishop Rutledge, completed under Bishop Young in 1865 and blown up on the river in 1885. From start to finish is twenty-four years. How did it vanish from history?"

Sam replied, "I first came across St. Dunstan's, as I told

you at St. George's, in letters in which Bishop Rutledge asked John Young to deliver a letter that requests the famous architect, Richard Upjohn, to design a church in Florida and then, a letter from Upjohn to Bishop Rutledge, accepting the commission. As you know, sometimes you discover an unexpected reference while searching for something else. I found a report in an old newspaper, dated 1885, of a towboat and barge with an unusual cargo destroyed by two mysterious explosions. I found a few reports and letters, not many, referring to St. Dunstan's and I pieced together a brief history. St. Matthews in San Mateo by comparison, is mentioned in few histories of the church in Florida. Built in 1880, the church declined in support and I found letters requesting bids to buy the church building and sadly, a final letter accepting a bid of twenty-five dollars to buy the wood for scrap. It is sad, but true. Without an active congregation and support from other churches, these wonderful [to you and me] small buildings are either moved or allowed to become a distant memory. My search for the assets of the Confederacy revealed more about St. Dunstan's or, it too, would literally have slipped away."

"O.K., Sam," Charlie said, "how do we start? We know there are twelve river churches from my list plus St. Dunstan's. Do we check them all? Seems to me the river, Upjohn's influence or design and the years of leadership by Bishop John Young would help us narrow our search. If we make a list of churches that meet those qualifications and compare J. J. Dickison's letters of his visits, we might have a good list of where to start."

"The place to begin," said Sam, "is Magnolia and St. Dunstan's. I realize there is nothing for us to see, but if we could walk around and somehow feel the presence of St. Dunstan's and the hotel, maybe even locate the old spring that was capped, we would be off to a great start."

"Before we go", said Charlie, "I'm gonna see if I can be lucky and find some old maps or plans of the hotel site." He headed for Green Cove Springs, twenty-five miles south of Jacksonville, to the Clay County Archives for a start. After a search through files of county drawings, a portion of an old survey of Magnolia was found that indicated "hotel ruins, the dock and boathouse." Charlie was pleased to also note a "cemetery" shown west of the hotel ruins. Since cemeteries, by law, retain the respect of subsequent land uses, any later drawings that continued to note the old cemetery could help Charlie locate the hotel on a current site plan.

From Green Cove Springs, Charlie turned north to Magnolia. A large apartment development occupied the riverfront site of the former village of Magnolia. One and two story buildings were comfortably spaced among palms, pines and oak trees; from the river on the east to U.S. 17 on the west and from Governor's Creek on the south then north on both sides of state road 209. A visit to the apartment manager's office produced a drawing that indicated the location of roads, buildings and, unexpectedly, the cemetery plot. A few hours of work on his drawing board, using the two site plans of different scales with the cemetery as a key and Charlie had a plan of the riverfront property with the hotel ruins shown as an overlay to the apartment building locations. Sam and Charlie reviewed all their notes describing the location of St. Dunstan's and decided on two or three possibilities to be checked out on their visit to Magnolia.

Charlie said, "Would it help to visit Magnolia by boat? Of course the dock is gone. After all we have read about Magnolia and with a little imagination, I can easily see us arriving by a side-wheel steamboat. We could tie up at a nearby public boat landing and walk to Magnolia." Charlie asked an old friend who owned a cabin cruiser to take the two men to Magnolia in return for gas, lunch at a local fish camp and a cold drink or two.

"Charlie was right," thought Sam. As the boat cruised slowly along the riverbank at Magnolia, the apartment buildings dissolved in his mind. There stood St. Dunstan's in the trees with the Magnolia Hotel, in all its glory, receiving new guests. Is that J. J. Dickison, Caleb and the Reverend Harold Alexander standing on the steps of the church? Reality returned abruptly as a jet ski roared by.

Sam and Charlie walked over from the boat landing, walked down a street and then between two one-story apartment buildings toward the river. The beauty of the sunlit property did little to dampen the optimism of the two men. Very old oak trees spread their branches over the sun-covered grass lawn that sloped down to the water. Gray-blue waters of the St. Johns softly disappeared into low underbrush at the riverbank. Sam spotted an old stump in the water, wondering to himself if that could be piling from the Magnolia dock. He looked at Charlie who shook his head in understanding Sam's thoughts. From Charlie's drawings of the property, the two men had discussed several possible locations for St. Dunstan's. Standing on the site, their search was narrowed to an area of higher elevation not quite as close to the water as they first thought.

"Where's the graveyard?" said Sam. "With the respect for cemeteries you described, I hoped a small plot surrounded by a rusting iron fence would have lasted through the years. Have 'the soldier' and the Reverend Harold Alexander's graves been forgotten?"

"We don't see the spring either," said Charlie. "I believe it might be at the head of this low area that slopes to the river from the west. It was capped many years ago after a brief attempt at bottling the waters. You know, I didn't really expect to uncover anything; certainly not an old sign pointing to the treasure!" laughed Charlie.

Returning to the boat, Sam said, "I think this visit helped me realize that what we are after has been lost for one hundred and fifty years! We have clues only; we'll need a little luck and a lot of time."

All the next day Sam thought about their trip as he visited

parishioners in their homes and hospitals. In the late afternoon, Charlie joined him and the two began planning for their next trip. A map was produced and eight churches were located and highlighted.

"Charlie," Sam said, "I'm scheduled to preach next week at Our Saviour in Mandarin and I'm looking forward to seeing the church and renovated chapel."

"Sam, you've got to get it straight. The church was destroyed by Hurricane Dora in 1964, when a large tree fell across the building. Yes, it was a wood frame church on the river, appreciated and loved by the residents of Mandarin but it was not an Upjohn design. The building, completed in 1883, was patterned after a church in New York, familiar to Harriett Beecher Stowe, who led the effort to build the church. Since Our Saviour was a parish in the Diocese of Florida, I'm sure Bishop John Young visited the congregation but that is the only connection in our search.

"The new Church of Our Saviour was completed and dedicated in 1966 and is almost twice as large as the original. I know the architects pretty well and after nearly forty years they are still proud of their design. The setting on the river is beautiful. I'm glad you're going but remember; except for the windows and salvaged furniture in the chapel, it's all new."

A week later, after the morning service, Sam sat alone in the Chapel at Our Saviour. He appreciated the simplicity and quiet dignity of the design but he was captivated by the center panel of the stained glass window above the altar. As the late morning sun illuminated the window, a deep feeling of sorrow touched Sam's heart as he saw two victims of a recent epidemic; a small girl introducing her brother to Jesus. From his seat in an old pew, Sam wondered if the altar from St. Dunstan's, J. J.'s responsibility, could have been similar to this altar. Where could any treasure be hidden in this three-sided shallow wood box? Sam walked forward to inspect the construction of the altar placed against the rear wall of the chapel [eastern, he noted with liturgical pleasure]. Tempted to slide the altar away from the wall, Sam was spared from any embarrassment by the voice of his Mandarin host reminding him of his priestly obligations.

Chapter 23

"Charlie, I've thought more about our process," said Sam. "I originally thought a telephone call from me, as a priest of the Diocese of Florida, would give us an entry to each church. For us to arrive, crawl under the building, move chancel furniture or even ask to remove a piece of a wall or siding, would raise questions after a couple of visits. I think now the best procedure is for you to use your professional identity as an architect, conducting a structural evaluation of wood frame river churches built in the late 1800's."

"That's good, Sam. I like it. I'll write you a letter describing my project and you can forward a copy along with a cover letter from you to each of the churches. I recommend we start with All Saints in Enterprise; on Lake Monroe across from Sanford."

The St. Johns, flowing north from its origin in South Florida, extended its banks to form Lake Monroe and at the same time provided sufficient depth of water for steamboat traffic. After the Civil War, freight and tourist traffic to and from Jacksonville, through Palatka and other stops on the river increased, bringing sportsmen and winter visitors as well as commercial business to Enterprise. Soon, Brock House, a two-story luxury hotel, was filled with visitors and by 1883 sufficient funds had been raised to answer a demand, by Episcopalians, to build a church. All Saints Episcopal Church followed the architectural design principles of Richard Upjohn, with a board and batten exterior enclosing a rectangular floor plan. Additional interior space was created by small transepts, or rectangular projections on each side and at the chancel, on the east-end, a straight-sided angled projection or apse. Later additions included a small sacristy and a covered entry porch.

Charles Gallagher, Architect, prepared and forwarded a letter to the Diocese of Florida describing his lifelong interest in the wood-framed river churches and asked for assistance in conducting a structural evaluation of a representative number. His letter was received, discussed and forwarded to seven churches with an appropriate cover letter from the Reverend Samuel Wood.

On a chilly morning two weeks later, Charlie arrived at All Saints, Enterprise. After a short visit to the office, he entered the small church. As always, entering one of these little buildings brought a smile of pleasure; just like seeing an old friend. Before turning on the lights, Charlie sat down in a pew halfway down the nave just to enjoy the quiet moment and to think about his search, with Sam, for the legendary treasure.

Charlie asked himself, why am I doing this? My family smiles politely with my tales of the lost assets of the Confederacy. I'm sure they believe I have moved into the early stages of old age. Sam has created a new interest in these churches turning my architectural thoughts in an historical direction. Maybe what we are looking for is not here but, it just might be. Anyway, here I sit looking at a familiar setting, wondering where Captain Dickison might have hidden something.

Charlie stood up and walked to the chancel. The wood altar had been moved forward; surely, someone would have noticed any unusual cabinet door, or box or shelf inside the framing. He slid the altar further away from the wall, checked the interior framing and found nothing. The pulpit and lectern were carefully inspected with the same result. Charlie turned to each stained-glass window unsure as to what he might discover in those wood frames.

J. J. probably visited each of the churches during construction, Charlie decided, so the roof trusses and the outside walls should be checked. Sooner or later I'm gonna have to crawl under this building, he thought. Retrieving his bag of tools and folding stepladder from his car, Charlie began his inspection of the steep-pitched rafters that supported the roof. He checked each rafter at the point of support at the wall plate and decided it would be too obvious a hiding place. He wondered if J. J. intended for a small piece of the treasure to be easily discovered. As he moved each pew to accommodate his stepladder, Charlie checked each wall stud and the inside face of the exterior wall, looking for a false piece of wood trim or unusual framing that perhaps could conceal a number of gold coins.

Outside, Charlie pulled on his coveralls. Holding his bag of tools [camera, flashlight, crowbar, small shovel], he decided to start at the chancel end, near the small apse. Pushing the low bushes aside, Charlie removed a small section of protective screen between two brick piers and crawled under the church. He turned on his flashlight, pulled his tool bag alongside and inched his way toward the center. Some evidence of mechanical and electrical additions plus the sacristy addition were obvious. Charlie was certainly not the first person to crawl under the church. He took several pictures in each direction for Sam, pulled his shovel forward and then pushed aside the damp earth. Reaching the summer beam down the center of the building, Charlie inspected the wood framing that raised the chancel floor. Just a little nervous about crawling in the dim light and meeting an animal, Charlie used his shovel to clear his way through masonry and wood debris. He reached up to touch, with appreciation, circular saw marks on the wood framing made over one hundred years ago by a steam powered circular saw. Reaching ahead with his hands and the shovel toward the area underneath the altar, Charlie pushed aside a small mound to reveal what looked like a corroded and blackened horseshoe. Looks pretty old. Sam might like to see this, he thought. Pulling his bag forward, the horseshoe was placed with his tools. Impressed with the condition of the wood framing and brick masonry piers, Charlie crawled on hands and knees around the perimeter of the foundation, back to the opening in the screen between two brick piers. After removing his coveralls, he made one last trip around the church looking at each triangular wood batten for any unusual mark that might be a clue.

On his way back home, Charlie placed a call on his cell phone to Sam. With a dignified soft bell, Sam's machine reported his absence and began a message. Charlie listened patiently to all the words of an active clergyman and then described his unsuccessful visit to All Saint's.

"I'll try to call Emmanuel Episcopal Church in Welaka to set up my next trip," he told the answering machine. "The office is hard to contact, but I'll let you know before I go. If you haven't been to Welaka, you might want to come with me or perhaps volunteer for a Sunday service. Welaka is a fisherman's joy, high above the river, not too far south from Horse Landing where Captain Dickison sunk the Columbine."

Since Emmanuel was not a self-supporting parish, Charlie called the Diocese and, after several calls to Welaka, made contact. He had not been to Welaka in several years, forgetting the attraction of the high bluffs overlooking the St. Johns as it disappeared in the distance around the curve of a projecting headland. The Timuqua Indian description of the St. Johns as Ylacco, roughly translated as "river of lakes", and pronounced as Welaka, was an appropriate name for the community. The streets were laid out many years ago in a rectangular grid oriented naturally to the water which provided access to the community. Palatka was only ten miles away but the meandering river doubled the distance. Over land, a rough and difficult trail led through hammocks and swamps. Near the turn of the century, steamboats from Jacksonville brought winter visitors and sportsmen and left loaded with cotton, corn, sweet potatoes, vegetables and citrus fruit. Today, Welaka remains attractive to sportsmen; boat sales and storage plus accommodations for seasonal and year-round visitors are located along the state highway that follows the curves of the river.

Charlie left the attraction of the river to return to the highway and Emmanuel Episcopal Church built in 1881. Shaded by a large oak tree and set back slightly from the road, the proportions and details of the church easily recalled the architectural principles of Richard Upjohn. The attractive entry porch, the lancet-shaped windows, the steep slope of the roof with decorative cut shingles in the gables, and a shingled bell tower looked familiar to a student of Richard Upjohn. He felt the addition of horizontal siding, probably over original board and batten, was unfortunate. Inside, Charlie remembered the words of Sam Wood about the presence of God in a silent church and sat quietly for a few minutes, thinking about the men and women who built Emmanuel; baptized their children, spent a lifetime of hard work here by the river and were buried from this small wood frame church. His thoughts returned to Captain Dickison. Did this church have any special meaning to him? Where would he place any coins or another portion of the treasure?

Charlie rose from the pew; then walked around the interior, checking the windows, frames and paneled walls. In contrast to the dark wood of the walls, the scissor-type roof trusses were painted white and the ceiling a faded blue. He stepped up into the chancel formed by a reduction in the width of the building. A small but well-proportioned wood altar was placed on the white painted east wall below three narrow stained glass windows. Charlie carefully slid the altar away from the wall to search the back. On the flat surface of the top of the altar, a low shelf supported two candelabra and a simple brass cross standing on a small square wood base. At first Charlie thought it was only used to increase the height of the cross. Then he noticed a front panel that was easily slid open to reveal a small cruet of wine and a wax paper-covered roll of unleavened wafers. Charlie remembered the container was called a tabernacle, used to hold in reserve unused elements from a recent communion service. Charlie decided other churches on his list would certainly be checked for a disguised sliding panel that could conceal a roll of gold coins.

Charlie repeated, from All Saints, his inspection of the walls, trusses and church furniture without success. As he stepped down from the chancel to the floor of the nave, he saw a loose corner of carpet. Carefully lifting the corner to expose the wood framing that raised the floor of the chancel, he decided to remove the wood panels and see what was under the floor rather than crawl under the building, which he noticed had settled more than All Saints. Charlie's letter had stated that his inspections would not include any destructive testing, but he felt he could easily remove three boards, look around and then replace the boards without disturbing anything.

"What are you doing?" a voice over his shoulder demanded, as he was half under the chancel floor. "You told us you would not tear anything up. I came in to check on you and find boards have been removed and you are practically under the chancel."

Charlie backed out of the opening and stood dusting his clothes and said, "Carpet was loose and I thought I saw a sign of decay in the wood framing and decided to check. I didn't see any problem of decay and I'll replace the boards. I hope I haven't spoiled the hospitality you have shown me."

The church secretary shook her head and said, "I will report this to our vestry. Please describe your actions in the written report you will certainly submit."

Charlie agreed, smiled as diplomatically as he could and began replacing the boards he had removed. He wished he had gone a little further under the chancel but felt he had seen enough and took pictures for Sam. He collected his equipment and thought of the two church visits. An old horseshoe and an idea to check for hidden sliding panels in all church furniture were not much to show.

Chapter 24

Susan Wood put down her cup of coffee, looked across the breakfast table and said, "Sam, I need to say I think you are going too far with this search for a treasure. You gave up a successful ministry in Richmond to come to Jacksonville and if I were your boss, I would tell you, as strong as I could, not to spend so much time in the archives of the Diocese."

"We've been through all of this before," said Sam. "Charlie and I have worked out a good scheme for visiting each of the river churches. I told you about it. His letter to me about a research project was certainly the type of request my office at the Diocese would receive. Charlie's been to two churches and he tells me of planned visits to two more. I don't think I have been neglecting my ministry. Frankly, I would rather be doing what he is doing, but I am a priest and I will continue to faithfully follow that call."

"O.K. Sam, just stop inspecting every stained glass window looking for what, I don't know. I know about St. Dunstan's in Magnolia, and the Magnolia Hotel, but we don't need a magnolia tree in our yard."

At his desk the next day, Sam considered the possible locations of St. Dunstan's altar. He recalled Bishop Young's letter closing the church asking J. J. "to take charge of the altar and to relocate it to an appropriate place." He thought J. J. probably took the altar to his plantation, storing it in his home to protect it. It is possible that some of the gold was stored inside the frame of the altar. Then what would he do? Move it at the right occasion to a church identified with Bishop Young or Richard Upjohn, probably on the river. Charlie has checked All Saints in Enterprise and Emmanuel in Welaka. He's going to St. Paul's, Federal Point and St.

Mary's, Green Cove Springs in the next few days and I'll hear about that soon.

Looking at a map of Florida and the St. Johns, Sam realized that Crescent City, on Crescent Lake, was only twelve miles east of Welaka. Steamboats from Jacksonville, entering the large lake by way of Dunn's Creek, served Crescent City, bringing mail, sportsmen and winter visitors, departing with citrus and vegetables. Sam recalled the yacht America was scuttled in Dunn's Creek by the Confederacy, just as the war reached Florida. He was surprised that Holy Comforter in Crescent City was not on their list of river churches. Charlie's original list was based on the influence of Richard Upjohn and Bishop Young but we have added J. J. Dickison and the Confederate treasure to our criteria. Certainly Holy Comforter was not on the river but river steamboats brought visitors and picked up a variety of freight and passengers destined for Jacksonville. Bishop Young sent occasional missionary priests to develop a congregation resulting in the construction of the small church in 1878. Photographs and drawings of Holy Comforter indicated the influence of Richard Upjohn so Sam added the church to their list. It was built before St. Dunstan's was lost. J. J.'s altar could be there; not likely, but possible.

Maybe if I take Susan with me to Holy Comforter she might understand some of the excitement I feel as I visit these small wonderful churches. Two phone calls later, the Reverend Sam Wood was scheduled to preach in Crescent City at the morning service. The influence of Upjohn was immediately apparent as Sam and Susan turned off U. S. 17 into a small parking area. The steep sloping roof, vertical board and batten siding, lancet windows and a simple entry porch on the narrow end certainly looked familiar. Sam recalled a drawing in the archives that indicated a south bell tower destroyed by a storm. A timber frame in the south church yard supported the original bell until a new bell tower on the north corner was built in 1942.

"Is this the church you told me about where the wife of the first rector was buried under the church?" asked Susan.

Sam said, "In 1876, the Reverend C. W. Williams from Brooklyn, New York, assigned here by Bishop Young, followed an earlier missionary priest conducting services in private homes. His wife died a year later as the church was being planned. She was buried where the future chancel would be located."

The appeal of a small church returned to Sam as he participated in the service. He had forgotten the satisfaction of being close to a congregation. The entire church interior here is smaller than the chancel at the Cathedral. After the service and the customary coffee hour, Sam left Susan with the Rector's wife and returned to the church. He had talked with Charlie about possible hiding places but felt inadequate this morning on his first visit to a river church looking for any evidence of a portion of the treasure. Where would Captain Dickison place something over a century ago that has not been discovered? Photographs in the archives showed a crowded altar area two steps above the nave floor with a small communion rail. Later photographs reflected new pews, carpet and relocation of the organ and choir to the back. Wall-mounted bracket lights between colored glass windows were replaced with overhead light fixtures suspended from the roof trusses. Sam had quickly determined that the altar was not from St. Dunstan's so where else should he look?

A lady from the Altar Guild entered the church from an adjacent sacristy carrying a small cruet of wine and a paper wrapped roll of communion wafers. Sam watched as she removed the altar cross from its place on a wood box, about ten inches square, slid open the front panel, placed the cruet and roll of wafers inside, slid the panel closed, replaced the cross, turned to Sam, smiled, and left the church. Charlie had told him to check the wood box, or tabernacle, and now he understood the possibilities.

Sam stepped up to the altar, removed the cross and lifted the wood box; actually a cube with the overall depth the same as the width and height. On the front panel, Sam noticed a carved, intertwined symbol of the first and last letters of the Greek alphabet; alpha and omega. On the rear panel the A was omitted and an upside down symbol for omega was inscribed in the wood. Even without a solid knowledge of woodworking or antiques, he could tell the tabernacle was very old. Turning it carefully to check all sides, he decided to remove the wine and wafers. Looking at the corners on the back, it was apparent the rear panel could not slide. Using his fountain pen as a measuring stick, Sam compared the depth of the inside compartment with the overall front to back dimension. Strange, he thought, the box is about two inches larger than the depth of the open section would indicate. He began to feel uncomfortable with his search and decided to replace the wine, wafers and cross, find Susan and be on his way back to Jacksonville. He picked up the tabernacle, pushed with his thumbs as he rotated the box back to its original position. Sam felt the left side give a little as he pushed. "I've broken it. I'm gonna be in big trouble," he mumbled aloud. The crack in the wood looked like a joint, Sam noticed as he placed the box on the altar. Charlie wouldn't stop now, he thought as he reached for the small knife attached to his car keys. Inscribing the joints on all four sides with the knife blade, Sam then pushed on the back panel. Nothing happened. He released the pressure from his right thumb and the panel moved outward with the pressure from his thumb on the left side. The secret of the release appeared to be the rotation of the box itself and thumb pressure on one side only. After years of handling, no doubt in one direction as the wine cruet and wafers were removed and replaced, through many cycles of humidity and layers of wax applied by the women of the Altar Guild, the joints on the back panel became less apparent.

Sam's fingers began to shake as he pushed on the panel.

The opposite side swung out revealing a small compartment crammed with paper. Sam carefully removed the scraps of paper yellowed with age to discover, wedged in one corner, a paper-wrapped cylinder of what appeared to be coins, larger than a quarter and about two inches high.

"My God," Sam exclaimed. "I never expected this. Now what do I do?"

Ten minutes later, Susan Wood entered the church looking for her husband and found him sitting in the first pew with his head bent.

"Sam," she said, "are you all right?" Sam raised his head, stood up, took her hand and guided her outside toward their car. Seated in the car, Sam said, "Susan, I think I found some of the treasure. A small roll of coins was hidden in a compartment in the back of the tabernacle on the altar. I happened to push one side as I looked at the antique small box and it swung open."

Susan looked at her husband in disbelief. "What did you do with the coins?"

"I removed the paper, put the coins in my pocket, closed the box and replaced everything on the altar."

"Sam, you can't do this. Those coins are not yours. How do you know they are part of your so-called treasure?"

"Susan, these coins have been there a long time. I agree that they do not belong to me and I intend to return them. But right now, somehow I am surprised but delighted to think Charlie and I are on the right track. I haven't unwrapped the coins and I'm not going to until Charlie and I can look together."

Chapter 25

Allison Gallagher, Charlie's wife, reached over to turn out her bedside light but then had second thoughts.

"What's the latest on the adventures of you and Sam?" she asked.

Charlie raised up from his pillow and said, "Alley, I've been to two churches, Sam was going to Crescent City to preach and take a look. All we've got is a lot of research, seven more churches to check, high hopes and an old horseshoe from St. Paul's, Enterprise."

"I'll tell you who else has high hopes, Charlie. Find that treasure or some part of it and I say we're outta here. Our kids have their own families and are doing fine. When you retired, I knew our lives would change and they have. We've settled into a routine that has all the signs of boredom with little to excite either of us. I'm ready to enjoy what you and Sam find. Maybe I'm dreaming about a wild chance but I have faith in you, and Sam, too, I guess."

The next morning, on his way to Palatka, Charlie thought about Alley's feelings. She's right, he told himself, maybe we need to get out of here and go do those things we've talked about even if Sam and I come up empty.

Arriving in Palatka, Charlie drove through town to make visual contact with the river. On the north side of the bridge, the St. Johns offered long vistas to the north. In contrast, on the south side, the river came from the south around a point called "Devil's Elbow." Just before the bridge, he turned north, circling two blocks back to St. Mark's Episcopal Church. Built in 1854, the wood frame church was the first in Florida designed by Richard Upjohn of New York City. The vocabulary of design for this building and the church plans and specifications presented in Upjohn's book, Rural Architecture, became the standard for the Episcopal mission churches developed by Francis Rutledge and John Young, the first and second Bishops of Florida, along the banks of the St. Johns.

Closed during the Civil War, reopened in 1866, St. Mark's has received several additions over the years. Soon after the war, an enclosed bell tower on the east side of the church replaced an open wood frame tower on the west. Not long after, the nave was expanded to the east and west to serve a growing congregation. Charlie felt Richard Upjohn would approve the architectural details of the additions. He wasn't so sure how Upjohn would feel over the apparent settling of the building. The church appears to be at ground level, the angled skirt board at the bottom of the board and batten siding was, in some places, touching the ground. Charlie wondered if the building had actually settled or had debris and backfill raised the grade around the church. Probably both, he decided. He knew now why his letter from Sam and his phone call had welcomed his visit, as he said, "to conduct a structural evaluation of wood frame churches."

A photograph of the church interior, dated 1884, before the nave additions, indicated a raised chancel, or altar area, created by a reduction in the width of the nave. On the wall about the chancel opening, painted words told the congregation to "Reverence My Sanctuary." The chancel furniture today appears to be from the same era. Wood rails with ornamental brass panels enclose the pulpit and form the communion rail. Charlie was told by the rector that the wood altar and paneled wall [reredos] behind the altar are not original. The location of St. Dunstan's altar, as relocated by Captain Dickison, jumped into Charlie's mind.

Charlie asked the rector, "Do you know where the original altar is?"

"The last time I saw the altar it was in pieces." said Charlie's guide. "The altar panels contain fleur-de-lis, beautifully carved."

From that description, Charlie knew the altar was not from St. Dunstan's. He recalled the description of the altar included symbol of the Greek letter, omega, in a design with horseshoes, open end up, without mention of any fleur-de-lis.

Charlie brought up his thoughts about the apparent settlement of the church and was surprised to learn of the existence of a crawl space under the floor framing. He was shown a small access door from the adjacent sacristy and an older access outside the north wall. After showing Charlie around the church interior, the rector excused himself as a tour guide, leaving Charlie to begin his work after assurance by Charlie that he would receive a copy of the investigation.

Charlie went first to the altar but decided it was too recent to have any concealed places. The pews and chancel furniture appeared to be very old but did not reveal any possible place to conceal any part of the treasure. The baptismal font, of smooth gray stone, had recently been relocated to a free-standing position beside the chancel opening. Blackened spots in the bowl itself were reported to be a result of Union soldiers using the basin to contain a cooking fire, but did not suggest any places for concealment.

Charlie retrieved his equipment from his car to prepare for a visit to the reported crawl space. He decided the sacristy access door was too tight so he went outside to the second access. He removed a wood frame screen, slipped on his coveralls, tied his bag to his waist, turned on his flashlight and crawled under. Due to the framing that raised the chancel floor, there was a little more room, but with the suspended duct work, it was still tight. To his surprise, his flashlight revealed a type of framing seen on most of the river churches. St. Mark's really was the prototype, he thought. Heart pine floor joists were supported by sill beams or girders on each side and down the center of the church, supported by individual piers. Some of the original brick piers remained at each end of the building with two foot square concrete piers poured as replacements for the original piers. The brick piers, unsupported by a solid foundation, probably were lost as water washed away the original compacted earth. Charlie crawled to the "summer beam" down the center, pushing the dirt ahead with his hands and small shovel. He turned to the north toward the chancel, working his way around and under mechanical duct work. Light from the access hole tempted him to leave but Charlie decided to move toward the area adjacent to the north wall and under the altar. To his disappointment, but not really sure what he expected, his flashlight did not reveal any old boxes or places that could conceal any type of container. Charlie dug around but all he uncovered was an old blackened horseshoe. Just like All Saints in Enterprise, he thought. Best take this one to Sam also, he decided.

With difficulty, Charlie made his way back to the access and climbed out. After thanking the church secretary, he was ready for a cold drink and lunch, before heading over the bridge to Federal Point.

After lunch, Charlie headed toward St. Paul's, Federal Point, across the river from Palatka, near Hastings, "the potato capital." It had been a few years since his last visit, and he'd forgotten how hard it was to find the church without good directions. This time, a few well-placed signs led Charlie along state roads through expansive potato fields to St. Paul's Church. The St. Johns River was closer to the church than he remembered, visible through side yards of houses to the north and west. Charlie was delighted to see the familiar shapes; steep roof, lancet windows and white painted board and batten walls shining in the sun. The cloudless blue sky of a Florida fall afternoon, the blue waters of the river, the green grass and trimmed landscaping made Charlie stand still for a minute or two as he left his car. A tall magnolia tree on the north side of the church gave Charlie a feeling of a hidden message. I know, I know, Sam, he thought. That tree is not a hundred years old, but I think it's a good sign.

Similar to the history of other river churches, a trading post, then a general store near the water's edge, were followed by steamboats bringing mail, sportsmen and winter visitors. Soon the popularity resulted in a small hotel and permanent residents. A mission to serve the small community was started by Bishop Young in 1880 with services in a barn surrounded by groves of orange trees. Charlie recalled, from the Diocesan archives, the construction of a church two years later, built for $1,000 with the provision of the contractor that the congregation carry the building materials from the dock on the river to the site of the church. Charlie often wished he could travel back in time to the late 1800's and watch how Bishop Young, guided by his friend Richard Upjohn, influenced the design and construction of these river churches. He felt today as he walked around the building that Upjohn and the Bishop would approve the relocation of the side entry porch to the west end of an expansion [in 1988] of the nave.

The double pointed arch design and the relatively low height suggested the entry doors were original. Stepping into the church, Charlie was immediately aware of the quality of light. The narrow lancet-shaped windows of purple and gray patterned glass set in diagonal lead frames with a variety of colored vertical bands down each side together with white plaster walls resulted in a most satisfying and serene feeling. Charlie imagined the church filled with people, wondering if any of the congregation was ever aware of this special experience. A red carpet down the center of the nave led to a wood communion rail and altar raised three steps above the main floor. Charlie felt the square vertical enclosures at each corner of the chancel were probably the result of compromises as the design was completed during the 1988 renovation. The usual wood scissor roof truss design was improved and probably strengthened with the addition of a horizontal brace formed with paired one by six boards.

Charlie went right to the wood altar placed against the

east wall of the chancel, attracted by the design and apparent
age. Checking all sides, he noticed a small brass plaque set
into the wood base on the narrow south face of the altar.
Excited, Charlie knelt down trying to read the inscription but
could not make out a single word of the Spencerian style
engraving. Frustrated, Charlie rose to his feet, headed back
to his car for reading glasses, hoping the plaque might offer a
clue to his search. Returning to the chancel, he laid down on
the floor but was still unable to read the words on the small
brass plaque. I'll have to come back with a magnifying glass.
Charlie smiled as he thought of the equipment needed by any
decent treasure hunter. How else would one read a hundred
year old plaque while lying on the floor of a small church?
From the altar, Charlie turned his attention to the two choir
pews, a small organ and a baptismal font on the first level of
the chancel. The polished stone font stood about forty-two
inches high with a pedestal base, a round column supporting
a stone cylindrical bowl about twelve inches deep. Carved in
the bowl was a shallow basin that would contain water used
for baptism. On impulse, Charlie carefully tilted the stone
font to check the weight and glanced at the bottom, noting a
hole probably used for drainage. Just a minute, he thought.
The basin did not have provision for draining the water.
After a baptism, the water that has been blessed is removed
and poured directly into the ground. Curious, he thought,
sticking his finger into the hole. Feeling an obstruction,
Charlie took his pocketknife, inserted the blade and pushed.
Retrieving the blade, a wad of paper fell out. Opening his
knife to a longer blade, he pushed again. This time a
yellowed crumpled wad of paper came out as the blade was
withdrawn. Running to his car for a screwdriver, Charlie was
nervous that someone from the church would be curious and
want to know what he was doing with the font. Which
reminds me, he thought, I told the people in Welaka that I'd
prepare a report of my investigation over there. No one
appeared so Charlie returned to the font. Carefully inserting

the screwdriver blade, he felt the movement of something solid inside the hole. Rocking the font from side to side, he was astonished when a roll of paper about two inches long containing what appeared to be rust-colored coins fell out onto the chancel carpet.

"I don't believe this," Charlie exclaimed. He suppressed a yell of excitement as he jumped up and down holding the paper-wrapped coins in both hands. Replacing the font, Charlie collected his equipment, ran to his car and grabbed his cell phone.

"Come on, Sam. Answer the phone. Where are you?" He listened to the message, not so patiently this time, then said, "Sam, I've found something at Federal Point. I've already been to St. Mark's in Palatka, but because of where I found something here, I'm going back to St. Mark's. If I don't hear from you, I will come to your house."

Charlie tried hard to hold down his speed, driving back to Palatka. Luckily, no police were nearby as he literally flew over the St. Johns River Bridge. With a deliberate effort, Charlie made himself calm down, easing into a parking place on the street beside the church.

"I'd like to go back in the church," he said to a surprised secretary. "This morning was informative, but I need to recheck a small item. Won't take but ten minutes."

"Since you were here earlier today, I'll let you use my key to the rear door. Please bring it back soon so I can close for the day. Sir, your hands are shaking. Are you O.K.?"

With a strong effort and a deep breath, Charlie made his hands stop shaking as he accepted the church key. Returning to the church through the sacristy, he headed directly to the stone baptismal font. The smooth carved gray stone looked similar to St. Paul's at Federal Point but heavier. He laid the font carefully on its side, delighted to see the same hole on the bottom.

No problem with tools this time, Charlie inserted his knife, then a screwdriver into the hole. An obstruction felt

more solid than paper this time. His flashlight revealed a
wood plug two inches into the hole. With his knife and
screwdriver, Charlie managed to work it loose. The plug was
not new, he thought, reaching for his flashlight. Trembling
again, he looked into the hole with his light to see nothing.
"It's empty", he said aloud. Whatever was placed in the hole
was gone. Kneeling on the floor beside the font, Charlie
knew his discovery at St. Paul's revealed where Captain
Dickison had placed some of Bishop Young's portion of the
treasure. Perhaps years ago, the priest or a worker or
somebody discovered the coins, maybe not. Charlie couldn't
ask the rector if any coins had been found. He knew, though,
where he would check first at the next church on his list.
Charlie carefully replaced the font, left the church and
returned the key to a waiting secretary.

"You certainly are not shaking now, Mr. Gallagher," she
said.

"No, I'm fine, thank you. I was afraid I had missed
something on my visit this morning," Charlie said. "I'm on
my way home now."

In his car, Charlie tried Sam's phone again, without
success.

"O.K. Sam, here I come."

Chapter 26

From his kitchen window, Sam watched Charlie's car turn rapidly into his driveway. He placed his coffee cup on the counter and went outside to meet him.

"Come in, Charlie, come in," he said. "I think I've found something."

"Me too, Sam. I've been trying to call you all the way from Palatka," Charlie said as he jumped out then reached back in the car to grab his bag.

The two men trotted through Sam's garage, into the kitchen, stood looking at each other, then began talking excitedly at the same time. Sam paused first, put his hand on Charlie's shoulder and said, "Easy, Charlie. Sit down. I'll get you a drink of water and then we'll tell our story. You go first."

Charlie smiled, took a long drink of water and sat down. "Sam, I found a roll of coins at St. Paul's in Federal Point in the base of the baptismal font."

Reaching in his bag, Charlie withdrew the small cylinder of coins. "I don't know what they are," he said. "I'm afraid to tear the paper."

He described his search and discovery at Federal Point after a morning visit to St. Mark's in Palatka. "After I found these," he said, "I went back to St. Mark's to look in their font, but found nothing.

Sam took the coins from Charlie, held them lightly in one hand, reached in his pocket with the other for a small cloth bag. "Look at this, Charlie. This roll came from Holy Comforter in Crescent City." Sam described his visit and discovery of the hinged back of the wood tabernacle that opened to reveal the coins.

"Charlie, I think without a doubt, that these coins were hidden by Captain J. J. Dickison, but I am not sure what we have. They look like twenty dollar gold double eagles to me. I guess I never really thought about what we would do if we found something; coins, gold or silver bars. Until we know more about these coins, I believe we should not unwrap them. Probably the best thing would be to put them in a safe deposit box for safekeeping. Just think, we have two more churches to visit; three, if we go back to Fort George. And Hibernia, St. Margaret's should be considered as influenced by Bishop Young."

"Sam, I need more than a drink of water," Charlie said as he held the two cylinders of coins.

Sam produced a bottle of scotch whiskey, poured more than a splash in Charlie's glass, reached for a glass and did the same for himself. With two matching smiles, Charlie and Sam raised their glasses in a silent toast to their success.

Charlie said, "At Enterprise, I was under the church and found a horseshoe. When I was under St. Mark's in Palatka, I found another that I put in my bag with the other. Should we keep these?"

Sam nearly dropped his glass. "Don't you remember the legend of Dunstan, the blacksmith, before he became Archbishop of Canterbury? Get the horseshoes out."

Charlie dug in his bag, pulled the two horseshoes out and placed them on the table. "Just look like old dirty horseshoes to me," he said.

"I know, Charlie, but look at the two. They are blackened but not rusty."

"So what," said Charlie. "They've been under the two churches in the dirt. No telling how long. Could be last week or last year."

Sam thought a minute and said, "Or a very long time ago." He turned to his kitchen catch-all drawer, pulled out a bottle opener that had a magnet attached to the back. "This might tell us something. The horseshoes are iron and should attract the magnet."

Sam took one horseshoe over to the sink and washed it off, rubbing the horseshoe with his hand to help the running water. "Looks like an old black metal horseshoe." He placed the magnet on the horseshoe and it slid off. He moved the magnet over the shoe without attraction from the magnet.

Sam looked at Charlie and said, "Do you suppose …?"

"Do I suppose what?" said Charlie. "Come on, Sam. What are you thinking?"

Sam picked up both horseshoes, looked at each closely and said, "Could it be possible that Captain Dickison melted down the bars of silver from the treasure and used a horseshoe mold to cast these, and maybe other, horseshoes. If so, I can't imagine how these two ended up under the chancels of the two churches. I'll check the dates the churches were built. Dickison could have visited the churches, as he told Bishop Young he would, and attached the horseshoes to the wood floor framing. The nails would have rusted and the shoes would drop into the dirt to be covered and pushed around by workers under the building over the years. As I recall, you didn't go under Emmanuel in Welaka. Maybe you should go back."

Charlie said, "If you think these two are silver, I will certainly go back. I'll mention the possible need to return when I write my report to the Vestry."

Sam said, "I have a friend who deals in antique silver. I'll talk to him and see what he says about very old blackened silver."

The two men sat back in the chairs around the kitchen table, smiling at each other, pleased with their discoveries. "Sam, you take the coins and old horseshoes, put 'em in a safety deposit box while I go look at St. Mary's, Green Cove Springs and Grace, Orange Park. That will complete the seven river churches we decided to check, plus Crescent City. I believe we should go back to Fort George, where we started; I'll see if the Vestry at Emmanuel in Welaka will let me return after I pulled up those boards in the church. We haven't been to St. Margaret's in Hibernia and I think we should go there, too. Captain Dickison could have gone there since Bishop Young was a friend of Margaret Fleming. Just look at the church and you can see the influence of someone who knew and cared about church architecture in Florida. If I can calm down long enough, I'll make the calls to set up the visits."

Sam said, "I can't help but think there is more to the Confederate treasure than a few coins and perhaps two or more silver horseshoes. All I have read about the assets of the Confederacy indicated gold coins with a monetary value, in 1865, in the thousands, plus bars of silver and ingots of gold. Legend has told us that Robert E. Lee took an ingot of gold with him when he left Magnolia in 1870. Where is the rest?"

Chapter 27

The next morning, the Reverend Samuel Wood walked into his office with a large smile on his face, pleased with himself, ready to go to the next river church. A note on his desk directing him to see the Bishop immediately wiped away his smile. Sam thought to himself that Susan had told me not to spend so much time in the archives and now, I suspect, the Bishop is going to point out, with displeasure, the frequency of my visits.

"Sam," the Bishop said, "we received this letter yesterday. Knowing of your interest in our history, please respond to the request of the gentleman from Maine. Copy me with your reply."

>Episcopal Diocese of Florida
>325 Market Street
>Jacksonville, Florida
>
>Dear Sir/Madam:
>
>I am interested in St. Dunstan's Episcopal Church. I have searched church registers and published histories of the Episcopal Church in Florida without success.
>
>My inquiry is based on a letter dated 1883, recently discovered in an old family history, from John Freeman Young, Bishop of Florida to Frank Sanborn, my great-great-great grandfather. In his letter, Bishop Young describes the windows given by my ancestor to St. Dunstan's. The church was to

be closed and he asked for instructions, by my family, as to the fate of the windows.

I could not find a record of any response by my family. Could you tell me if St. Dunstan's still exists and, if so, what happened to the windows.

I anxiously await your reply.

Yours truly,

Frank Sanborn

3116 St. Charles Avenue
Brunswick, Maine   04033

Mr. Frank Sanborn
3116 St. Charles Avenue
Brunswick, Maine

Dear Mr. Sanborn:

It is my pleasure to respond to your request for information on St. Dunstan's Episcopal Church. The church was designed by the architect, Richard Upjohn of New York after a request by the first Bishop of Florida, Francis Rutledge. Construction started in 1861, walls were erected and roof shingles were nearing completion when Bishop Rutledge stopped the work as the Civil War came to the St. Johns River.

In 1867, Bishop John Young, second Bishop of Florida, authorized the original contractor, Ed

Foley, to resume work. A letter from Frank Sanborn of Brunswick, Maine, authorizing the purchase of appropriate stained glass windows, without any dedication, is in the files.

Diocesan files indicate the closure of St. Dunstan's in 1883 with a copy of the letter to your family asking for instructions with respect to the windows. The files do not include any response.

I can report to you my research efforts, on another facet of St. Dunstan's, indicate the church was placed on a barge to be relocated to an unknown site on the river. I assume the windows were placed on the barge or possibly removed for use in another mission church.

In my research, I found a description of an explosion on the St. Johns in 1884 describing "an unusual cargo", that I believe was St. Dunstan's Church. All records of St. Dunstan's stop at that point.

I hope I have answered your questions. Please contact me if I may be of further assistance.

Sincerely,

The Reverend Samuel Wood

The Reverend Samuel Wood
Diocese of Florida
325 Market Street
Jacksonville, Florida

Dear Sir:

Thank you for the information on St. Dunstan's
and the fate of the windows. I am intrigued by the
possibility the windows were removed and relocated.
It is my plan to travel to Jacksonville, in the near
future, to search for the sword of my ancestor,
Ensign Frank Sanborn, United Stated Navy,
surrendered during the war to a Confederate officer.

On arrival, I will contact your office to express
the appreciation of my family for your efforts.

Yours truly,

Frank Sanborn

Sam put down the letter. Sword? What sword? Who was
Ensign Frank Sanborn? He put aside his notes on Diocesan
history and turned to his books on Jacksonville and the St.
Johns during the Civil War. With interest, he read how the
war began to affect the lives of the people in Jacksonville
and up the river. Historians described the activities of a small
fleet of steam-powered gunboats, ordered by the U. S. Navy
to locate and assist any Union sympathizers and to stop all
Confederate traffic on the St. Johns. Most important, the
gunboats were directed to seek out and capture Captain J. J.
Dickison, commanding a troop of Confederate cavalry
continually and successfully attacking Union troops in North
Florida.
Then he saw the name: Frank Sanborn, Ensign, U. S. Navy,
Commanding Columbine, the gunboat made famous as the
only warship of the U. S. Navy captured and sunk by a troop
of cavalry. The sword offered in surrender by Ensign
Sanford to Captain J. J. Dickison had to be the sword sought

by his descendant, Frank Sanford of Brunswick, Maine.

Sam forwarded the letter to the Bishop with a note identifying Mr. Sanborn and offering to meet him if he visits Jacksonville and makes contact with the Diocesan office.

Sam decided he would not be concerned about any possible interference with his own search but would let Charlie know in case their paths should cross.

Chapter 28

The polished black sedan turned from the busy street into a small parking lot beside a one story brick building. Frank Sanborn from Brunswick, Maine, sat for a moment gathering his thoughts. Since the successful sale of his business, Sanborn found the transition from his office into an active pursuit of family history both interesting and satisfying. He had spent most of the day in the Jacksonville Public Library, leaving with a recommendation to visit the Museum of the Confederacy. Sanborn hoped it wasn't too late. Cars were in the parking lot and lights were on.

Inside the museum, a group of men stood beneath a large, wall-mounted map of the Confederate States of America, talking with enthusiasm about the increasing number of visitors. Just as a staff member began to turn out the lights, the entry door swung open. A well dressed, tall, gray haired man stepped through the doorway.

"I hope I'm not too late to speak with someone about the Civil War on the St. Johns River. My name is Frank Sanborn and I live in Brunswick, Maine. A reference librarian at the library downtown directed me to this museum in search for two things. The first is a navy sword apparently lost on the river in 1864. Perhaps you have a collection of swords from those days that would include a sword of this type that could show me, better than a picture or a written description, what I'm looking for."

Smiling, a heavy set, bearded man stepped forward from the group. "Welcome, Sir. Please come in." Extending his hand, he said, "My name is Brewster Adams. These gentlemen with me, supporters of the museum, are always anxious to talk about the history of The Civil War, especially here in north Florida. Can you give us any further details?"

Sanborn said, "Research in the history of my family tells me the ancestor, also named Sanborn, was in command of a Union gunboat on the St. Johns in 1864. All I know is the boat was sunk in a battle on the river. His sword was offered in surrender to a Confederate officer. One account described this person as a cavalry officer but that doesn't sound right. I believe the boat was named Columbia. I am looking for his sword." He looked around the room at the small group of men. Somehow, he didn't see what he expected. All looked and dressed like businessmen that he had dealt with for many years, each appearing ready to help a late visitor.

Three men started to speak at the same time. "The gunboat was named Columbine, not Columbia, and was indeed sunk by gunfire from a troop of cavalry, led by Captain J. J. Dickison." Motioning to the other two, one man continued. "The battle happened south of Jacksonville and Palatka at Horse Landing, just north of where the Oklawaha River joins the St. Johns." He turned to the map on the wall, pointed out the location telling the story of how Captain Dickison and his men followed the Columbine as she headed south, then waited on the west bank to attack the gunboat on her return north.

Sanborn was then escorted, by Brewster Adams, through the museum to a display of gleaming swords mounted on dark cloth. His host pointed to three weapons and said, "The longer sword with a slightly curved blade was used by the Union army. The Confederate sword is basically the same but of poorer finish. The third sword is a Union navy sword with a shorter blade that meets a "cut and thrust" requirement; the guard is marked USN and you can see the hilt is decorated with dolphins and an eagle. The blank panel on the blade was for the owner's name."

Sanborn said, "Up until today, I did not know the difference between an Army and Navy sword. Obviously this particular weapon was not my ancestor's but you have graciously shown me what I need to look for."

"You mentioned two concerns," said Adams. "What was the second?"

Reaching for his notes, Sanborn said, "I found a letter, dated 1883, to my family from the Episcopal Bishop of Florida, John Young. He asked for instructions regarding stained glass windows given by my family to a church scheduled to be closed. Located in Magnolia, on the St. Johns, the church was named St. Dunstan's. I am looking for the church, the windows and even the town of Magnolia. I have been in touch with the Diocese of Florida. They offered little help in locating the church and I can't find Magnolia on any map."

Pointing to the map, Adams said, "Magnolia was located just north of Green Cove Springs. A large resort hotel was built on the river during the age of steamboats and burned in 1882. General Robert E. Lee visited Magnolia after the war; for what reason I have never understood." He shook his head. "Can't help you any more with your last concern. The only man I know who could possibly help you with the church is a retired architect named Charlie Gallagher."

Sanborn noted the name, shook the hand of Adams, smiled and left.

Adams turned to his associates and said, "I didn't mention any legends about Robert E. Lee. He'll hear all of them soon enough."

Chapter 29

On his way to Green Cove Springs, Charlie thought about the dates of construction for the river churches. He had started his search for the treasure at All Saints in Enterprise, built in 1883; St. Paul's in Federal Point had been built one year before that; and today he was going to St. Mary's, built approximately four years before either one. Sam and Charlie believed St. Dunstan's was dedicated in 1866 and was the first. When Captain J. J. Dickison began his visits to the churches of Bishop Young, St. Dunstan's was still active. From his study of the Captain, Charlie felt Dickson would have been inclined to start with the earliest and then visit each church, perhaps while construction was in progress or upon completion. So after the departure of Robert E. Lee from Magnolia in 1870 and Bishop Young's refusal of any share of the balance of the treasure, Captain Dickison would have gone first to St. Mark's, Palatka, an Upjohn design and certainly within the interests of Bishop Young. Then he would have gone to St. Margaret's in Hibernia, completed in 1875. While only a family chapel, not yet an Episcopal parish, the small church was certainly a statement of the Bishop's architectural preferences and an expression of his friendship with Mrs. Margaret Fleming. Next, Dickison would have gone in 1878 to Holy Comforter in Crescent City, where Sam found the tabernacle and the small secret door. Then to St. Mary's in Green Cove where Charlie was headed this morning. He wondered continually about the treasure. If J. J. Dickison was placing coins or silver horseshoes at each church, where was the balance? He was doing this with Bishop Young's share; where was his own? Did Dickison want the churches to find their gift easily? So far, Charlie decided, the clues are there; tabernacles, baptismal fonts, silver horseshoes under chancels, fleur-de-lis window designs, altar panels and crosses, plus the repetitive triangular wood battens at churches designed by different architects and built by different contractors.

As he headed south from Jacksonville on U.S. 17, Charlie was aware that his route would follow the river, passing side roads that led to four river churches; Grace in Orange Park, St. Margaret's in Hibernia, the site of St. Dunstan's and his destination today, St. Mary's in Green Cove Springs. A few miles after crossing the Black Creek Bridge, Charlie passed through the community of Magnolia, identified today only through street names, business titles and a country club. Looking toward the river, Charlie recalled that in 1880, the Magnolia Hotel was in full operation as the largest hotel on the river. St. Dunstan's nearby, with a loyal congregation of local residents including J. J. Dickison and a few northern visitors, was led by the Reverend Harold Alexander.

Crossing Governor's Creek into Green Cove Springs, in only a few seconds by bridge today, Charlie imagined the difficult access between the two towns by private boat or a small open ferry, hardly more than a raft. Both communities enjoyed visitors from the north arriving by railroad with regular stops on the route between Jacksonville and Tampa or by steamboat on the river. The choice of hotels depended upon the desire of the visitors to bathe in the flowing waters in Green Cove Springs with a wide choice of hotels or to enjoy the Magnolia Hotel, the largest on the river, with multiple attractions and a smaller flowing spring that offered medicinal qualities. In contrast to the loyalty and backing of a predominately local congregation at St. Dunstan's, St. Mary's enjoyed the enthusiastic support of northern visitors and clergymen to Green Cove Springs. After receiving a gift of land and other positive expressions, Bishop Young turned first to his old friend Richard Upjohn and his shared vision of the proper design for Episcopal churches. Finding that

Upjohn had retired, Bishop Young selected Charles Haight of New York, an experienced and talented architect who shared the basic principles of a revival of Gothic architectural details, perhaps adding a few more decorative details than Upjohn.

Turning toward the river as he left his car, Charlie immediately recalled that this church was truly a river church, with the entry facing the river less than twenty-five yards from the water's edge. At the local historical museum, Charlie found a lithograph, dated 1885, that showed multiple docks extending into the deep waters of the St. Johns and a walk from the springs and hotels along the waterfront all the way to Governor's Creek. In earlier visits, Charlie had searched for evidence of this walk and had decided, based on contemporary photographs of the town, that it was probably a walk made of wood planks. Interestingly, the lithograph referred to the walk as "lovers' walk" while other references describe a "St. David's Path". Charlie imagined the well-dressed northern visitors and the local members of the congregation in their Sunday best, walking along the path to St. Mary's as the church bell called them to the morning service.

St. Mary's has grown old gracefully with loving care for over one hundred and twenty-five years. Approximately sixty feet long raised above the ground on spaced brick piers, the church appears larger than other river churches. The white painted vertical board and batten exterior, eleven symmetrically placed narrow lancet-shaped windows, the pitched roof and steeple beyond demonstrate the proportions necessary for a well-designed building. Charlie recalled that the architect, Charles Haight, also designed Good Shepherd in Maitland, near Orlando, completed in 1882.

The height of the building and the open areas between the piers attracted Charlie to begin his search under the church. Pushing his equipment bag ahead, Charlie crawled under the north end, looking closely now for horseshoes. He felt

Captain Dickison would not place any coins under a church unless he had a disguised location, so Charlie checked the perimeter sill beams and the summer beam down the center for any unusual framing. He smiled at the sight of circular saw marks from a long time ago still evident on the wood timbers. Working carefully around twentieth century mechanical equipment on his way toward the chancel, Charlie noticed pants and shoes walking along the side of the church. A face appeared and said, "Hello, under the church. Will you be coming out soon? I haven't found anyone else around today and I have a couple of questions you might be able to answer."

"Hold on," said Charlie. "I'll be out in a few minutes. I'll meet you on the river side."

Doesn't sound like a church member wondering what I'm doing like the lady in Welaka, Charlie thought. So he continued his search under the chancel, noting the additional framing necessary to raise the floor level. All beams and joists looked standard. He did see two rusty nails that could have supported a properly hung horseshoe but digging and moving the dirt around led only to debris and deposits left by visiting animals. Charlie thought that any encounters with animals under the churches could lead to Sam taking over the next adventure into a dark crawl space.

Charlie recognized the pant legs and shoes he had seen from under the church. An older man with gray hair, dressed in creased khaki pants and a blue golf shirt, stood as Charlie walked around the corner of the church. Extending his hand, he said, "Good morning. I saw the sign that the church is open, but I felt uncomfortable as a visitor to just walk in. I hope I didn't disturb you from whatever you were doing under the church. My name is Frank Sanborn."

Charlie offered his hand, introduced himself and said, "I'm a visitor myself, although I've been here many times. The door sticks and might discourage a more casual visitor. Are you familiar with St. Mary's?"

"I only know this is one of the so-called river churches and I'm interested in the windows. Many years ago, soon after the Civil War, my family made a gift to one of the churches and I'm looking for the windows. I was in Magnolia earlier today. I was told a large hotel and small church were there many years ago but I saw no evidence of any old buildings, just a bunch of apartments."

Charlie pulled open one of the two entry doors and the two men entered the church. Sanborn glanced around and with little apparent appreciation for the church interior, turned immediately to the windows on the north end, pausing only long enough to read the dedication. Then, glancing at the narrow leaded-glass windows on each side of the nave, he walked to the chancel end to inspect the windows above the altar. After a brief moment, he turned to Charlie and said, "Nice, but not what I'm looking for. Can you tell me if Green Cove Springs has a museum of local history that might include weapons?"

Charlie thought to himself that this man, who Sam had told him about, is really in a hurry. He wanted to ask if Sanborn knew what dedication was on his family's windows, or, what about the leaded-glass with the fleur-de-lis designs at the nave? Did he know this design appears on other river churches, probably produced in New York, perhaps a result of a gift? And he is asking about old weapons? His search is as mysterious as mine. Charlie directed him to the local museums he knew about, here and in Jacksonville.

Sanborn said, "Thanks for your help. One last question. Will you give me directions to Federal Point?"

Charlie gave him further directions, pulled the door closed as Sanborn left and turned to continue his own search.

The architectural influence of Richard Upjohn through his friend Bishop Young is apparent on the interior of St. Mary's. However, the architect Charles Haight demonstrated his own more Victorian abilities. To architecturally define the chancel, at the roof truss above the first step leading to the altar, he eliminated the tie beam across the nave, placed a timber column from the floor to the sloping roof rafter and connected the column to the wall timber with a horizontal wood brace, creating a simulated hammer beam. In the open area below the hammer beam, Haight placed a pointed arch. Carrying his theme further, he placed pointed arch wood trim on the north and south walls. The pointed arch theme was also expressed in the chancel rail. Charlie was sure Captain Dickison was unaware of these additional details and would probably stick to his pattern in honoring his friend by placing a silver horseshoe under the church or gold coins somewhere in the chancel furniture. First he checked the altar to be sure the altar of St. Dunstan's had not been relocated here at St. Mary's. The altar, placed slightly away from the rear wall, was covered today with a frontal, a heavy ornate cloth that hung on three sides. Charlie carefully lifted the cloth to be sure the design and wood trim did not include the omega or horseshoe of the St. Dunstan's altar. Satisfied the altar was not St. Dunstan's, he turned to a wide shelf, called a retable, on the rear wall, below the stained glass windows. An ornate cross on a stepped base stood at the center, silhouetted against the color of the windows. Charlie looked for a tabernacle, a box, as described by Sam, or any container that could hold a roll of coins. Without success, he turned to the lectern and pulpit, beautifully crafted in brass, searching for possible hiding places for Dickison's gold coins.

Charlie then turned to the baptismal font, a favorite hiding place of Captain Dickison, in the rear of the church. He recalled, from his research on St. Mary's, one list describing the gift of a font; a second list not mentioning the font. Charlie felt the description of memorials on both lists presented by benefactors identified as seasonal visitors, indicated chancel furnishings and stained glass windows, fabricated in northern more experienced workshops and studios. The baptismal font, however, was of a more humble design in wood possibly presented by a local craftsman.

The baptismal font stood about forty-two inches high; a hexagonal-shaped cabinet containing a polished metal basin, topped with a removable wood pyramidal cover that added twelve inches to the height of the font. The cabinet was supported by a faceted wood column with flared brackets standing on a wood base formed with three hexagonal planes, one horizontal to support the column, one sloping and one vertical.

Charlie removed the pyramid cover and checked it thoroughly. He decided to check the font for a false drain hole, carefully placing the font on one side. At first glance Charlie was disappointed with the absence of any holes on the bottom. He ran his fingers over the flat surface and felt, in the center, a faint outline of a letter or symbol. Remembering his lesson from St. Paul's, Federal Point, he removed a magnifying glass from his bag. Charlie's heart skipped a beat or two as he saw, through the glass, a faint image of the Greek letter omega, or as Charlie saw it, a horseshoe in reverse. Charlie took a deep breath, moved to an adjacent pew and sat staring at the font, his pulse racing as a smile of pleasure appeared on his face.

"Captain Dickison," he said aloud. "I gotcha." The symbol was a positive clue, he felt, but where was the gold? Charlie stood the font back up and returned to his pew to consider any possible hidden compartments.

From Sam's discovery of the hidden panel at Holy Comforter, in Crescent City, Charlie realized that a very good craftsman had worked with Captain Dickison. He recalled the name of Will Hendry as the woodworker who built the altar for St. Dunstan's. Charlie decided the two stone fonts he had seen were early locations for the gold coins. Captain Dickison must have planned alternative locations and asked Hendry to create hidden panels in gifts to be made to the river churches as each was complete. Charlie wondered if the hiding place here at St. Mary's had been found. The gold was part of the share of Bishop John

Young and was intended to be found. As Sam and Charlie discovered, the coins were hidden better than J. J. Dickison probably intended. Charlie ran his hands over all the surfaces of the font, pushing and pulling, but nothing popped or slid open.

Charlie hoped the privacy would continue, although no one would see anymore than a man sitting in a pew at the rear of the church. He hoped the sticky door at the entry would offer enough warning to be able to disguise his further search.

Charlie thought Sanborn had gone but he had not. Sanborn had walked to the riverfront and realized his notes were on the table inside the entry. The sticky door was not closed. Sanborn opened the door and saw Charlie at the baptismal font.

Charlie picked up the font. Although portable, it was heavier than he thought. The font had to be stable, presenting a positive support for the basin of water during a service of baptism. Pushing the font back and forth, Charlie decided the upper cabinet depended on a heavy base for stability. Wood blocking, he felt, was not enough. With a silent prayer that the church door would really be difficult for a visitor to open, Charlie braced the base with his feet, placed his arms around the upper cabinet and turned. Nothing happened. He repeated the same motion while bracing the cabinet and attempting to rotate the base. The result was the same.

He removed the water basin. The current basin was supported by flanges on the rim of the basin. A wood framed box about eight inches deep suggested that other basins, of varying sizes, could have been used. The sides of the box formed an open square on the top surface of the font with flush joints barely discernable. Sam had described similar joints on the hidden door he found at the tabernacle in Crescent City. Years of waxing had hidden the sides of the open box. On all four sides of the box Charlie noticed round holes about one inch in diameter. Inserting a finger in two of the holes on opposite sides, Charlie took a deep breath and pulled up. He felt a slight movement. Moving his fingers to the opposite pair of holes and pulling produced more movement and then, all of a sudden, the open box came loose. Looking into the cabinet Charlie saw the open end of the faceted wood column connecting the upper section to the base. Reaching into the opening, he was able to remove a tinplate cylinder about twelve inches long that felt heavy enough to provide stability to the font. Probably filled with sand, Charlie thought. Holding his breath, he reached in again and withdrew two cylinders of coins.

Sanborn had stepped inside to retrieve his papers and closed the door. He noticed Charlie handling the font and moved into a shadow to watch. When Charlie withdrew the cylinders, Sanborn was astonished. He decided to make a hasty exit, hopefully unnoticed.

Charlie reassembled the font, unaware he had been seen. Walking up and down the aisle to calm down, he said aloud, "Captain Dickison, I don't believe you wanted Bishop Young's share to be found."

Holding tight to the two cylinders of coins, he left the church with the confidence of a successful treasure hunter. He decided to see next what Grace Church, in Orange Park, revealed.

Chapter 30

On his way north, toward Orange Park and Grace Episcopal Church, Charlie decided the best way to lower his level of excitement was to park his car near Grace Church and walk down to the river before visiting the church. Looking east across the broad river, he thought about his wife, Alley, and their future. Would the discoveries of gold coins and silver horseshoes offer any change in their lives? It certainly had affected his life. All he thought about was small wood frame river churches and a clever Confederate captain. He hadn't thought of playing golf in quite a while. Charlie wondered about the value of what he and Sam had uncovered. As pleased as he was with their effort, he realized once again that Captain Dickison's portion was still hidden. Did he ingeniously hide a portion of the gold and silver in Bishop Young's behalf, intending to retrieve the treasure at a later date if the church did not find their gift? Where is his share, Charlie asked himself again. Did he simply enjoy his riches after the war?

Charlie stood on the bank above the river watching, in his imagination, the arrival, by boat, of a visiting priest or perhaps Bishop John Young himself together with church members as they gathered for Sunday services in the early 1880's. He remembered a presentation, enjoyed many years ago, dramatizing the search for a suitable name for the new church in Orange Park. References to oranges and groves, along with biblical references were rejected by the congregation. One Sunday, at the conclusion of a visit, Bishop Young, standing in his boat, raised his hand in a farewell blessing and said, "Grace be unto you." Exchanging smiles and nods of approval by church leaders, Grace

Episcopal Church was born.

Rain clouds were building in the west as Charlie walked back to the church. An early photograph, dated 1879, showed a small building of simple design; a rectangular structure with a steeple, pitched roof standing alone in an open field. A fence is in the distance. A young oak tree is nearby. The narrow path to the river shown in the photograph has grown into two paved single lane roads separated by a landscaped island. The oak has grown to full maturity, casting shadows on the church. One story buildings surround the church, now referred to as a chapel. A large handsome church stands across the street in evidence of the growth of the congregation.

Development of Grace Episcopal Church followed the same basic pattern of other river churches: the river, a long wood dock reaching into deep water, farming and citrus groves, winter visitors, then a hotel (The Park View, long since demolished) and a missionary Bishop. His architectural preferences were faithfully executed here in Orange Park by Robert S. Schuyler, formerly of New York, an active churchman and a prolific architect. Churches in Waldo, Fairbanks, Earleton on Lake Santa Fe, St. Peter's in Fernandina, St. George at Fort George, and St. Andrew's in Jacksonville demonstrated his understanding and affection for Bishop Young's principles of church architecture.

From the street, three carefully designed building forms identified the church; a steep-sloping gable roof topped with a bell tower supported by wood brackets below the edge of the roof, a triangular stained glass window above the ridge of the gable roof of an entry porch and a pair of wood doors in a single lancet frame. Schuyler placed a transept on each side of the nave and reduced the width of the chancel area, creating a cruciform-shaped building plan. The width of these smaller spaces resulted in three lower gable roofs. The old photograph indicated vertical board siding as compared to the present wood shingles darkened by stain and age, pleasantly contrasted with glossy white trim of the exterior doors and windows.

Charlie wondered how J. J. Dickison felt, back in 1880, as he stood in front of the plain wood church holding a roll of coins and perhaps a silver horseshoe. What could have been his inspiration for a hiding place? Today, even with the darkening skies, Charlie thought the setting of this small church would result in a more interesting hiding place. He hoped, however, to visit the church thinking like J. J.

Charlie entered the church, carefully securing the wood doors behind him. Standing in the back, he was delighted, as an architect, to see a creative mind at work. In his own projects, Charlie had often followed an old design principle: to leave uncovered the framing members, or the "bones" that form the basic structure of the building. This church was different from other river churches. Where Charles Haight at St. Mary's, Green Cove Springs, demonstrated an inclination for decorative expressions, Robert Schuyler's structural design was there for all to see. Wood columns braced top and bottom with diagonal braces, forming a "Y" at each column and a triangle at the base. Charlie noted the backside of the exterior board siding supported by horizontal ledgers attached to the columns. Scissor-shaped wood trusses reached across the nave, receiving wood purlins and roof decking, even in the low level of light the three-dimensional quality of the exposed structure contributed to the feeling of being in a special place.

Charlie went forward to first check the altar to be sure that St. Dunstan's had not been moved here. This altar, without the omega and reversed horseshoe of St. Dunstan's, was built of pine in a simple design placed against the rear wall. A brass cross stood on a retable beneath three lancet windows, similar in design to the nave windows. As he walked up and down the center aisle looking at the windows, Charlie wondered if Sanborn, his visitor this morning in Green Cove, had been here. He felt Sanborn might be missing a clue that could help him in his search if he failed to notice the similarity found in most of the river church windows; a border of bright colors surrounding a field of diamond-shaped small panes of glass with a stylized flower design. The windows, similar in design in many of the river churches were probably designed and fabricated in the same glass shop. Charlie felt Sanborn might not have realized the necessary coordination between church builders over a relatively short time. Even if selected from a catalogue, he felt it was possible that a single donor (Sanborn's family?) had initiated these designs. Under each window in the nave, evidence remained of the small access doors used for ventilation in hot summer months. From the exterior, wood shingles covered the old openings but on the inside, Charlie could see the doors still in place under each window probably forgotten. Charlie felt certain that Captain Dickison would have planned the placement for his gifts at each church, perhaps even in a custom-built location. Since the building was currently used for a church service one day a week, the tabernacle and baptismal font, missing from the chancel, could be across the street in the big church. Charlie heard the rain begin as he looked in familiar places and a few new spots; in the altar construction, in the delightful exposed wood framing, even under the pews. Once again, he began to realize he might have to go under the church. Not today, for sure, with the rain. As he sat in a pew near the front thinking of possibilities, even a search across the street, he looked again at the small ventilation doors under each window. Apparently, pulls and hinges had been removed, leaving only a section of wood paneling that hardly looked like a door. Using his knife, he worked at the perimeter joints. Finally he was able to slip a blade into the joint. With a silent prayer, he twisted the blade, the panel moved slightly and then came loose. On the bottom of the opening, at the wood sill plate, Charlie noted a round plug, a little over one and a half inches in diameter. "Just like the fonts", he said aloud. Using his knife and an ice pick, the plug came out with amazing ease. He wondered how many hot days had this door been opened to catch a breeze? How many restless children had crawled through the door during a lengthy sermon? How many years had the door been opened and closed without noticing the plug? Laying the plug aside, he reached into the opening and withdrew a cylinder of yellowed paper-wrapped coins. Charlie sat back on his heels, taking deep breaths and smiling with pleasure. He wondered if the Captain had placed a roll under each of the windows or had he, with luck, picked the right one. He carefully replaced the wood panel forcing it back into the original position. He went to the window directly across the nave and then to the two middle windows, repeating his process without success. In the rear of the church, on the west side, the search came up empty. On the east side, after removing the door, Charlie found a wood plug similar to the first doorway which led to a second roll of coins.

Not being a carpenter, Captain Dickison certainly had help in placing his gifts. Together the two men had hidden the coins in the wood font at St. Mary's, Green Cove Springs. Maybe Dickison felt the interior of the font was too hard to find. Perhaps they looked for a place that would be less difficult; like a doorway opened occasionally. The door sill worked so well that Dickson concealed a second roll.

Charlie closed and locked all the doors at the small church and walked out into a pouring rain, oblivious to everything except what he held in his hand. Smiling with pleasure at his discoveries today; two rolls from St. Mary's and two more from Grace Church. Charlie paid no attention to the rain or the black sedan parked next to his car. Sanborn waved through his rain streaked window, wondering why Charlie was smiling, apparently in no hurry in the heavy rain. Charlie had two thoughts: one, Sam didn't think any treasure would be found and two, Captain Dickison told Bishop Young that the coins "would be hidden in a place he would recognize from their experiences together." Charlie remained unsure if Dickison wanted the gold and silver, as part of Bishop Young's share, to remain undiscovered this long.

Chapter 31

Charlie's excitement seemed to be endless. Standing in Sam's kitchen, he felt Sam's offer of coffee was not appropriate for successful treasure hunters. He reached for the scotch and poured more than a splash into an ice-filled glass and added water. Stirring his drink, Charlie nodded his head at the same tempo. Smiling to himself at this ridiculous pair of synchronized movements, he said, "I am glad you told me about Sanborn. He seemed to be in a hurry."

"I haven't heard anymore from him either," said Sam. "You are right about his lack of curiosity about the repetitive window glass designs. I have a feeling we haven't seen the last of Frank Sanborn."

Sam collected his drink, picked up a delicate wood box, directing Charlie to his nearby small den. "We should be in deep shadow, perhaps have a storm raging outside as we talk of treasure", he said.

Charlie reached into his coat pocket for the paper-wrapped rolls of coins retrieved earlier at St. Mary's, Green Cove Springs, and Grace Church, Orange Park. Sam placed the four rolls in his wood box and said, "So far, we have six rolls of twenty coins each from seven river churches, plus two horseshoes that I believe are silver. The coins appear to be twenty dollar gold pieces, called double eagles. The name comes naturally from a smaller ten dollar gold coin referred to as an eagle. The double eagles were the largest denomination of gold coins issued by the government and proved to be the coin of choice for trade and commerce. I'm certain the confederate treasure contained primarily circulated coins of different dates and marks from different government mints. Some could be in non-circulated condition. Somehow,

Charlie, I doubt it as the coins have been worn and scuffed pretty well as they traveled from Richmond to Gainesville and on to Magnolia. My research tells me that the value of what we have would best be determined by numismatic experts. The value would be based on the condition, the date and the mint identification. In any event, you and I should handle the coins as little as possible. I know, I know, Charlie. You want to know how much I think the coins are worth. When J. J. Dickison placed the coins, each was worth twenty dollars. If he put twenty coins in a church, the gift from Bishop Young would be $400.00. In the late 1800's that was a nice sum of money for a small church. I took four coins from those I found at Holy Comforter, Crescent City, carefully wrapped in cloth and separated by paper to a local recommended coin dealer. In the privacy of his office, I uncovered the coins and he nearly jumped across the desk. He determined two were dated 1860 from the New Orleans mint, and had been circulated. He estimated the value to be between $3,000 to $7,000 each. The other two coins were from the Philadelphia mint, dated 1862, valued in his opinion between $750 to $1,700 each. These four coins, selected by me arbitrarily, could be worth as little as $7,500 or as high as $18,000. The gold in the coins is worth about $700 each. You can see what we have so far could be worth nearly a million bucks."

Charlie jumped to his feet with a loud cry. "Sam, we did it. Let's cash in tomorrow."

"Charlie," Sam said. "These coins are from seven churches. We know Captain Dickison is placing the coins in Bishop Young's behalf, but where is the balance of the treasury? I think we should visit St. Margaret's in Hibernia and then return to where we started; St. George at Fort George. Those two churches might reveal more coins and possibly a clue that will lead us to Captain Dickison's share."

Chapter 32

Driving south past Orange Park on U.S. 17, Charlie turned east onto Hibernia Road. He was glad Sam was along, about to visit St. Margaret's for the first time.

"You missed a sign, Charlie," said Sam pointing to the north.

"No, that's for the new church. We'll go straight ahead on this dirt road to the original church."

Overhanging branches from old oak trees formed a canopy, punctuated by magnolias and pines, as Church Road headed east and then turned north.

"Where's the river?" asked Sam.

"About a hundred yards to the east," said Charlie, pointing to his right.

"Created by a Spanish land grant bounded by the St. Johns on the east, Black Creek to the south and westward for hundred of acres, George Fleming named his plantation Hibernia after his native Ireland. His first house near the river was destroyed by marauding Indians. His son, Lewis, built the second house in 1856, considerably larger, to accommodate his growing family. Carefully located further back from the river, under shading oak trees, Fleming built wide porches on two floors to catch any breezes from the river. A long dock extending into deep water, citrus groves, cotton fields, and vegetable gardens were slowly added to his growing plantation. His second wife, Margaret, brought energy and beauty to Hibernia as visitors arrived by steamboat from Jacksonville.

"The death of Lewis Fleming and the Civil War brought many sorrows to Margaret Fleming. Prosperity was gone, Union gunboats had replaced the steamboats, and Margaret was forced to leave Hibernia, seeking refuge in Lake City. Returning after the war, she found her home in ruins."

"Why are you telling me about the Fleming family, Charlie?" asked Sam. "What did they have to do with the church?"

Charlie pulled his car over to the side of the road and said, "Sam, the church is named for Margaret Fleming. After the war she rebuilt Hibernia and enjoyed great success as the plantation became a popular destination for guests. She had dreamed of building a chapel and I believe, spoke at great length with Bishop John Young about the design. I think you will quickly see his influence on the architecture of St. Margaret's."

He drove ahead smiling as he saw Sam's reaction as the small church came into view.

"My gosh, Charlie. You didn't tell me enough. I think you saved it for the last. The setting is wonderful; the dirt road, the trees, the picket fence, the scale and proportions for a river church with a well-tended cemetery beyond are perfect."

Charlie said, "St. Margaret's was originally about three hundred yards to the south. Construction started in 1875. After Margaret Fleming died in 1878, her funeral was the first service in the church. Records indicated the church was relocated to its present location in 1881. Stained glass windows in her memory were placed above the altar. By 1881, Bishop Young's missionary efforts had resulted in churches in Crescent City, Green Cove Springs, Orange Park and San Mateo. Emmanuel in Welaka and St. Paul's in Federal Point were under construction. I'm sure the Bishop, in his travels, visited St. Margaret's to check on the relocation of the church and to enjoy the results of his architectural recommendations. If Captain Dickison was inclined to place any gifts here, I figure it had to be in 1881 or 1882. What is interesting to me is that St. Margaret's remained a family chapel until 1886 when it became an

Episcopal church, ironically one year after the death of Bishop Young."

In their walk around the church, Sam and Charlie stopped for a minute by the fence along the dirt road. "Charlie, I remember the pleasure I felt at St. George as I learned from you about the river churches. The wood siding with triangular battens, the steep roof, the details around the entry porch, even the small belfry appear on many of the churches. Same vocabulary but each is unique."

"I agree, Sam," said Charlie. "Each church uses the same materials and remains distinctive. The use of the triangular wood battens remains a mystery to me. River churches, built over a twenty year period, designed by different architects and built by different builders have used this unusual detail. I think you could bevel the edges of a rectangular wood board for joint covers, as Richard Upjohn specified, rather than split a square block of wood. The triangular shape may be a sign for you and me in our search, but I haven't figured it out."

Sam asked Charlie about the shutters at each of the lancet-shaped windows. Charlie said, "I have a marvelous old photograph of the church on Sunday morning. A horse-drawn buggy is passing by as well dressed members of the church arrive for a service. Four of the windows on the east side are glazed with small diamond-shape panes of glass. The chancel window contains what appears to be stained glass. One of the windows is tilted open, rotated by a pin in the center of the window. The shutters you see today, functional not just decorative, were added in recent years to protect the stained glass windows."

Entering the church, Sam directed Charlie to a pew. The two men sat quietly; Charlie knew that Sam would break the silence when he was ready.

Just like at St. George, about the time silence was becoming uncomfortable, Sam said, "Bishop Young's influence is certainly obvious to me. The elements are here;

lancet windows, raised chancel, and wood trusses with just enough detail to satisfy the architect or the builder's desire for decorative expressions. I have a vision of Bishop Young standing here describing his architectural requirements to the builder."

The two men admired the stained glass; three individual lancet-shaped windows above the altar dedicated to Margaret Fleming. One window on the east side of the nave pictured the Fleming house at Hibernia; all the windows being memorials to the Fleming family and church leaders.

Charlie pointed out to Sam the five scissor-shaped wood trusses reaching across the nave plus the two trusses at each end wall; all seven supported by wood columns on the exterior walls. Two additional columns were placed at the chancel steps to define the altar area, somewhat similar to St. Mary's in Green Cove, but not quite. A Greek cross [all four arms the same length], appears on the rear wall at St. Mary's, built into the wood truss framing. Here, at St. Margaret's, the same cross is found in the truss framing at the chancel steps. Charlie said, "Sam, the architect for St. Mary's, built in 1879, was Charles Haight. The architect for St. Margaret's, built in 1875 and relocated in 1881 is not identified. The common element in the architectural details of the two churches is Bishop John Young."

"Charlie, I'm overwhelmed at the history I feel around us today." said Sam. "I think we should look for any evidence of a visit by Captain Dickison. I see the tabernacle used as a stand for the altar cross is similar to Holy Comforter in Crescent City so I'll start there."

Charlie replied, "The baptismal font is similar in design to St. Mary's. Doesn't look as large or as detailed but you never know. Check the altar while you're there. I would be surprised if the Fleming family would accept a second-hand altar."

Sam determined quickly that the altar was not from St. Dunstan's. The Greek letters for alpha and omega were on the front but no horseshoe or an upside down omega. Carefully removing the brass cross from the retable behind the altar, he placed the tabernacle on the flat surface of the altar. On the retable, Sam noticed a cruet of wine too tall, he guessed, to fit inside the wood cabinet. The tabernacle would be used primarily to store communion wafers, perhaps even a small cruet. The overall size suggested that it was possible to have a hidden compartment. The joints at the corners looked familiar. After scribing the joints with his penknife, he very slowly pushed on each side.

Charlie pushed, pulled and twisted. Even stood the font upside down searching for a false drain hole. He was about to give up when he heard a loud intake of breath from Sam.

"Come quick, Charlie. Captain Dickison has been here," he whispered.

Charlie watched as Sam pushed open the back of the tabernacle and reached in to retrieve a paper-wrapped roll of rust-colored coins. He said, "Hold the coins. Put everything back exactly as you found it."

"I am taking these coins reluctantly, Charlie. Captain Dickison's mind and heart must have been filled with sadness as he hid the coins in the tabernacle, probably made by Will Hendry. Fire had consumed the Magnolia Hotel, the Reverend Harold Alexander was dead, and St. Dunstan's was in pieces on the bottom of the river. These coins don't belong to us. After we visit St. George, our final church, we need to have a serious discussion about our future plans."

"We'll talk, Sam," said Charlie. "For now, put the coins with the others for safekeeping. I'll call St. George to set up a visit under my original inspection plan. But I believe there are more than silver horseshoes and gold coins carefully hidden somewhere on the river, waiting for us."

Frank Sanborn was also captivated by St. Margaret's. After visiting the church, Sanborn stood in the shadows of the cemetery watching Charlie Gallagher and another man arrive. "Now what?" he wondered. "I've seen Gallagher at two churches, watched him take something at St. Mary's in Green Cove and left Orange Park smiling in the rain. What is he looking for? Who is this new guy?"

Chapter 33

A few days later, Charlie and Sam met for the second time at St. George Episcopal Church on Fort George Island. While checking in with the church office, the two were surprised to hear a report, from the church secretary, of a recent visitor who mentioned Charlie's name. She said, "His name was Sanborn and he wanted to see the windows. He stayed about an hour and left."

Entering the church, Charlie knew what Sam would do. Sure enough, Sam ran his hand over the back of a wood pew and sat down, motioning Charlie to do the same. After a brief silence he looked at Charlie and said, "Many of the details you pointed out before mean more to me this time. Over the years, I've seen many styles of architectural expressions in church design, but I'm beginning to be in complete sympathy with the ideals of Bishop John Young from so many years ago. The white plaster walls, the stained glass windows and the exposed wood framing combine in a setting so satisfying for a house of God. I would like to serve at this church."

Charlie said, "You haven't been to all of the river churches. Regardless of how our search turns out, go see each one. I'll bet St. Dunstan's, if it were still around, would be as perfect as St. George." As they got up, Charlie continued, "You go check the altar and tabernacle. I'll look elsewhere. Maybe Captain Dickison was attracted to the baptismal font or the ventilation doors under each window."

Charlie turned first to the baptismal font standing in the rear of the church. Running his hands slowly over the smooth surfaces made of stone, more simple in design than St. Mark's in Palatka, or St. Paul's, Federal Point, Charlie hoped to find a carved Greek letter omega that could be reversed for a horseshoe. Feeling none, he carefully laid the font on its side. His ice pick and flashlight failed to reveal any hidden treasure. Studying the exposed wood framing under a window, Charlie noted that any evidence of a small door had been covered on the exterior by recent renovations. He checked each opening, head, jamb and sill, looking for round plugs similar to those he found at Grace in Orange Park. Charlie's expectations had been high. To check these two familiar places and find nothing was disappointing. Surely Captain Dickison had visited St. George to hide a portion of Bishop Young's share. Maybe he used a new location. Charlie noticed Sam standing on the chancel steps staring at the windows and moved to join him.

"I hope our friend Sanborn looked closely at these windows," said Charlie, "especially in comparison with other river churches. Not the windows in the chancel and high on the rear wall, but the nave windows. They appear, at first glance, to be similar to other river churches with a colored border and diagonal panes of glass containing a floral design. These windows are not in a fleur-de-lis pattern and approximately at eye level; the panes are square and tinted blue. I don't believe these nave windows are from St. Dunstan's but were possibly selected by a benefactor who chose this design rather than a standard pattern."

Sam and Charlie turned their attention to the three lancet windows above the altar. In the center frame, below the image of St. George, the design included the Greek letters for alpha and omega entwined in a monogram. "Charlie", said Sam, "I've been looking at this window for ten minutes, trying to reverse the omega, but it becomes a stretch. I've checked the tabernacle also. Now, I'm trying to get up my nerve to remove the altar cloth.

Sam carefully lifted one end of the cloth draped on three sides of the altar, hanging over the edge about twelve inches. Sam lifted the other end and then folded the cloth back. He said, "Look at the five crosses carved into the flat surface of the altar. Somehow I recall the crosses symbolize the five wounds Jesus received on the cross. I'm not sure altars made today include this symbolism. Perhaps it is telling you and me that this is an old altar."

"Sam, look at the carved design on the wood trim below the flat surface of the altar", Charlie exclaimed. "There is a repeating omega and horseshoe. I think this might be St. Dunstan's altar, built by Will Hendry and placed here by Captain J. J. Dickison. The dates would be right. St. Dunstan's was placed on a barge and lost to exploding mines in the river in 1884. St. George was completed the year before. About this time cabinetmakers delighted in creating secret compartments. My family has an old Victorian dresser that has a hidden drawer in the wood base that surprised us all. At an exhibit, I saw several cabinets where an expert had revealed cabinets behind drawers and vice versa. Perhaps Will Hendry concealed one or two hiding places behind false fronts just for Captain Dickison."

"Charlie, I think we should slide the altar away from the wall. Most of the wood frame altars I have seen are simple three-sided boxes. I think this one may have a back," Sam said.

The two men went to the ends and took hold of a corner, slowly pulling the altar away from the wall. Charlie started thinking of a valid reason for what they were doing if a visitor or church official appeared. Sam was right. The altar was more than a three-sided box. In addition to the heavily carved trim around the top, the face and sides of the altar were built of pine boards, obviously selected with care, placed vertically with the joints covered with triangular battens, smaller in scale, but similar to the exterior walls. Each was shaped at the bottom to stand on a beveled wood base.

Sam said, "Look at the design on the end panels. A symbol of the trinity, a triangle, is entwined with a reversed omega. You can't tell me that is not a sure sign this altar came from St. Dunstan's."

Charlie pushed, pulled and tapped the altar. Sam followed, running his hands slowly over the top and sides. At one end Charlie noted the triangular battens seemed to penetrate the apron trim. He placed his hands on the batten and pushed up. He felt the wood give slightly and pushed harder. The batten slid up into the trim above. "Sam," he said. "Go stand at the door of the church. Lock it if you can."

Sam went to the lancet-shaped double doors to make sure the existing wood barricade was dropped in place across the opening. Returning to the chancel, he watched Charlie push a second batten up. "I think these triangular trim pieces locked a drawer in the base of the altar," said Charlie. He placed both hands under the trim around the base of the altar and pulled. Nothing moved. "It's not going to be easily moved, Sam. If it is a drawer, it has been in place in all sorts of conditions for a long time. You go to the other end and see what happens there."

Sam reported the same resistance at the other end. Charlie took his knife and scored the joints on all sides and still the drawer, if that is what it was, refused to move. "Sam, I can't get a good grip 'cause I'm sweating so much. Why don't we both pull together at this end?"

Wiping their hands as dry as they could on pant legs and handkerchiefs, the two men sat on the floor at the west end of the altar, put their fingers under the base and pulled.

Suddenly, the drawer came free. Sam and Charlie backed up quickly and slid it open. On the bottom of the drawer was a small wood box.

The two men looked at each other, smiling with pleasure at their discovery. With care, Sam picked up the box. Charlie closed the drawer, pulled the battens back in place and moved to the other side. Sam said, "I think we should move the altar back against the wall in case someone with a key comes in through the sacristy."

After sliding the altar in place, Sam restored the cloth frontal to its proper place leaving the east side folded on the flat surface. The triangular joint covers on this side did not move as easily. Charlie scored the sides of each batten, wishing for a can of spray lubricant. Finally the wood slid up into the apron trim. Once again the two men sat on the floor and pulled. The drawer took their best efforts, before sliding open to reveal another small wood box.

Sam said, "Charlie, do you think these two boxes are the balance of the treasure?"

"No, I don't. Depending on what we find in the boxes, I'll bet this is only the balance of Bishop Young's share."

Charlie and Sam replaced everything around the altar to its original position. Charlie went to unlock the front doors. Sam held the two boxes tightly as he sat in a front row pew. Charlie joined him, expecting Sam to sit quietly. The two men had been to nine of the eighteen river churches; Charlie or Sam alone or together looking for the gifts of Bishop Young through the efforts of his friend, Captain J. J. Dickison. The remaining nine churches from their original list had been destroyed, relocated, rebuilt or forgotten after the years of leadership by Bishop John Young.

After a few minutes, Sam said, "By good fortune, we started and finished our search here at St. George. I believe Captain Dickison concealed a portion of Bishop Young's share over a period of eight years beginning with St. Marks in Palatka after the war ended and finishing here at Fort George in 1883. Bishop Young died in 1885."

"O.K. Sam," Charlie said. "I think the balance of the Confederate treasury is somewhere on the river, but like the man says, we done good. Let's go to your house, lock the doors, have a stiff drink and see what Captain Dickison left at St. George."

Chapter 34

In Sam's den, Charlie placed the two boxes from St. George side by side on the desk. He was disappointed that the boxes did not reflect the craftsman's skill of Will Hendry as seen in the baptismal fonts, tabernacles, wood framing and altar. These two boxes were identical in design and shape, apparently weighing the same. Charlie opened one box carefully. Inside, he recognized the familiar shape of two rolls of paper-wrapped coins placed end to end between two oblong-shaped parcels, tightly enclosed in yellowed paper. "Sam," he said, "I'm afraid to touch what I see. I recognize the coin wrapping but do you think what I think is in those two packages?"

Sam removed the coins. Rubbing his hands together in anticipation, he picked up one package and placed it on his desk. Slowly he unfolded the paper. He knew his heartbeat became audible as he looked at Charlie. "It's gold," he whispered.

Charlie lifted the shiny ingot. Smaller than a brick but much heavier, he turned it over and over in his hands, then passed the ingot back to Sam.

"Charlie," Sam said, "the coins have been exciting; a dream that I wished for and never really expected, but I'm telling you, this is unbelievable. In my hand is a part of history, placed in a box with other ingots of gold on a train in Richmond, Virginia, on April 2, 1865. From Virginia, this bar traveled to North and South Carolina, Georgia, into Florida and then was brought by Bishop Young and Captain Dickison to Magnolia and St. Dunstan's church. Hold it, Charlie. A small part of the Confederate States of America is in your hand."

Captain Dickison and Will Hendry's second box was opened to reveal the same contents, arranged in a similar manner. Sam and Charlie left the paper-wrapped coins and ingots undisturbed and placed the box beside the first. The two men sat silently for a minute; then Charlie said, "Do you have any idea of the value of what we have?"

Sam brought out his inventory that listed coins and horseshoes uncovered to date. Adding the recent discoveries from St. George, his list indicated:

St. Paul's, Federal Point	20 double eagles
St. Mary's, Green Cove Springs	40 double eagles
Grace, Orange Park	40 double eagles
Holy Comforter, Crescent City	20 double eagles
St. Margaret's, Hibernia	20 double eagles
St. George, Fort George	80 double eagles
Total	220 double eagles

All Saints', Enterprise	1 silver horseshoe
St. Mark's, Palatka	1 silver horseshoe
Emmanuel, Welaka	0
St. George, Fort George	4 gold ingots

"I don't know why three churches received twenty coins while forty or more were found at three others. I also wonder if Captain Dickison placed a silver horseshoe at all nine river churches and we have found only two," said Sam.

He continued. "The value of the double eagle coins is difficult to estimate. The gold alone would be worth, at the price today, $634.00 per ounce. The coins weigh slightly over an ounce each, so I estimate the value of 220 coins times $634.00 to be $139,480.00 - say $140,000.00. The value to coin collectors is based, my research tells me, on what a collector would pay. Published prices, estimates really, are available. Based on condition, date and mint mark, each coin would have its own value. Since the double eagle, before and during the war, was the coin of choice for most commerce, I'm sure the Richmond banks would have a variety of coin dates from 1850, the first issue of double eagles, right up to 1865. Most of these would be circulated grades; some could be of a higher grade stored in the vaults of the Richmond banks.

"The four coins I took to a coin dealer indicated a range of $3,000 to $7,000 for those double eagles. It is possible that a few could be worth more, many worth less. With the quantity we have, some dealers might offer a price for all the coins. I believe a fair value of what we have could be as low as $200,000 or as high as over a million. Remember, Charlie, each double eagle would have its own price."

Charlie smiled with delight.

He said, "The horseshoes were cast, I think, by Captain Dickison from silver bars in the treasure. An expert would have to determine if the shoes are silver and what percentage is pure. Maybe Dickison placed one in each church; I came across one by accident and searched for the second. If seven more are found, the value would be more as part of the Confederate treasure."

Sam said, "As far as the gold ingots are concerned, I never thought we would find anything like this. Bars of gold sound like treasure of some pirate buried for safekeeping, never recovered and lost for generations. And here on my desk are four gold bars, discovered in no small part to your hard and imaginative work." Sam unfolded the paper-wrapping of a single ingot. Holding it in his hand he said, "We need to weigh the gold bar. It's probably too heavy for my postal scale, so don't laugh if I use a bathroom scale for our estimate. From the paper today, gold is bringing $650.00 per ounce. Our ingot weighs about ten pounds. So ten pounds times sixteen ounces per pound equals 160 ounces. Using the price per ounce today, I would estimate our ingot is worth approximately $104.000.00; or $416,000.00 for four."

Charlie grinned and added the figures:

220 gold coins	$200,000 average
4 gold ingots	$416,000 average
2 silver horseshoes	$1,000 curiosity
	Total $617,000

Charlie said, "Sam, that's a pretty good number for all our work. It could be higher, much higher if gold prices go up or the double eagles have more numismatic value than we have estimated. Sam, I think we have solved the mystery of the disappearance of the Confederate treasure. Let's have a drink of your best to celebrate our good fortune."

After several drinks, exchanging smiles of triumph with Sam, Charlie asked, "Do we tell our wives or wait until we find the rest of the treasure?"

Sam said, "Charlie, I have thought about this moment, even prayed a little. I believe what we have found is the entire treasure. To me, the four gold bars from St. George confirmed my opinion: this is all the treasure of the Confederacy. Captain Dickison placed the balance in the secret drawers you found at St. George in the altar that came from St. Dunstan's in Magnolia."

"Why would he give up all that money, Sam? Place in a compartment and just forget it? If it is the balance, which I doubt, I'm sure Dickison would return from time to time to retrieve some for his personal use. I can't accept that he would just walk away from all that gold. Did he intend for the people of St. George to find the money? He used Bishop Young's share to place coins in the river churches. Perhaps the four bars of gold were the balance of Bishop Young's share. What we know is that 220 gold coins, four bars of gold are in our hands. Your share and mine, so far. I believe there are more coins and ingots of gold and some silver still somewhere on the river."

"Charlie, we haven't talked about dividing what we have found. I've thought of what I would do with my share of the gold. I intend to return twenty gold coins to each church, including those where you found only a horseshoe or even nothing. I don't know how but I plan to anonymously mail or place in the offering twenty double eagles in memory of Bishop John Freeman Young. You saw the letters in the Diocesan files that Captain Dickison wrote to the Bishop after each of his visits. Those double eagles belong to the churches. I'm proud of what we have done, the process you have used to locate the coins and I'm asking you to understand what I feel I must do."

"You're crazy, Sam. When you and I first met at St. George, after I described the river churches, you had come to Florida to look for Confederate gold. The evidence you put together in Richmond and here in Florida led us to riches we didn't expect. Now, you want to stop searching when we are close to Captain Dickison's share of the treasure. In plain language, you return your share, not mine. I intend to claim one half of what we have and keep looking."

Sam said, "I have read of Bishop Young and the hardships he faced in Florida. Responsible for finding Episcopalians who moved to Florida and to find new ones, encouraging them to worship together, perhaps to even build a church. Then he met Captain Dickison and General Breckinridge in Gainesville and was asked to 'protect certain items' that you and I believe was the treasure of the Confederacy. Bishop Young could not accept any portion of what he agreed to protect. Captain Dickison hid some of the Bishop's share at each mission church he built, and I feel I must follow that missionary direction. I plan on using only my share to return, somehow, twenty gold double eagles to all nine river churches."

"I admire your faith," said Charlie. "But I don't agree with your missionary spirit. I'm anxious to hear what happens as each church finds gold coins in their collection plate. If you give twenty to the nine churches, that will leave forty coins and four ingots. I will claim the coins remaining and two of the ingots. Keep them all in our safety deposit box; plan on renting another, even bigger, because I'm gonna find the rest of the treasure."

Chapter 35

After his discussions with Charlie, Sam spent the next few days thinking about his decision. In the early days of his research about the war in Florida and on the St. Johns River, he thought only of the thrill of finding treasure most historians believe had disappeared into legend. At Holy Comforter in Crescent City when he opened the tabernacle, all his planning, research, and even the move to Florida were justified. And yet, when he got into his car, showed the coins to his wife and she said, "Sam, those coins are not yours," uncertainty began to displace the thrill of what he and Charlie had found. He wanted to return the coins, but how? At first he thought all he had to do was place twenty double eagles in the offering plate. The ushers would probably recall the stranger who placed the heavy envelope in the collection. Then Sam thought of returning the coins to the various churches when he served as a visiting priest. Removing the roll from his pocket under the vestments during the service would be awkward; if he waited until after the service, someone might notice his placement of a bulky envelope. Perhaps by Federal Express, UPS or a delivery service but paperwork would have to be generated. Susan helped him with his decision when she offered to make nine small bags of cloth. Sam found boxes that would contain the bags. Wrapped in plain brown paper, the coins could be mailed from various postal branch offices with no return address.

To test his decision, Sam mailed the first box to Holy Comforter in Crescent City. Leaving the post office he was not sure what reaction, if any, he could expect. After several days, then a week, Sam checked every possible newspaper without finding any report. He thought I'll just have to wait and see what happens.

In Crescent City, Mrs. Joyce Donald, part time secretary/treasurer for Holy Comforter, came to work for the second of her three days at the church. Unlocking the door, she picked up the pile of accumulated mail deposited through the slot on the door, placed it on her desk and turned to make the coffee. Most of the mail, she saw, was routine; nothing from the Diocese. Only a small package addressed to the church. Curious, she removed the paper wrapping, opened the box and then the small bag. Twenty rust-colored heavy coins fell across her desk. Reaching in the bag, Mrs. Donald discovered a slip of paper with a typewritten note, "In memory of John Freeman Young, Second Bishop of Florida." Grabbing the phone, she tried to call her husband, the rector of the church and the senior warden of the Vestry all at once.

Sam paid close attention to all forms of local news for a week. After ten days with no reports of gold coins, he decided to continue with his plan to mail twenty coins to each of the remaining eight churches. For All Saints, Enterprise and St. Marks, Palatka, Sam decided to use a larger box to include the horseshoe found by Charlie under each church. No further explanations would be included except for the same memorial note in all nine bags.

Two weeks later, Sam found an article in the Orange Park newspaper reporting a gift of twenty gold coins to Grace Episcopal Church. The story identified the coins as twenty dollar "double eagles," offered to the church anonymously in memory of a former Episcopal Bishop of Florida, John Freeman Young. According to the article, the gift had created excitement and curiosity in the congregation, anxious to learn of the value of the mysterious gift.

A week after that article appeared, the writer Annlynn Jones was looking in the Crescent City weekly newspaper for details of a popular fish festival and was astonished to read of a similar gift to Holy Comforter Episcopal Church in

Crescent City. A telephone conversation with the church office confirmed the duplicate gift. Annlynn then contacted the Diocese of Florida to learn Bishop John Freeman Young served from 1865 to 1885 and had lived in Jacksonville as a young missionary priest from 1845 to 1848, returning seventeen years later after election and consecration as Bishop. Intrigued with the possibilities of a larger story, she began checking newspapers in central and north Florida.

Within two days Annlynn learned, through the Palatka newspaper, of two more recipients; St. Paul's, Federal Point and St. Mark's in Palatka. In addition to the gold coins, each of these two churches received a blackened horseshoe. Her follow-up story, featuring the mysterious addition of horseshoes and complete with photographs brought collectors and coin dealers to the four churches eager to see the coins and extend offers to buy.

After two weeks, just as the story was fading to the back pages, Emmanuel Church in Welaka and St. Mary's in Green Cove Springs released details of similar gifts. All Saint's in Enterprise contacted the Orlando Sentinel, resulting in a page one feature. Then St. Margaret's in Hibernia called Annlynn to tell of their gifts; St. George at Fort George made page one of the Florida Times Union and a full blown media frenzy was underway. National television correspondents and cameramen, magazine writers and wire service reporters descended on North Florida and the river churches. Emphasis was first placed on the small wood frame buildings as a common element in the gifts. Attention then switched to the life of Bishop John Young. What part could he have played in the gift to river churches? Where did the coins come from? Visitors to the churches went from occasional to frequent. Attendance at Sunday services strained the seating capacity of the churches. The mystery deepened with the discovery the horseshoes were silver and with publication of the value of each of the coins as estimated by experts.

Sam called Charlie when it seemed every day brought a

new approach or theory about the coins. "I feel good about returning the coins, but I never expected this reaction. Do you think any reporters will connect the coins with the Confederacy?"

"Who knows?" said Charlie. "I disagree now, more than ever, with your sharing. I'm going to hold off any further search until all this calms down. If anything exciting develops, you can find me on the golf course or in my boat fishing."

As the excitement over the appearance of the coins increased, Sam knew a summons from the Bishop would soon be expected. The invitation did not take long.

"Sam, what do you know of all this?" asked the Bishop. "I am aware of your interest in the history of our Diocese, and I know John Freeman Young was the second Bishop of Florida, and I know he served at Trinity Church in New York and also in Jacksonville in his early ministry. I know he has never received the honor he should in bringing the Christmas hymn, Silent Night to American churches. What could his relationship to the gold coins be? I want you to help me answer the many questions I have been asked. On top of calls from television and newspaper reporters, I have received requests for advice from each of nine churches.

"I want you to find out more about Bishop John Young and any possible relationship to these coins and now silver horseshoes, for heaven's sake. Somewhere in his biography, our archives or library are answers. My office cannot remain silent and I need your input as soon as possible."

Sam quickly prepared an interim report to the Bishop that summarized the life and ministry of John Young. He decided to also include what he had learned about the twenty dollar double eagle gold coins; the importance of dates of issue, mint marks and condition of each coin. He recommended the nine recipients pool their gifts for an evaluation of all 180 coins and then decide to sell and divide equally. Sam did not mention the silver horseshoes. In a final comment, Sam reported he would continue to develop more detailed information about John Young.

For someone who enjoys history, any occasion to visit the archives is a pleasure. On official business today, Sam enjoyed himself even as he reviewed familiar material; the biographical file on Bishop Young, the individual folders on each of the mission churches developed through Bishop Young's missionary visions and annual reports of the Diocese during John Young's administration.

All of this contained nothing new, so Sam decided to see if the Diocesan library offered any further insight. A frequent visitor to the library, Sam was attracted to a section that contained a collection of prayer books used by the Episcopal Church. Protected by glass doors, the selections included an English prayer book of 1662 and subsequent revisions published by the church for use in America. Sam thought of the dates of John Young's ministry in Florida and reached for the 1801 Edition of the 1789 prayer book. As with the coins, Sam was reluctant to handle the leather-bound book. Remindful of his adventures with Charlie at St. George, Sam took the plastic envelope and moved to a nearby table. Using his handkerchief, he carefully opened the plastic envelope to retrieve the book. Opening the prayer book, Sam noted, on the inside front cover, a dedication to John Young, by his wife, on the occasion of his ordination. Slowly turning a few pages, Sam said a silent prayer as he read so many wonderful phrases, used for hundreds of years and still in use today as common prayers, in a singular order, all over the world.

From the same envelope, Sam withdrew a slim book, bound in leather to match the prayer book. His heart jumped when he realized it was a journal of Bishop Young containing his impressions, dreams, frustrations and joys entered, no doubt, during the long intervals of travel to his congregations. Sam was drawn to pages dated 1865, as Bishop Young expressed his bewilderment of a personal letter of invitation to meet General John Breckinridge in

Gainesville and his subsequent displeasure of being asked to protect his "luggage". Sam could not believe his eyes when he turned to the next entry, dated 1870, describing the visit of Robert E. Lee to Magnolia and St. Dunstan's. Bishop Young's impressions and notes of a final conversation with General Lee and Captain J. J. Dickison answered many questions.

Sam felt little comfort as he read of General Lee's direction for John Young and J. J. Dickison to accept the balance of the treasury upon receipt of the phrase "strike the tent". Having been given from his deathbed, the expression has been a mystery to historians. Now Sam knew why Captain Dickison distributed the coins as Bishop Young refused to accept his share.

I have done what Bishop Young wanted, thought Sam. Twenty coins have been returned to each church. I'm not certain my conscience will let me "strike the tent" and keep the balance of what Charlie and I have found. The notes in the journal could apply to me and Charlie; accept the gold and use it wisely. There is no doubt in my mind what Charlie would say.

Two days later, Sam prepared two versions of his report to the Bishop. In the draft of the first, he described the relationship he had found, in Bishop Young's journal, between John Young and Captain J. J. Dickison, a most successful leader of Confederate cavalry in central and north Florida during the Civil War. Sam wrote of the letter he found inviting John Young to travel to Gainesville to meet Confederate General John Breckinridge as the war ended.

Sam's report continued with his discovery of St. Dunstan's in Magnolia; what he found in the archives of the construction and, in 1883, Bishop Young's reluctant closure of the church, followed in 1884 with the loss of the building on the river. Sam concluded this version, offering his opinion that someone held the coins a long time; someone who knew of John Young's ministry, perhaps a descendent, who wanted to make an anonymous gift in his memory.

Sam pushed the print button on his computer thinking about John Young, J. J. Dickison and his own efforts to find the legendary treasure. Sam reviewed the report and sat back at his desk wrestling with his conscience about what he had not told the Bishop in this draft.

The next morning, Sam walked to the Bishop's office and asked for a meeting.

"Bishop", he said. "I have prepared a report as you requested. I took it home yesterday, spoke at length with Susan about it, prayed a little and decided to tell you today what I believe Bishop John Young would want.

"Sir, the coins are part of the treasure of the Confederacy that disappeared in 1865. When I lived in Richmond, I became fascinated with the legend; finding reference after reference that mentioned Florida and the St. Johns River. I accepted the call to come to work for the Diocese, hoping to find an answer to the disappearance."

The Bishop stood, walked over and closed his door, picked up his phone, directed his secretary to cancel his morning appointments, and then motioned Sam to continue.

Sam began again. "I was attracted to the small churches along the river; in the archives I learned of St. Dunstan's in Magnolia, how it was started and how it was lost."

The Bishop interrupted Sam to confess his lack of knowledge of St. Dunstan's and asked for background information on the life of that church. Upon completion of that part of the story, Sam described his friendship with Charlie Gallagher, their search of the nine churches, under the guise of structural inspections by Charlie, and the discovery of gold coins and two horseshoes. Sam described his delight in finding Bishop Young's journal with the notes of the words of Robert E. Lee telling John Young and Captain Dickison, upon receipt of the phrase "strike the tent" to accept what was left of the assets of the Confederacy and to "use them wisely."

"Go over the story again, Sam," directed the Bishop. "Give me more details. We have all day. I've got to digest what you have told me and the impact it will have on the Diocese of Florida."

Sam started again, offering details of St. Dunstan's, Magnolia, Captain Dickison, the war, the history of the Confederate treasure as it left Richmond and where he and Charlie found the coins. "I decided," Sam said, "to return the coins and horseshoes to each of the churches in memory of Bishop Young. I am telling you all this today because I believe Bishop John Young would want me to use wisely what has been found." Reaching into his briefcase, Sam took the two paper-wrapped ingots and laid them on the desk.

The Bishop of Florida sat back in his chair gasping as the ingots were uncovered. "My God," he said. "It's true. I can't believe it." After a long moment of staring at the gold, he said, "Now what to we do?"

"I recommend we let the current commotion subside a bit before you release the news of receipt of gold bars also in memory of Bishop Young. I have not told you where the bars were found. I believe it is necessary to keep that knowledge private to prevent a response that could get out of hand. I recommend your announcement of the receipt of the gold cover the coins as well. Someone held the coins and gold bars a long time; someone who knew of John Young's ministry, perhaps a descendant, who wanted to make an anonymous gift in his memory."

The Bishop stood, offering his hand to Sam. "I know how hard it was to share this story with me. Your faith and respect for history brought you to an appropriate decision."

Sam left the office wondering what Charlie would say.

Chapter 36

Two months later, directed by the Bishop, Sam had visited all nine churches, telling each vestry all he knew about the coins and recommending that their gifts be pooled and appraised as a collection. After considerable discussion, the leadership at each church agreed, asking Sam to coordinate the selection of a national numismatic organization. This process had begun and all anxiously awaited the results.

The original furor over the coins had subsided until the Bishop announced the receipt of two gold ingots as a gift to the Diocese with the same memorial. Each ingot weighed ten pounds with a Richmond, Virginia assayer's mark. Speculation and excitement rose to a new level.

Today, Sam sat in his office concerned with the fact he had not heard from Charlie. When he called, Allison Gallagher said he was playing golf and working on a new project, and she would have him call. Sam figured after all the announcements he would have heard from Charlie, but he never called. His secretary interrupted his thoughts to announce the arrival of Frank Sanborn. Sam had not heard from Sanborn after his initial letter. Charlie reported two contacts, so he was surprised when Sanborn called to ask for an appointment.

Sam smiled and extended his hand to greet the tall well-dressed man. Sanborn said, "I'm on my way back to Maine and stopped by to thank you for the information on St. Dunstan's. My search for stained glass windows and the sword of my ancestor has been in vain. It was a pleasure to learn about Jacksonville and the river. The beauty and charm of the St. Johns were enjoyable, certainly not expected. I visited the Confederate Museum and found Brewster Adams and his associates most helpful.

"Ensign Frank Sanborn, my great-great-great-grandfather, surrendered his sword to Captain J. J. Dickison after his gunboat, Columbine, was sunk in 1864. I have visited historical museums, military weapon shows, gun shows, antique dealers and flea markets looking for his sword without success. I ran into your colleague, Charlie Gallagher, early in my search and most recently as I attempted to locate Captain Dickison's home, camp locations or battle sites in north Florida.

"After Dickison died, his widow moved to Jacksonville and I found her house. Dickison is buried in Evergreen Cemetery and I visited his grave hoping, I suppose, for some insight."

Sanborn continued. "All of this publicity about the coins and gold bars, with a memorial to a man who, I am sure, knew Captain Dickison, is somehow connected to the churches on the river. On my next trip, when I can stay longer, I may expand my search. Anyway, I believe your conclusion that the windows of St. Dunstan were destroyed is correct, but disappointing to me. I looked at many small churches. Some of the windows appear to be from a single source. At St. George, the pattern is slightly changed and could be from a different benefactor. I would like to think the gift of my family many years ago would be unique and with a theme for each window."

Opening his briefcase, Sanborn brought out a small rectangle of stained glass, mounted in a wood frame. "I bought this from a fisherman who claimed he found the glass in a mud bank on the west bank of the river. It is possible to be from St. Dunstan's but I doubt it. In any event my family will have a small piece of stained glass found in the St. Johns that could serve as a memento of the service of my ancestor.

Sam noticed a blackened horseshoe in Sanborn's open briefcase and asked about the source. Sanborn replied, "I bought the horseshoe in a flea market after I learned of the origin of the name of the church, St. Dunstan's. Looks dirty, but cleaned up, I'll place it beside the glass."

Sam thought to himself that when Sanborn discovers the horseshoe is silver, he'll be back. He said, "Don't hesitate to contact me if you return. I have no doubt we haven't seen the last of you."

Sam returned to his desk, still telling himself he had done the right thing in telling the story to the Bishop and presenting the two gold ingots. With a diminishing sense of guilt, Sam opened his desk drawer to touch the key to the safety deposit box that held his twenty gold double eagles. He said, "Strike the tent, General Lee."

Chapter 37

Charlie Gallagher decided he had enjoyed his boat and played enough golf. After reading about and listening to reports of the "mysterious" gifts, he decided it was time to resume his search. Charlie recalled the discussions with Sam over the few facts they knew and what they established as a chronology of the assets of the Confederacy as it entered Florida:

1865 - Bishop Young meets John Breckinridge in
       Gainesville. Joined by Captain J. J. Dickison.
       Asked by Breckinridge to "protect and hold certain
       items of luggage". Could be the assets of
       Confederacy.
1866 - Treasure hidden where? Probably at St. Dunstan's
       or somewhere in Magnolia.
1870 - General Robert E. Lee comes to Magnolia and St.
       Dunstan's. Meets with Bishop Young and Captain
       Dickison.

Sam and Charlie decided the treasure was uncovered for the meeting and then placed in the secret drawers of St. Dunstan's altar where it remained untouched for seven years. Letters found in Diocesan archives by Sam indicated the first letter from Captain Dickison to Bishop Young was dated 1877 and referred to a visit to St. Mark's, Palatka. The letters continued each year starting with a visit to St. Margaret's, Hibernia and ending with St. George at Fort George in 1883.

In that year, Bishop Young closed St. Dunstan's. Captain Dickison, Charlie believed, presented the altar to St. George. It was possible that the balance of the treasure was concealed in the altar; Captain Dickison had previously distributed coins and horseshoes to eight churches. Sam and Charlie both agreed the amount in the secret drawers was intended, by Dickison, for St. George and other churches to be started by Bishop Young. The death of Bishop Young in 1885 changed the Captain's plans. Sam believed the eighty coins and four gold ingots were the balance of the treasure. Charlie thought Dickison left that amount for St. George, moving the balance to a location that offered easier access to the gold and silver. But where?

Charlie decided he needed to find out more about Captain Dickison; where he lived, fought and died. He started by visiting Dickison's homes, his battle sites and camps, if he could find them. He searched first for a location for his home on the west bank of the St. Johns. Present day Wilkie Point, north of Magnolia seemed a likely place for Dickison and his young family as the Civil War appeared on the horizon. The community of Magnolia was growing; St. Dunstan's Episcopal Church was started by the first Bishop of Florida, Francis Rutledge. After the war began, northern gunboats patrolled the river searching for Union sympathizers, offering sanctuary to all slaves while repeatedly harassing those who claimed allegiance to the Confederacy. To protect his family, Dickison possibly moved his family to a larger home on Orange Lake, south of Waldo and southwest of Palatka.

Next, Charlie visited Quincy, near Tallahassee, where Dickison lived after the war, maintaining an active interest in military affairs. He served as adjutant general for the state and as commander of the Florida division of a Confederate veteran's organization. Captain Dickison died in 1902 at "Sunnyside", his Orange Lake plantation. Following his final request, he was buried with full honors in Evergreen Cemetery in Jacksonville.

Charlie read of Dickison's orders during the war "to find the enemy and attack whenever conditions and terrain are suitable". Obviously, his camp sites were many; an outpost near Palatka, a large camp referred to as Camp Baker located near Waldo and others near Welaka and Volusia on the river. Charlie visited Horse Landing, the site of Captain Dickison's famous victory over the U. S. Navy gunboat <u>Columbine</u>. Standing on the river bank, Charlie could easily imagine the boat heading north around the bend and Dickison's men opening fire on a surprised gunboat. He read, once again, the plaque describing the battle, placed by individuals and a state organization dedicated to preserving historic sites. As he had laughed with Sam, there was no sign with an arrow pointing to hidden treasure. The life of Captain J. J. Dickson offered little to Charlie in the way of a new direction. Dickson was a leader in his community before and after the war. During the war, he proved to be an exceptional tactician planning attacks on both sides of the river by men and horses in heavy underbrush, probably not receiving the recognition he deserved as commanding officer of Company H, Second Florida Cavalry. Charlie felt the key to the location of the treasure had to be on the river in the area known as Magnolia or, on some maps, Magnolia Springs.

Standing on the property under shading oak trees with the river glistening in the distance, Charlie tried to imagine how the site looked in 1861 when Francis Rutledge, first Bishop of Florida laid out the foundation for St. Dunstan's located in a cluster of homes, barns, groves and a trading post. His imagination then rapidly moved to the late 1800's as the elegant Magnolia Springs Hotel stood on the river, the last and largest of three hotels built on the site, filled with 800 guests enjoying the beauty of Florida and the St. Johns.

Today, sixteen one-story small buildings set back generously from the water follow the curve of the river. Docks and boat houses from earlier generations are gone; the pleasure of viewing the ever-changing river is all that remains today at Magnolia.

Charlie unrolled the site plan he had prepared, using an old partial survey that indicated "hotel ruins, cottages, dock and boathouse" and an indication of a cemetery. The building locations today were shown on a drawing of a larger scale but surprisingly also showed a cemetery. Using the cemetery as a base Charlie had laid out a plan that indicated the present buildings and with dotted lines, the hotel, dock, cottages and boathouse.

Perhaps the cemetery, shown on both drawings, was the key. Charlie was aware that early congregations often located their cemetery near the church. St. Margaret's, Hibernia, and Our Saviour, Mandarin, are good examples but Charlie was not sure this small cemetery had any connection to St. Dunstan's. A local historian suggested the genealogical department of the Mormon Church might tell him more about the ten by fifteen foot plot of ground. It did not take long for the Mormon Church to reply. Official records identified the small burial ground as a Methodist Episcopal cemetery containing six graves. During World War II bulldozers, clearing the ground for government housing, were stopped by local citizens who managed to salvage a number of headstones. Two well worn stone slabs inside the wrought iron fence are all that remain. Charlie tried to lift each one of the stones without success. He returned to his car for his tool bag deciding, with a smile, not to use a shovel in a graveyard in broad daylight. A crowbar would be less likely to draw a crowd. He carefully inserted the bar under four sides of the smaller stone, testing the resistance around the perimeter. One narrow end gave way slightly, drawing Charlie to his knees. Carefully lifting the stone, Charlie was astonished to see a dirt-filled figure of a horseshoe. Realizing he had been holding his breath, Charlie exhaled with excitement as he sat back on the ground.

"St. Dunstan's", he mumbled. "But where would the church have been?"

The location of cemeteries has been carefully respected and identified by law over many years. For this small plot of ground to be left alone since the Civil War and then for local citizens to stop the bulldozers in 1941 in respect for the men buried here is amazing. Charlie admitted to himself that the church has been long forgotten; his own experience in studying river churches missed it. The church would have been located near the cemetery but all he could see today was asphalt and apartment buildings. He decided to call Sam.

"Sam, it's Charlie. I know, I know. I should've called, but I've been looking. A little while ago, in that small cemetery shown on our drawing of Magnolia, I found a headstone with a horseshoe carved above a name that had been worn away. I'm sure it is a tie-in to St. Dunstan's and it might help if we had an idea of who might be buried here."

"I'm glad to hear from you, Charlie. I can't imagine who could be buried there but, like you said, the connection is obvious. When I prepared my report to the Bishop, I used an old journal of Bishop Young. Maybe his notes will tell us more. I'll call you when I find something."

Anxious to continue his search, Charlie decided to learn more about the construction of St. Dunstan's. He had told Sam, at their first meeting, of typical construction details used in the wooden churches but realized he would need more to find the location at Magnolia. To prepare a foundation and floor plan, Charlie reviewed his photographs, plans, construction drawings and sketches produced during his years of architectural practice. Returning to the architect Richard Upjohn's book, Rural Architecture, to confirm his conclusions, he noted Mr. Upjohn had specified a continuous footing and foundation wall. His experience with river churches indicated individual brick piers. Charlie decided, with anticipation, that it was time to draw.

Back home, on his drawing board, Charlie began his latest project: St. Dunstan's Episcopal Church of Magnolia. He knew most of the river churches were about the same size, 1,000 square feet more or less. Laying out pew capacities, aisle widths, baptismal font areas and altar arrangements, he decided St. Dunstan's could have been approximately twenty feet wide and thirty-six feet long. A sacristy or robing room, ten by ten, added to one side would result in an area of 820 square feet. Using his rule of thumb, he decided the chancel or altar area would have been about one third the length of the nave. Using this hypothetical floor plan, Charlie then laid out a continuous footing and foundation wall plan, according to Upjohn and then he drew, according to his own experience, a series of brick piers, twenty inches square, equally spaced from the corners down each long side plus a row down the center of the church. Charlie placed the entry at one narrow end, locating the sacristy adjacent to the altar area. He then reduced his design to the scale of his overall site plan; now he was ready to locate the church beginning with the cemetery as a link to St. Dunstan's.

In the midst of his design drawing for a wood frame church built in 1861, Sam called. "Charlie, Bishop Young's journal for March, 1882 mentions a funeral he conducted for "H. Alexander". He also notes a promise to Mrs. Alexander to place a horseshoe on the headstone. That could only be the Reverend Harold Alexander, the first and only rector of St. Dunstan's who died saving others in the Magnolia Hotel fire. I guess you are trying to find the location of St. Dunstan's. I hope this helps. Don't wait so long to call."

Chapter 38

Expressing an interest in preparing a history of the hotel and Magnolia, Charlie received permission from the apartment management, to walk over the property and particularly the river front on approved occasions. Site plan in hand, Charlie tried to place St. Dunstan's on the ground first using the cemetery as a base. Smiling and waving to the apartment tenants, he wandered over the property considering the cemetery, proximity to the river plus a desired eastern orientation for the altar. Charlie remembered the legend of the first Bishop, Francis Rutledge, as he traveled the St. Johns by boat, stepping ashore with axe in hand as he located each mission church. Charlie figured the Bishop placed the church near the spring guarded by magnolia trees while maintaining access to the town dock. Considering erosion patterns as a clue to the old spring, he paced off several possibilities with an east west orientation without any positive feelings of success. The old cemetery must have been located further away from the church than he thought. The spring, either capped or dried up, couldn't be accurately located. All Charlie had was the river. The town dock would have created an east west axis for town growth, he felt, but maybe that's the way planners today would think. Magnolia had grown from a trading post into a small community with buildings and homes located under or near shading oak trees. Of course the trees were gone so the river and the land remained as his only clues. Finally, Charlie brought his boat up the river to Magnolia, drifting with the current, trying to think like the Bishop. High ground was desirable so Charlie believed the church would have been somewhere toward the south on a higher elevation than the water's edge. From his boat, he selected two possibilities; then docked at Governors Creek, walking around to check. Either site could be the location, he decided. Frustrated, Charlie returned to his boat and headed down the river toward Jacksonville. All the way home he thought about Harold Alexander's grave in the cemetery, St. Dunstan's foundation and floor plans, the forgotten spring and his futile searches back and forth over the apartment property. All that remained was a strong feeling that a large part of the treasure of the Confederacy was near St. Dunstan's. And then again, he thought, maybe Sam was right; the four gold ingots and eighty coins we found in the hidden compartments of the altar at St. George were the balance.

As his boat eased through the waters of the St. Johns, Charlie went over his travels and discoveries. After St. George, he recalled, we had four gold ingots and 220 gold coins. Sam gave away two ingots and returned 180 coins. I have two ingots and twenty coins. History of the assets describes multiple bags of gold coins and ingots. "I know there is more and it has to be in Magnolia," he mumbled.

Charlie reluctantly returned home to an old routine: reading, playing golf, fishing a little, thinking about churches and lost treasure, while occasionally driving through Magnolia.

Two months later, Charlie was awakened just before dawn by heavy rain, lightning, and sounds of thunder. The forecast for the day had been for wet weather brought to north Florida by a hurricane just off the east coast, gaining strength from the warm waters of the Gulf Stream. A bathroom night light and electric clock went dark as power failed. Alley, his wife, turned over, looked at Charlie and went back to sleep. Fully awake, Charlie got up to check on any leaks or wind damage. Grabbing his flashlight, he went from room to room as the power flickered on and off. Charlie thought how his morning routine was not going to be changed even without lights, coffee or newspaper, so he just sat in his favorite chair, grumbled a little bit and waited. The sound of the newspaper bouncing and sliding up the driveway woke him up. A very wet, gray dawn greeted Charlie as he ran to retrieve his paper. With power now restored, he could return to his standard early morning rituals; coffee, newspaper and then television with a bowl of cereal.

The senior television weatherman, C. M. "Millibar" Thompson, grabbed Charlie's attention as he described the effects of the storm, excitedly reporting on a small tornado that touched down during the night just north of Green Cove Springs, in Magnolia. Charlie jumped to his feet as live pictures revealed heavily damaged apartment buildings and many uprooted large trees. He dressed in a hurry, grabbed his old baggy rain suit, woke Alley, and headed for Magnolia.

Heavy rain continued as Charlie turned into the apartments. Power crews were already at work repairing fallen wires while warning local residents of the danger. Tenants of the apartments wandered in shock, soaking wet as they searched for family and friends. Charlie parked his car out by the highway, managing to slip by police barriers as he headed for the river. He noticed the cemetery fence supported numerous small branches but seemed O.K. The tornado had demolished five of the one-story frame buildings; many roofs were gone, windows and doors were smashed at other buildings. Trees were down everywhere. Some pines were snapped in half. Others had crashed to the ground sending branches in all directions. Strangely, cedar and magnolia trees appeared to be only windblown but still standing. Oak tree branches covered the ground. The river looked angry today. Strong winds pushed white-capped waves over the banks, flooding lower elevations. Charlie looked for people trapped by collapsed walls, moving debris aside as survivors climbed out, thankful to be alive. It didn't take long for the people of Magnolia and Green Cove

Springs to respond. Soon police, firefighters and medical personnel arrived to guide rescue operations. Charlie helped where he could and found himself at the south end of the apartment site near one of the two possible locations he laid out in his mind for St. Dunstan's. Charlie was astonished to see a very large old oak tree on the ground. Large branches snapped from the trunk by the fall, created a small mountain of wood, moss and leaves. The roots of the tree were spread in a huge circle of broken and tangled pieces covered with mud. Charlie stood on the edge of the mud-filled hole, considering the power of nature, when he spotted a familiar shape in the mud.

"It's a horseshoe", he cried. Charlie jumped into the mud, waded across the rapidly filling hole and grabbed the horseshoe. Beside it in the mud, he stared at a small pile of rust-colored, muddy, round flat shapes protected by a broken clay pot. Charlie placed the horseshoe and all he could find of what had to be coins in his rain suit pockets and climbed out of the hole. The shapeless baggy jacket never did much to keep out the rain but it certainly held what he had found.

"Captain Dickison," he said. "Now, I know where to start."

Walking to his car through the rain with baggy pockets full, Charlie felt like one of the senior citizens seen on his golf course, pockets full of balls retrieved from ponds and creeks, attempting without success to be casual as they walked to their cars. He thought of his next step; the horseshoe and coins could have been placed before the oak began its growth. After all, it had to be at least one hundred years ago. Captain Dickison could have buried the horseshoe and coins in the ground beneath the place of the altar at St. Dunstan's or buried the treasure under or beside a brick foundation pier that remained after St. Dunstan's was placed on the barge ready to begin a fateful trip down the river. Charlie still felt strongly that the Captain buried the treasure so he could retrieve portions from time to time.

Charlie realized very quickly that he was dealing with treasure buried on private property. "I'll have to think about that problem," he sighed.

After the storm passed, Charlie waited a week before returning to Magnolia. Tree removal, cleanup and rebuilding were in progress, and he was delighted to hear that minor injuries and property damage were the only results of the tornado. He tried to be casual, but concerned, as he stepped over broken pieces of wood wall framing, plywood sheathing and small branches, heading for the downed oak tree. The hole had been backfilled with dirt; the trunk lay on the ground ready to be reduced by saws into moveable sections.

With the foundation plan in his mind, using the location of the horseshoe as a center; he paced off a possible layout on the ground of St. Dunstan's. Standing at the assumed position of the altar, Charlie reminded himself that was all he could do on private property. It was time to call Sam.

Once again the two men sat in Sam's kitchen. Sam's fingers followed the shape of the horseshoe, washed clean and given the magnet test. He knew he should handle the coins as little as possible, but he could not resist the urge to stack and then restack the double eagles listening to Charlie's tale of the tornado and the discovery of the horseshoe and coins in the root hole. Charlie stood and walked over to Sam's bar to refill his drink. "Sam", he said. "I know there is more to be found and it has to be buried at Magnolia. I watched the papers and television to see if newsworthy items had been found. When I returned to Magnolia this morning, I'm sure I would have heard if anything unusual had been uncovered. I thought, on the way here, about using a metal detector. That might work. A number of companies I have checked on offer a wide variety of underground searching devices, but we can't use any deep-seeking technology because we would be on private property."

Three weeks passed as Charlie tried to figure a solution to

the dilemma of what he felt with certainty was that what he and Sam had been seeking was there at Magnolia, on the property of someone else. One day after a trip to Magnolia, Charlie sat in his kitchen, eating lunch. "Charlie," said Alley. "Sam Wood is going to preach Sunday at church and I think we should go."

"O.K. Alley, I got a call from Sam telling me that I should be there for a special sermon. I can't imagine what he could be talking about, but we'll go."

On Sunday, Alley and Charlie sat down in their regular pew then knelt to individually offer a prayer. Charlie thought of the joy and love he felt for his family and friends, expressed his gratitude and sat back, waiting in silence as Sam had taught him, for the service to start. The congregation stood as the processional hymn began. Following the acolytes, choir and other clergy, the Reverend Sam Wood entered the church, looking for Alley and Charlie. Halfway down the center aisle, Sam smiled in recognition as their eyes met.

During the reading of the Gospel, Charlie stood with the congregation, but was not properly attentive until he felt Sam's eyes were focused directly at him from the chancel. He nodded slightly, deciding to pay closer attention to what was being read. When he heard the words, 'field' and 'treasure', he looked up briskly, then asked Alley in a whisper if she heard which book of the New Testament, chapter and verse, was being read. Alley shook her head, looking at Charlie in surprise at his request.

Ever a church architect, Charlie counted the steps as Sam stepped up into the pulpit for his sermon. After a brief prayer, Sam waited until the congregation was seated, then looked right at Charlie and began:

"The Lectionary, in our prayer book, directs the reading of portions of the Old and New Testaments for each Sunday of the church year. This morning the Gospel reading was from St. Matthew, Chapter 13, verse 44."

"The kingdom of heaven is like a treasure hidden in a field, which a man found and covered up; then in his joy he goes and sells all that he has and buys that field."

Charlie sat up straight and reached for a Bible from the rack at each pew.

Sam continued, "Most preachers depend on the appointed readings as a basis for their sermon. As I prepared for today, all of my thoughts were for those treasures that have been buried and are lost and forgotten. Today we celebrate the feast day for Dunstan, Archbishop of Canterbury in 988; a man who has been forgotten by all except those who prepare the church calendar. Dunstan rose from blacksmith to become a Bishop of the church and became the basis for the legend of good luck associated with a horseshoe. One day while working with his hammer and anvil over a red hot fire, the devil appeared asking to be properly shod with new shoes on his cloven hoofs. Dunstan grabbed the devil, tied him to his anvil, beating him severely until the devil cried for mercy, promising to never enter a door where a horseshoe was placed, open end up, ready to receive the blessing of heaven.

"On the St. Johns River, a small mission church named for St. Dunstan was built in 1861, just as the Civil War began. This wood frame mission church was one of eighteen river churches organized by Francis Rutledge, first Bishop of Florida, and John Freeman Young, his successor. In 1884, St. Dunstan's Episcopal Church of Magnolia was lost as the building was being relocated by barge. This treasure of the Diocese of Florida was forgotten until research by a local architect developed the history of St. Dunstan's and returned this small wood frame river church to us."

At the mention of St. Dunstan, Alley reached over to squeeze Charlie's hand. Sam continued his sermon, frequently looking directly at Charlie. Charlie was paying closer attention to a sermon than he had all his life; holding a Bible open to the passage from St. Matthew. The words "…found, …covered up, …joy, …sells all, …buys" ignited a fire in his mind, telling him, through Sam and the Bible, what he should do.

Sam explained, in the sermon, his interpretation of the parable told by Jesus, with emphasis on lost and found, forgotten then remembered. Charlie heard only the inspiration he needed to continue his search. He sensed Sam was speaking directly to him but all Charlie received was the way to find the treasure.

After the service, Charlie asked Alley to locate Sam's wife, Susan, while he searched for Sam. He found him removing his vestments in the sacristy of the church.

"Sam," he said. "You were talking to me all morning, but what came through was "buy the field!" That's our next step. I know the balance of the treasure is there at Magnolia and the lesson and your words today told me what to do."

"Charlie, we can't just "buy the field." That beautiful riverfront land is worth more than I, or you and I together, can handle. It may not be for sale."

"You preached to me, Sam. St. Dunstan's was lost, we found it but brought the church and its history back for own use. As much as I have come to think of St. Dunstan's of Magnolia, without the possibility of treasure it would soon, as you preached, slip away from my memory. I'm gonna borrow the money, Sam. I'll sell all that I have; stocks, bonds and my boat. Cash in my IRA, mortgage my home. Do whatever I need to buy that property. Are you with me, Sam?"

After days and nights of deliberation plus hours of prayer, Sam agreed. The two men knew they now had to convince their wives; discussions and the final decision took longer than expected. Some serious arguments took place. Marriages were on the line until finally, one Sunday afternoon in Sam's kitchen, the two wives were presented with the evidence; four gold ingots (two given to the Diocese), 250 gold double eagles (180 returned to nine churches. Sam kept twenty, Charlie had twenty plus thirty from the root hole) and four silver horseshoes. Impressed with the efforts of Sam and Charlie, Susan Wood and Allison Gallagher reluctantly agreed to the enterprise. An important condition of the joint approvals of Sam, Susan and Allison was for Charlie to take charge. He started by authorizing his attorney and accountant to begin the preparation of the agreements necessary to buy the land. To begin fundraising Charlie then contacted mortgage holders, brokers, bankers, financial consultants, realtors and real estate appraisers.

Charlie soon found the purchase of a moderately successful apartment project was not easy. Under normal circumstances, he and Sam could fund the purchase price by combining a bank loan with money available from the sale of their stocks, bonds, IRA's, boats or houses. The problem developed that the Magnolia apartment property was not generating sufficient cash flow to support what Charlie felt was a more than adequate purchase price.

The gap between the partner's equity and the amount a bank would loan required an additional element of structured financing. He and Sam would not raise any more capital on their own and conventional lenders would not underwrite a larger loan, so it became necessary to find alternative sources. Contact with institutional lenders and venture capitalists did not produce any worthwhile offers until one day, their mortgage broker brought a proposal from a wealthy investor in Maine, interested in properties in north Florida.

Lengthy negotiations between Charlie and Sam's representatives and the unidentified lender's organization finally resulted in an agreement. Charlie and Sam would contribute 40% and the Maine investor would contribute 60% of the equity necessary to meet the amount to be underwritten by the bank, with an understanding that cash flow and any future value produced by the property would be shared on a pro rata basis.

Finally, the property belonged to Dunstan and Associates. After an exhaustive closing of the loan, Charlie, Sam, Susan and Allison stood together looking across the St. Johns as the western sun brushed the far shore. Charlie started to say something, then paused, knowing Sam Wood would tell him to be quiet.

Sam said, "I ask you to silently pay your respects and offer a prayer of thanksgiving for the lives of Francis Rutledge, John Freeman Young, Bishops of Florida and for the Reverend Harold Alexander, Captain J. J. Dickison and for the people of Magnolia. I hope that we, in our efforts on this land from this day forward, remember them with respect and affection."

Chapter 39
Six Months Later

As rental leases expired, Dunstan and Associates occupied one of the first riverfront apartments to be vacated, establishing what appeared to be a standard developer's office. Realtors and local officials were curious for the future use of the property but were told the new owners would use the multi-family zoning classification for their projects. Sam and Charlie felt Dunstan and Associates had only a single project in mind; find the treasure of the Confederacy.

Using the engineering survey that defined the limits of the property, indicated all easements, rights-of-way and existing buildings, Charlie commissioned the same engineering firm to add topographical information plus the location and specie of all trees over six inches in diameter. On his drawing board, Charlie prepared an overlay indicating the probable location of the old Magnolia Hotel and the location of the horseshoe and coins uncovered during the tornado.

Charlie stood on the porch of his new office thinking of Captain J. J. Dickison. All he had to begin his search was a single horseshoe and a handful of coins, trying to imagine where the Captain hid the balance. His first assumption was the gold and silver would have been divided into smaller amounts and hidden separately, allowing access for distribution to future churches of Bishop Young and for Captain Dickison's own use. St. Dunstan's was still standing as J. J. hid the coins and horseshoes at nine river churches. Charlie tried to visualize how the gold or silver would have been uncovered while the church building remained.

Was there a second cemetery, forgotten and unmarked? Charlie felt it was possible but not likely. The Captain would have to excavate from time to time; in daylight, questions would be asked, at night would be ridiculous.

Perhaps a clue existed in the area of the spring enjoyed by hotel guests. Charlie spent days looking for any sign of the spring. Contour lines on the topographical survey indicated drainage slopes toward the river. Two creeks toward the north and a single narrow waterway to the south offered the best possibilities. Charlie found two old bottles partially covered at the south creek, possibly confirming the local story of a bottling plant that used the spring as a source for the water. This location seemed to be too remote from the location of the hotel to be valid. Using a steel rod, Charlie went from south to north looking and probing for any suggestions of a hiding place for the treasure. After slowly and carefully walking over the property without any serious prospects, Charlie decided the time was right for the next phase.

He had watched metal detectors in use but had no idea of the capabilities of the latest and very sophisticated models. Using a wide range of sound frequencies transmitted through a coil mounted on a hand-held aluminum frame, the size and depth of metal objects could be located precisely and displayed on a liquid crystal screen. During an awkward learning experience with a rented model, Charlie found drink cans, pull tabs, bottle caps, nails, keys, nickels, dimes and one ring just below the surface of the ground. Adjusting the frequency for a greater depth and the diameter of a double eagle, Charlie got serious in his search. He started out where he found the horseshoe and coins walking slowly in a straight line first toward the river, then west, north and south recording the direction on his topographical drawing. Expecting instant success, Charlie was disappointed with only a few signals that came through the headphones producing older drink cans and bottle caps. Sam Wood regularly took his turn on the detector with similar results. Alley began to be concerned with finances.

"I realize we can't hurry and I think I'm still optimistic, Charlie, but I'm getting discouraged pretty fast", she said. "The rings and coins are interesting but we need to find a double eagle or even another horseshoe."

Charlie increased the depth of the signal on the detector, deciding to walk in a spiral pattern from the horseshoe/coin location. Using small flags stuck in the ground, he marked his progress while slowly increasing his circular path. Days turned into weeks without a promising signal. Raising the signal coil from the ground occasionally, Charlie and Sam mimicked the movements of the nearby blue herons slowly walking in shallow water pecking with their long beaks search for small fish.

Charlie thought once again of the foundation plan he had prepared. Based on his knowledge of the wood frame churches and the architecture of Richard Upjohn, he knew this layout had to be a key to the treasure, fully realizing the brick and mortar would have disintegrated long ago. Individual brick piers, twenty inches square on a grid of approximately nine feet; three piers wide by five piers long covered 680 square feet. Using his overlay of the topographical/tree survey, Charlie marked, with a small flag, the corners of the two possible church locations he had selected from his boat. Multiple slow passes with the detector did not produce a signal of any strength.

Frustrated, Charlie then moved his grid to the horseshoe/coin location. Assuming Captain Dickison would not have buried any portions of the treasure under the building, Charlie placed small flags again at the corners of the grid, picked up his detector and began his sweeps. Very slow, overlapping passes up, down and across the grid were completed with the same negative response.

At lunch, two days later, Charlie sat at his drawing board sliding his grid overlay back and forth over the topographical/tree survey. Suddenly, two trees jumped into focus through the transparency. A double trunk magnolia was close to the limits of his grid and a second magnolia, equally large, appeared two grid squares away. Charlie dropped his sandwich, grabbed his detector and ran to the double trunk tree. On his third circle around the tree, his earphones began to ring. He stopped, standing very still as the ringing increased. As the readouts materialized on his screen, Charlie yelled, dropped the detector and ran for the shovel and post-hole digger. Carefully working at the indicated area, Charlie dug to about three feet below the grade. He found a horseshoe first that probably produced the strong signal, then a broken clay pot containing the remnants of a rotted bag full of loose gold coins. Under the clay pot was a small corroded metal box containing two gold ingots.

Sitting back in the pile of dirt, Charlie reached for his cell phone. "Sam, where are you? I'm sitting on top of what we were looking for. Come quick."

Without attempting to isolate the coins, Charlie placed coins and dirt in two canvas bags. In two trips, Charlie moved the treasure to the office. Returning to the magnolia tree, he refilled the hole and tamped the earth as well as he could to disguise the spot.

Holding a cold beverage, Charlie sat staring at the bags on the floor, breathing hard, waiting for Sam. After a while, just as expected, he watched Sam hit the curb as he turned into the parking area, stopping diagonally across the indicated straight-in marked spaces and jump from his car with the motor still running. The two men shook hands and with triumphant smiles stood looking at the treasure.

"Where was it?" Sam asked.

Charlie described his grid system and then his realization the church would not necessarily be located in an open space. He told Sam of his hunch, noticing two large magnolias close to his grid that led to his discovery.

"You were right after all," Sam said. "There was more than in the altar at St. George. Don't you think this is all?"

Charlie said, "No, now that I have two points, I believe I

can come close to laying out a foundation plan on the ground. I believe Captain Dickison buried a portion of the treasure by the side or near each brick pier of the church."

Sam shook his head. "We should be happy with what we've got. I can't believe there is more."

"You and I owe a lot of money on this land, Sam. I know that our equity partner in Maine will have demands, as we expected. With what we have it is possible the loan could be paid and even sell the land for a little profit but I'm not satisfied. There's more here, I'm certain."

After washing the dirt from the coins, Sam and Charlie were delighted to count 200 double eagles, not new, but in good condition. They decided to take the coins, ingots and horseshoe to their safety deposit box before joining Alley and Susan for a proper celebration.

The next day Charlie returned to his overlay and the second large magnolia. In a circle around the tree, with great anticipation, he slowly continued his routine. By lunch time, nothing. Not a single signal of any volume. Disappointed, he returned to his grid, ignoring for now tree locations. He had two positive points on his assumed foundation plan, rotating and sliding his grid around these two spots.

One week later, Sam was handling the metal detector, criss-crossing the site between the two points where he heard a strong signal in his headphones. He marked the spot with a flag and ran to find Charlie. Taking turns on the shovel, about three feet down, eight horseshoes, black and dirty, were found.

"These have to be silver," said Sam. "Why would anyone bury plain iron horseshoes?"

Charlie said, "The best part of this find is now we have a third point. If my assumptions are anywhere close to the actual foundation plan, I think we can locate the church, then check each pier location." Charlie plotted the three points on the survey and overlaid his grid transparency. After moving the grid around, the most likely arrangement resulted from placing the first horseshoe/coin location at the center just outside the altar end of the church. The second point appeared on one side and the last, or exclusively horseshoes, was located near a front corner. As the sun set, Charlie placed flags where each individual brick foundation structure appeared on his assumed plan, then took a cold beverage down to the edge of the river and looked southwest to see if the site was logical or anywhere near the two possible church location he had picked out from his boat. The next morning, after an anxious and sleepless night, Charlie lifted his detector and went right to work. As he moved around each flag, the liquid crystal screen lit up, accompanied by a positive signal through the earphones, almost as loud as Charlie's shouts of joy.

Two months later, standing at the end of the recently completed dock, Dunstan and Associates, Charlie, Sam, Allison, and Susan looked back to Magnolia. Charlie pointed out the location of the hotel; Sam described St. Dunstan's as it served the community through happy and sad years. He said, "You all know how I feel about the sound of silence. Stand quiet now and listen in your heart for the whistle of an approaching steamboat bringing the excited residents of Magnolia to where we now stand, anxious for mail, visitors and necessary supplies. In my imagination, I just heard, far in the distance, the crack of a whip signifying the presence of the circuit riders of Captain Dickison protecting the community. Standing over there near St. Dunstan's is the Reverend Harold Alexander talking with his Bishop, John Freeman Young."

After a period of quiet, Charlie looked at Sam and said, "Strike the tent."

Chapter 40

In midstream of the St. Johns, aboard his yacht Columbine II, Frank Sanborn of Brunswick, Maine, lowered his binoculars and smiled in anticipation of the first meeting with his new partners!

Comments and Endnotes

Francis Rutledge and John Freeman Young, first and second Episcopal bishops of Florida are not imaginary. I have added dialogue that I believe would be appropriate to their character and behavior in my story.

However loyal I feel to the creation, St. Dunstan's Episcopal Church did not exist. The eighteen other river churches are real. Nine remain with us today. I have attempted to describe them accurately.

Richard Upjohn, architect, designed many churches after his most famous project, Trinity church, New York City. His book, <u>Rural Architecture,</u> did serve as the basis for design and construction of an unknown number of small wood frame churches.

Over many years, I have been intrigued with numerous incidents that actually occurred in North Florida; the yacht <u>America</u>, the U. S. Navy steam gunboat <u>Columbine</u> truly sunk by a troop of cavalry, and the visit of Confederate General John Breckinridge to Gainesville and Waldo as he escaped Union patrols searching for the Confederate cabinet member.

Captain J. J. Dickison lived and served as I have written. From Magnolia, raids across the river into Yankee territory, the successful attack on the <u>Columbine</u> and his friendship with Bishop Young, I have involved the famous cavalry leader in my story, giving him leadership, dialogue and in my imagination, involvement with the treasure.

The visit by Robert E. Lee to Jacksonville and the river took place as I have written except I moved his destination across the St. Johns from Orange Mills to Magnolia.

The Magnolia Hotel, the third hotel and largest on the

river, burned many years later than the tragedy in my story.

As an appendix to <u>St. Dunstan's and John</u>, I offer an essay on the magnificent St. Johns River. From a spring in a swamp in south Florida, the river flows north hundreds of miles to the Atlantic Ocean, slowly expanding from a narrow waterway in to wide bays of water defined by headlands on alternating sides of the river.

Thank you for visiting St. Dunstan's and the St. Johns with Captain J. J. Dickison, Bishop John Young, the Reverend Sam Wood and Charlie Gallagher. Any shortcomings or errors are all mine.

Appendix: The St. Johns

Two herons glide in the wind, banking around each finger of land as it reaches out into the river.

"We have followed the river south for many days," said the younger. "Surely this large lake ahead must be the beginning."

"Fly on," says his older friend. "We may find food here but the river begins in a lake in the middle of a swamp far away!"

The morning sun moves across the marsh as the shadows of night become lighter and lighter. Cypress and palm trees are touched with gold. The grasses in the distance appear as brown fur slowly moving in the early breeze. Up close, the marsh grasses appear as knives with a central fold and saw-like stems along the edge. This grass-like plant, called sawgrass, has roots below the water with stems and brown leaves rising above the water. Water lilies, cattails and iris add texture and color to the sea of grass.

Overhead, hawks, ospreys and an occasional eagle watch the marsh as herons and egrets tip-toe through the shallow water looking for breakfast. A black and gray alligator slips into a pond causing ripples in the silent water.

These fresh water marshes are flatlands with poor drainage created by the relatively flat topography of Florida. As the subsurface bedrock or porous limerock dissolves in contact with ground water, lakes, ponds, sinkholes and caves are formed. The Florida aquifer, an underground source of water for most of Florida, moves through the limestone from north to south. Caves and interconnected streams flow beneath all of Florida, portions of Georgia, South Carolina and Alabama. Water from this marvelous stream of water is available through artesian wells, shallow in a few cases, more often hundreds of feet deep. Above the aquifer, a subsurface water table is created by a variety of confining soils. As rainwater is absorbed by the earth, it is directed by this water table and flows to lower elevations creating lakes, ponds, rivers, and creeks in Eastern Florida, and ultimately, to the St. Johns River.

Water flowing through the aquifer occasionally breeches the water table and literally springs to the surface. Amazing quantities of water are produced. Authorities rate springs on the measurable amount of water produced. "First magnitude" springs exceed 65 million gallons of water per day. Four springs alone [Blue Springs, Silver Springs, Silver Glen Springs and Alexander Springs] that flow to rivers and on to the St. Johns produce over 700 million gallons of water per day! Smaller springs contributing to the flow of the St. Johns contribute an additional 150 million gallons of water per day![1]

From the northern border of St. Lucie County, into Indian River County and extending north to Brevard County lies St. Johns marsh. West of Melbourne, this poorly drained flatland becomes Jane Green swamp. In contrast to flatlands, swamps are poorly drained river floodplains that support flood tolerant trees such as palm, cypress, bay, myrtles, maple and some species of dogwood. The subsurface limerock has dissolved creating a 400 acre lake called Helen Blazes. From here, the St. Johns begins its slow descent to the Atlantic Ocean. The river moves north in a series of "S" curves through marshes and swamps, occasionally gathering itself into lakes and ponds.

Wildlife is abundant, people are not.

As the St. Johns falls ever so slightly toward the north, ultimately to the Atlantic, the river becomes narrow as it follows the contours, flowing between higher ground elevations, looping on itself to form hammocks, or spreading out over lower elevations into lakes that gradually increase in size.

Between the lakes, the river twists and turns through swamps and marshes. Along the edges of the slow-moving dark water, palm and cypress trees stand as sentinels protecting the dark forest beyond. Osprey nests balance precariously on dead trees. Hawks, eagles and cormorants rest on dead tree limbs. Water and live oaks, pine, magnolias, hickory, bay and gum trees form a beautiful and practically impenetrable barrier to the land beyond the river.

Clearings are hard to find. Overhanging limbs, dripping with moss, a multiple variety of vines plus cypress "knees" make access to the river difficult.

Determined fisherman, searching for a variety of fish; bass, bream [pronounce brim], shell crackers, speckled perch and catfish to mention a few, have found their way to the river by narrow unimproved roads leading to the water's edge.

On the eastern border of the Ocala National Forest, the St. Johns meanders into Lake George, ten miles long, five miles wide, covering 46,000 acres; the second largest lake in Florida [Lake Okeechobee, in South Florida with 500,000 acres is the largest].[2] As the river continues north, twists and turns are fewer. More bridges and highways provide easier access to the river. On the west side, south of the town of Welaka, the Oklawaha River enters the current of the St. Johns, as its main tributary. The Oklawaha has been joined east of Ocala by the Silver River increasing the volume of water dramatically. The source of this increase is Silver Springs, a first magnitude spring with a flow of over 500 million gallons of water per day.[3] The Oklawaha runs north from the junction of the Silver River, and makes a gentle turn to the east and, after meeting two dams, enters the St. Johns.

Five miles north, the ill-fated cross Florida Barge Canal joins the St. Johns. The canal was excavated in 1960 in an effort to join the St. Johns with the west coast of Florida.

Construction or the Rodman Dam, as part of this effort, created a large reservoir with shallow, slow-moving water, plentiful vegetation and accents of dead trees above and below the surface of the lake – a paradise for fishermen.

South of Palatka, Seven Sisters, Murphy, Polly and Rat Islands interrupt the current of the river. Dunns Creek, on the east side, provides access to Crescent Lake. Early maps of Florida refer to this body of water as Dunns Lake. This 16,000 acre lake, named for its shape, is fed by small springs and water run-offs from nearby low lands and is another popular destination for fisherman.

As the river passes "Devil's Elbow," a sharp U-turn south of the U.S. Highway 17 Bridge, tidal currents from the Atlantic Ocean, over 60 miles to the north, begin to affect the St. Johns. A measurable high and low tide are found in the now brackish water. The Jacksonville Florida Times Union reports a seven to eight hour time difference. As the river flows past Palatka, the slate gray and dark blue waters have become wider. The twisting and narrow river, only barely navigable to small boats, has spread its banks.

From Federal Point to Tocoi, a small community west of St. Augustine, swamps and marshes are still seen with dense forests of pine, palm, oak, magnolia, bay and cypress trees lining the river overlooking grass flats. Docks and boat houses appear more often searching for deeper water as they reach out into the river.

Below Tocoi [in a northern direction since the river flows south to north] points of land form distant edges of the river creating the appearance of a series of wide lakes. As one headland is reached, another is revealed on the opposite shore. Banks of the river appear as gray and green walls, dappled with sunlight and highlighted by dead trees. An occasional glimpse of the majestic length of the St. Johns is seen as the headlands recede. The Timucuan Indians described the course of the river as "Ylacco" or Welaka, translated by many writers as a "river of lakes".[4]

Just past Green Cove Springs, the dark and mysterious Black Creek enters the river. The waters are black; legends speak of many sections of the twisting creek as bottomless. The mighty Seminole chief Osceola camped on its banks in a grove of magnolias on the south side of the quiet black waters.[5]

Below Black Creek, swamps and creeks to the west and Doctors Lake to the north form Fleming Island, named for George Fleming, an Irishman who served in the Royal Spanish Colonial Army and, for his service, received a grant of 1,000 acres on the west bank of the St. Johns. On this land, Fleming built a home called "Hibernia", named for his birth place.[6]

Doctors Lake, after a relatively narrow entry from the St. Johns, extends approximately five miles to the southwest. Similar to Crescent Lake to the south, this large body of water is fed by small springs and ground water.

Across the St. Johns from Doctors Lake, Julington Creek offers comfortable anchorages at its mouth, then rapidly shoals and narrows to the east.

North of Julington Creek lies Mandarin Point. In 1867, Harriet Beecher Stowe, author of Uncle Tom's Cabin, was so impressed with the climate and beauty of the river that she purchased a house and orange grove for a winter residence.

After Mandarin Point, the river stretched its banks to a width of over three miles. Interstate Highway 295, the Buckman Bridge, crosses here from north of Orange Park on the west bank of Plummers Point on the east. Even with this visual interruption, the alternation of headlands from east to west recall "the river of lakes".

Approximately six miles to the west, between the towns of Marietta and Baldwin, McGirts Creek begins a slow descent to the south, meandering through the swamps and heavy underbrush, beneath U.S. 90, I-10 and State Road 228 [Normandy Boulevard] emerging as the Ortega River. Near the intersection of I-295 and State Road 21, Blanding

Boulevard, the Ortega takes a northerly turn and gradually begins to widen its banks.

Just north of the bridge at State Road 134 [103rd Street], a small but navigable creek flows to the east. Once called Mary's Creek, this small waterway continues by culvert under Roosevelt Boulevard [U.S. 17], into a small pond and then underground again into Pirates Cove and the river. Although barely noticeable today, these waterways formed the Island of Ortega offering isolation and protection for early settlers.

To the north, the Ortega River is joined by Fishing Creek, Butcher Pen Creek and the Cedar River, makes a turn to the east and merges with the St. Johns at Ortega [or Sadler] Point.

The flow of the St. Johns continues north until downtown Jacksonville is reached. McCoys Creek passes under Riverside Avenue at the Florida Times Union Building through culverts and enters the river just south of the railroad bridge. As the river turns to the east, the banks narrow and a deeper waterway is created. After the sharp turn under the railroad and Acosta Bridges, the river passes through downtown Jacksonville. Office buildings, hotels, theaters, restaurants and entertainment centers connected by boardwalks are found on both banks of the river. The dark water is never still as boat traffic, commercial and pleasure, moves in all directions. People, cars and trucks are everywhere. In contrast to the busy scene of today, early writers describe both sides of the river with gentle sloping banks and occasional marshes.

At the foot of Liberty Street and high rise condominium apartments on the opposite shore, the Timucuan Indians forded the river, naming the place <u>Wacca Pilatka</u>[7] where cows could be herded across.

On the north side of the St. Johns, an Indian camp, called Ossachite,[8] was located near a spring-fed creek surrounded by oak, pine and palmetto plants. From the camp, a trail to the west crossed a ridge of sand hills, still identified on many maps as Trail Ridge. The single narrow trail continued to Olustee Creek and the Suwanee River, Aucilla, Lake Wiccosukee and Tallahassee in the territory of the Apalachee Indians.

Near Hemming Park in downtown Jacksonville, the trail to the west split with a branch heading north toward the St. Mary's River, crossing into Georgia east of Folkston near Colerain. On many maps, an intersection of two roads at the river is identified as Kings Ferry. From Wacca Pilatka, Indian trails continued on the south bank toward St. Augustine.

After Britain acquired Florida from Spain in 1764, the crown encouraged settlement in the new territory. To learn more about Florida, the royal botanist, John Bartram, together with his son William and a group of writers and mapmakers visited east Florida. One of the writers described the place of crossings as "cow ford, from the multitude of cattle [that could be] drove through here."[9]

The name was appropriate and Cowford was born.

To assist both settlers and soldiers traveling south from colonies in Georgia and South Carolina, work began on a graded road from the St. Mary's River following the Indian trail south to Cowford. This highway, referred to as Kings Road crossed the St. Johns by fording or by ferry, then continued on to St. Augustine and south to New Smyrna.

Kings Road remains in Jacksonville today following U. S. Highway 1 on the southside and continuing on the north side of the river as U. S. Highway 23. Near the junction of U. S. Highway 1, Kings Road splits into New Kings Road and Old Kings Road merging again near the Duval/Nassau County Line. Evidence of Kings Road remains on many maps today.

North of downtown, the floodplain of Hogan's Creek gathers groundwater run off and flows south from near 11th and Jefferson Streets, under several bridges, two viaducts and the Hart Expressway, through an industrial area, under a low bridge at Bay Street and into the St. Johns.

At Commodore Point, under the Hart Bridge, the river turns north again. The Arlington River, its banks lined with private docks, boathouses and riverfront homes, is joined by Big and Little Pottsburg Creeks and then enters the current of the St. Johns at Empire Point.

Soon after, the river is divided by Exchange Island, identified on some maps as a park but is not currently developed and is accessible only be boat.

From the Matthews Bridge [U. S. Highway 90A] north, the river offers two identities. On the east bank, a high-rise building [Jones College], a boat yard, marina and a public boat ramp quickly give way to relatively high banks, gently sloping down to the river punctuated by lengthy docks and boathouses. Waterfront multi-family and single residences and the campus of Jacksonville University are shaded by cedar, magnolia, bay, pine, oaks of all sizes and an occasional palm.

On the west side of the river, anchored red and green buoys indicate a channel dredged to a depth of approximately thirty-four feet to permit passage and anchorage of large ships.[10] Tall blue cranes designed to unload containers appear to match their name: long legs and neck with a straight bill that bobs up and down as containers are lifted from anchored ships. These steel framed machines stand as sentinels for the industrial and commercial activities. Concrete silos, petroleum storage tanks and chimneys punctuate the riverfront. At the north end of the shipping channel, Long Branch Creek enters the river as a gradual curve to the northeast begins. The Trout River, fed by the Ribault River, joins the flow at Sandfly Point. Channel buoys and range markers bring large ships close to the north bank. Islands created by dredging and shifting river currents overlook wide expanses of shallow water to the south. The Broward River and Dunn Creek flowing from the north became part of the St. Johns.

Dominating all views, the Dames Point Bridge sweeps across the river with thin white cable arranged in a chevron pattern supporting a roadway 160 feet above the flowing currents.

Leaving the shadow of the bridge, channel markers indicate an easterly path to the Atlantic. Closer review of the nautical chart shows a second channel to the north. This channel follows the original course of the river, curving from Dames Point to the north. Dredging of a direct course to the ocean created Goat Island, later called Blount Island, and offered Jacksonville a large industrial site with docking facilities for ships of all types. Deep water is available on all sides of the island interrupted only by an automobile bridge with low clearance.

From Blount Island east, the dark blue water appears to move more swiftly almost in anticipation of joining the ocean. High banks on the south side form St. Johns Bluff with occasional saltwater marshes and small river plains. Small strips of land along the north side separate the flowing river from a maze of creeks and saltwater marshes. These flats are alternatively drained and fed by each change in the tide and are home to a large variety of bird and aquatic life. Creeks and tidal channels turn on themselves to create hammocks of oak, pine, magnolia and cypress. This maze extends to the north towards the Nassau River and Fernandina. To the east, Sisters Creek forms one leg of the Intracoastal Waterway; beyond, marshes and the barrier islands and sandy beaches define the edge of the sea.

In late April, 1562, leaders of the Timucua Indians of northeast Florida, Alimacani[11] on the north side of the river and Saturiwa on the south, were no doubt surprised to see sailing vessels in the Atlantic anchored near the mouth of the river. European explorers had been here before. In 1513, Ponce de Leon had landed north of present day St. Augustine [the Spanish Admiral recorded his location at 30 degrees, 8 minutes North latitude or approximately one and one half miles north of Micklers Landing on Ponte Vedra Boulevard.][12] A second Spanish explorer, Juan Quexo, paused at the mouth of the river in 1520 but it remained for Jean Ribault, searching for a place to establish a French Hugenot colony, to overcome breaking surf and strong tides and entered the river on May 1, 1562.

In command of an expeditionary squadron of three ships, Ribault had been exploring along the coast of Florida and had anchored the night before. In three shallops [rowboats or dinghies], he entered the "goodly and great river."[13] To commemorate the occasion, he named the river "Riviere de Mai" or the River May. On the south shore he planted a hexagonal stone column "carved and engraved with the arms of France." The exact location of the monument is unknown; a similar column was erected in 1924, but was not accessible to the public upon construction of the Mayport Naval Station. The replica was moved to a high bluff overlooking the river, Sisters Creek, Mayport and Fort George and is maintained by the National Park Service.[14]

In 1564, Jean Ribault's second in-command, Rene de Laudonniere, returned to the St. Johns to establish a permanent French colony in the New World. After searching for a suitable location as far north as the Carolinas, Laudonniere decided to place his settlement on the south bank of the river below the high bluffs. To protect themselves, the French colonists constructed a triangular-shaped fort, named Fort Caroline in honor of King Charles, on flat land with a moat on two sides. Visitors to the fort today see only a reconstruction based on educated guesswork. The exact size and location of the original fort is not known. Old drawings indicate an expanded triangular "arrow shape"[15] with the point of the arrow facing east. Fort Caroline, under the protection of moats, high battlements and timber palisades, was not to endure. It was only a matter of time before Spain, in St. Augustine, learned of the settlement. In late September, 1565, Pedro Menendez de

Aviles led a force of 500 soldiers from his headquarters in St. Augustine, overland in a rainstorm, attacked and destroyed the fort.

In 1587, on the north bank of the river, San Juan del Puerto was established by Franciscan missionaries. From St. Augustine in the south, north to the Carolinas and west toward Tallahassee, Catholic missions were built to Christianize the Indians, possibly enlist them as allies and to establish claim to the land in the name of Spain. San Juan del Puerto flourished and became one of the most successful missions. "The church constructed of hand-hewn wood planking…was very ornate…, had a set of bells and perhaps even a bell tower."[16] Aligned with the Creek Indians in their continuing conflict with the Timucua and Apalachee Indians, British raiders destroyed San Juan del Puerto in November, 1702.

Challenging Spanish claims to northeast Florida and supported by the Creek Indians, the British moved south from their colony of Savannah, established in 1733 by General James Oglethorpe. Following the inland passage formed by creeks, inlets and rivers, Oglethorpe selected English names for various coastal islands, Santa Maria became Amelia, Sarabay became Talbot, San Juan, the location of the Catholic mission, became St. George Island, and San Juan, the river, became St. John's.[17]

After landing on St. George Island, Oglethorpe and his men climbed an unusually high dune, gaining a view of the inlet and over Talbot Island to the Atlantic beyond. Cannon and swivel guns were mounted and Fort George was established.[18] Although obvious from a defensive standpoint, this location has not been confirmed by archeological evidence. Recent theories locate the fort at Mile Point, on the north side of the river opposite the entrance from the St. Johns to the present day Intracoastal Waterway.

Across the river from Fort George Island is the village of Mayport, originally accessible only by boat; a home for fishermen and bar pilots. Wind, tides, strong currents resulted in constantly shifting sandbars with a channel often disguised. An experienced pilot was necessary to bring a vessel into the river.

To open Jacksonville as a port it was necessary to overcome these difficulties. Ships waiting for days to enter the river would be easily persuaded to carry their freight to a more accessible port. Vessels loaded with timber and citrus from Jacksonville could not leave without waiting for the shifting sands to open a channel.

The slope of the streambed is low; the flow velocity of the current is approximately five to seven knots. The river is basically a constructed channel with tidal action reversing the current four times in a period of time based on a lunar cycle.[19] In contrast to an alluvial river that carries silt, small stones and sand along its path, reaches a larger body of water with lesser currents and fans out into a delta, the St. Johns is a non-alluvial river carrying spring and ground water runoff.[20]

Attempts were made through regular dredging operations to create a dependable channel but met little success. In 1880 construction of two jetties began at the mouth of the river. Resting on a foundation of logs and brush, large blocks of rock [originally granite from South Carolina and from New York, later limerock from Florida] were placed to create a wall in the Atlantic on either side of the river. The north jetty extends 3 miles and the south 2 ½ miles into the ocean. Completed in 1895, the jetties produced the scouring action necessary to create a deep regular channel.[21] Shipping could easily enter and leave the river and Jacksonville became a seaport.

The St. Johns River has had many names. The first European explorer came upon "a place where the waters were boiling and tumbling as if over rapids." Attributed to Juan Quexo, a Spanish explorer, the river was appropriately named <u>Rio de Corrientas</u> [river of currents].[22] On May 1,

1562, Jean Ribault overcame the tides and strong surf, entered the river and landed. To recognize the date, he named the river Riviere de Mai [River of May]. Two years later in late September, the Spaniard Pedro Menendez de Avilez, marched overland from St. Augustine, attacked and captured Fort Caroline. In honor of his victory on the feast day of St. Matthew, Menendez renamed the fort and, following Spanish custom, the river, Rio de San Mateo [St. Matthew].

Across the river, the location of the mission, San Juan del Puerto, gave its name to the river. Many maps of the 1700's show both names: San Mateo and San Juan. When Florida was ceded by Spain to Great Britain in 1763, the name of the river was anglicized to St. John's. It is interesting to note that the apostrophe remained in the name until Florida became a territory of the United States in 1821.

A description of the flow of the water, a date, a fort, settlement or mission, to honor saint or king have each been the basis of naming the St. Johns. The majestic and distinctive beauty of this river is best described by the Indian name, Yllaco. Pronounced Welaka and interpreted by many as River of Lakes.

Appendix: Footnotes

1. Emmet Ferguson, Jr., <u>Springs of Florida</u>, Saratoga, NY, Saratoga Publishing Group, 1997 p. 13
2. Ferguson, <u>Springs of Florida</u> p. 235
3. Ferguson, <u>loc. cit</u> p. 128
4. Dena Snodgrass, "A River of Many Names,: Papers V. Jacksonville Historical Society, 1969. P. 1-4
5. Margaret Seton Fleming Biddle, <u>Hibernia: The Unreturning Tide</u>, New York, Vantage Press, Inc., 1974, p. 33
6. Ibid, p. 24
7. T. Frederick Davis, <u>History of Jacksonville, Florida and Vicinity, 1513-1924</u> Gainesville, Florida, 1964, Facsimile Edition of the 1925 Edition p. 25
8. Ibid, p. 24
9. James Robertson Ward, <u>Old Hickory's Town</u>, Jacksonville, Florida Publishing Company, 1982, p. 62
10. National Oceanic and Atmospheric Administration, Nautical Chart 11491, St. Johns River Atlantic Ocean to Jacksonville, 32 Edition, April 2000
11. Ward, <u>loc. cit</u> p. 36, 37
12. Davis, <u>loc. cit</u> p. 1
13. Davis, <u>loc. cit</u> p. 4
14. Pamphlet, National Park Service, Fort Caroline National Memorial
15. Charles E. Bennett, <u>Fort Caroline and Its Leader</u>, Gainesville, University of Florida Press, 1976
16. Ward, <u>loc. cit</u> p. 47
17. Ward, <u>loc. cit</u> p. 54

18. Wayne W. Wood, <u>Jacksonville's Architectural Heritage</u>
    Jacksonville, University of North Florida Press, 1989
    p. 309 citing Francis Moore, <u>A Voyage to Georgia</u>
    London, 1744
19. National Oceanic and Atmospheric Administration,
    <u>Currents in the St. Johns River, Florida Spring and
    Summer 1998</u>, NOAA Technical Report NOS CO-OPS
    025, 1999
20. Department of the Interior, United States Geological
    Surveys, 1979, Cape Canaveral, Orlando, Daytona
    Beach, St. Augustine, Jacksonville, Florida
21. George E. Buker, <u>Jacksonville Riverport - Seaport</u>,
    Columbia, University of South Carolina Press, 1992,
    p. 93 - 95
22. Ward, <u>loc. cit</u> p. 36